LESSONS
FOR A
WEREWOLF
WARRIOR

Jackie French

Angus&Robertson
An imprint of HarperCollins*Publishers*

Angus&Robertson
An imprint of HarperCollins*Publishers*

First published in Australia in 2009
by HarperCollins*Publishers* Australia Pty Limited
ABN 36 009 913 517
www.harpercollins.com.au

Text copyright © Jackie French 2009
Illustrations copyright © Andrea Faith Potter 2009

HarperCollins*Publishers*
25 Ryde Road, Pymble, Sydney, NSW 2073, Australia
31 View Road, Glenfield, Auckland 0627, New Zealand
77–85 Fulham Palace Road, London W6 8JB, United Kingdom
1–A, Hamilton House, Connaught Place, New Delhi – 110 001, India
2 Bloor Street East, 20th floor, Toronto, Ontario M4W 1A8, Canada
10 East 53rd Street, New York, NY 10022, USA

National Library of Australia Cataloguing-in-Publication data:
French, Jackie
  Lessons for a werewolf warrior/Jackie French; illustrator, Andrea F. Potter.
  ISBN: 978 0 207 20076 2 (pbk.)
  Series: French, Jackie. School for heroes ; Book 1
  Target Audience: For primary school age. I. Heroes – Juvenile fiction
  II. Werewolves – Juvenile fiction III. Supernatural – Juvenile fiction
  Other Authors/Contributors: Potter, Andrea F.
A823.3

Cover design by Darren Holt
Internal design and layout by Agave Creative Group
Printed and bound in Australia by Griffin Press
70gsm Classic used by HarperCollins*Publishers* is a natural, recyclable
product made from wood grown in sustainable forests. The manufacturing
processes conform to the environmental regulations in the country of
origin, Finland.

6 5 4 3 2 1   09 10 11 12

To all the heroes.

Contents

THE BEST ICE-CREAM SHOP IN THE UNIVERSES

MENU

POODLEPOPS
FROZEN RAT SURPRISE
(BIG, MEDIUM OR MOUSE)
ICE CREAM:
KITTENLICIOUS
WORMY RIPPLE
DOGGIE CHOC
CRUNCHY CRUSHED COCKROACH
SNAPPED-FLY SUPREME
AND, OF COURSE, ON SPECIAL ALWAYS:
THE BEST ICE CREAM IN THE UNIVERSES!
ALSO: MAGGOT SMOOTHIES, DRIED-FLEA SCONES,
BUMBURGERS, SNAIL AND SALAD SANDWICHES

ALL FRESHLY MADE!

1

A Stuffed Poodle Christmas

It was a frosty Christmas Eve in Sleepy Whiskers. Even the tiny flying pigs wore little red and green jumpers. Icicles hung like daggers from every branch, and the wind smelt of cold bones mixed with warm Christmas pudding.

For Boojum Bark, one of the best things about being a werewolf at Christmas was that you got to eat a wolf-type Christmas dinner of stuffed poodle and squashed-fly pudding, then the grown-ups Changed into human form and everyone ate a second dinner with plum pudding and mince pies.

Yum, thought Boo, drooling slightly as he bounded over a snowdrift. Mum made the best stuffed poodle in Sleepy Whiskers, as well as her famous ice cream. Only one more delivery today, then back home to the Best Icecream Shop in the Universes to have a (shudder) … *bath*. Then help Mum stuff the poodle for Christmas dinner!

Where do pigs get their jumpers from? Boo wondered. The tiny pig tried to land on his nose again. He batted it away from his nose with his paw. 'Woof! Go and stick your snout into a flower, you silly pig!'

'Oink,' said the pig reproachfully. It fluttered off, its little wings poking out of its jumper.

Boo lifted his leg on old Ms Shaggy's gate post, watched the yellow drops trickle down into the snow, then trotted up to her front door and pressed his nose against the woofer.

'Woof, woof, woof, woof, woof!' The woofer's noise jangled down the hallway.

'Coming!' Boo listened to the shuffle of Ms Shaggy's slippers flapping down the hall. She must be

in human form again, he decided. All werewolves started out as puppies, then as they grew older learnt how to Change to human shape whenever they wanted to.

Huh, thought Boo, hopping from one paw to another so they didn't freeze on the cold path. *If* they wanted to! Human shape was boring!

Ms Shaggy peered down at Boo. She wore long trousers and a cardigan, to cover up the bits that a werewolf's fur kept warm and hidden.

'Oh, it's little Boojum Bark. Woof! How sweet of you to deliver my ice cream! It wouldn't be Christmas without the Best Ice Cream in the Universes.'

Boo tried not to growl. Cat guts! Sweet?! If one more person called him sweet he'd bite them. It wasn't his fault he had a curly tail! He had the sharpest fangs in Sleepy Whiskers!

But he wouldn't bite old Ms Shaggy. He wouldn't even lift his leg on her doorstep. Ms Shaggy was nice.

'Woof!' said Boo politely instead. 'One carton of the Best Ice Cream in the Universes, Ms Shaggy, and four frozen Rat Surprises. Mum said it was too icy for you to come this afternoon,' he added. 'You might slip. Especially on only two feet.'

Ms Shaggy beamed as she held the carton of ice cream. 'My great-nephews just love your frozen Rat Surprises. Especially with chocolate-coated beetles on top. I don't know how your mother manages to make such delicious ice cream! It's magic!'

Boo grinned. 'Thanks, Ms Shaggy. I'll tell Mum.'

Ms Shaggy bent down and scratched his ears. Boo endured it.

'Have a lovely Christmas, Boo dear.' She handed him the money, then a small parcel wrapped in red paper, with a ribbon tied round it so he could carry it in his jaws. 'Just a little Christmas gift,' she added. 'It's a nice smelly chicken neck.'

Boo's tail wagged against the doorpost. Ms Shaggy's chicken necks were nearly as good as Mum's ice cream!

The Bark family had been ice-cream makers forever. Great-great-Grandma Bark had come up with the famous Rat Surprises, and Grandad Bark had thought of Kittenlicious and Choc-coated Maggots. But it was Mum who had invented the recipe for the Best Ice Cream in the Universes, when she took over the shop after his grandparents and dad died, when Boo was a tiny puppy. No one was really sure what the Best Ice Cream in the Universes tasted like — every mouthful was different. But they *did* know that they adored it.

And only she and Boo knew the recipe. Boo grinned, sending a little dribble of drool around the package of chicken neck. One day he'd come up with an even better recipe! They'd have to call it Better than the Best Ice Cream!

Suddenly he pricked up his ears. 'Grrr! Can you hear something, Ms Shaggy?'

Ms Shaggy shook her head.

Of course not, thought Boo. Ms Shaggy was in human form. Humans couldn't hear as well as wolves!

5

'It's a sort of … grinding noise.' He could feel it, too, he realised: a faint throbbing under his paws.

It felt a bit like the way the ground vibrated when a tortoise train brought supplies in from the outlands. But even the biggest tortoise train in Sleepy Whiskers didn't make the ground vibrate like that.

Boo shivered. Whatever it was, it was time he went home.

'Woofy Christmas, Ms Shaggy,' he said politely. He turned away to pad down the icy path.

'Tell your mum Woofy Christmas too!' called Ms Shaggy.

But Boo hardly heard her. The strange noise was even louder now. It felt … *wrong*, he decided. He didn't even feel like lifting his leg on the gate post again. But he did. Wolves *always* lifted their leg on every gate post, even if they only left a couple of drops. A wolf had to do what a wolf had to do.

Boo trotted down the road towards the ice-cream shop. It was growing darker now. Brightly lit windows showed glimpses of families enjoying themselves: dads lifting their legs against Christmas trees and puppies chewing their parcels, trying to work out what was inside.

Boo shivered again. He wanted to get home fast, to the shop and his basket by the fire. Maybe Mum would whip up a frog and milk for them both …

He broke into a run.

'Woof, young pup! What's the hurry? Can't wait for Christmas?'

Boo skidded to a halt. Mr Bigpaws was the Mayor of Sleepy Whiskers. His wife trotted beside him with their pups, each dressed in long doggie socks and a little red coat. One of them grinned at him. It was Spot. Spot's nose was already scarred in a most interesting manner, and one ear was ragged, where her brothers had chewed on it, too. No one would ever call Spot cute, thought Boo enviously.

'Woof,' answered Boo politely as Mr Bigpaws sniffed Boo's bum — it was just plain good wolf manners to sniff another wolf's bum — then paused to scratch his ear with his back paw. Boo gave his ear a quick scratch too. That was the trouble with fleas — as soon as you saw someone scratching you just *had* to scratch too, even if you'd just had a … a … (bleugh!) *bath* and half a tin of flea powder or could feel a weird vibration with your paws …

Mr Bigpaws looked at him curiously. 'Everything's all right, isn't it?' he asked.

'Of course, Mr Bigpaws,' said Boo automatically, trying to speak clearly over the chicken-neck package in his mouth. He hoped Mr Bigpaws hadn't learnt too much from sniffing his bum, like how he'd forgotten to tidy up the bones under his bed even though Mum had told him to, and how he'd fallen over every time he Changed at Two-Leg class last week. That was the trouble with bum-sniffing — it was hard to hide *anything* from a wolf who'd sniffed your bum.

Mr Bigpaws frowned. 'You smell worried, Boo.'

'Well …' Boo hesitated. 'I can hear something.'

Spot giggled. 'So can I. Someone's howling Christmas carols.'

'No, I mean something strange. Something I've never heard or felt before.' Boo frowned. 'I can smell something too. Like ... like popcorn.'

Mr Bigpaws pricked up his ears. He stood still for a moment, his nostrils wide, his paws feeling the ground, and then he nodded. 'You know, I think I know what you mean. But I've never smelt a popcorn scent quite like that! It feels like something is digging, too ... Something enormous ...'

'But that's impossible!' said Mrs Bigpaws. 'Who'd be digging on Christmas Eve?'

Suddenly the hackles rose on Mr Bigpaws's neck. 'Right, you pups. Home!' he barked. 'Now!'

'But, Dad —' began Spot.

'Go!'

Spot began to run, her tail between her legs. The other pups ran after her. Mr Bigpaws turned to Boo. 'You'd better go with them.'

'But why —' began Boo.

'Because those vibrations are coming from the ice-cream shop,' growled Mr Bigpaws quietly.

'What?! Then I'm coming too! Mum's in there!'

'This is no business for puppies,' growled Mrs Bigpaws. 'Sit, boy! Sit!'

Boo sat automatically. 'Maybe the ice-cream mixer has gone bung,' he suggested hopefully. 'Or maybe ...'

Suddenly the vibrations stopped. The digging sounds stopped as well. Boo felt the breath seep back into his body. It was going to be all right!

But both the Bigpaws had already begun to creep up the icy path to the shop. Boo padded after them, catching up just as Mr Bigpaws pushed the door open with his nose.

'Woof?' enquired Mr Bigpaws softly as he stepped into the shop. Mrs Bigpaws followed him.

The hairs lifted on the back of Boo's neck. He could smell strawberries too. Like strawberry jam! He raced up the steps after the Bigpaws.

The shop was empty.

'Mum?' he yelled. 'Mum, where are you? Mr Bigpaws? What's happening?'

He glanced around. Everything looked all right — the wooden counter, low enough for wolves to get their noses over, the big display freezers, empty of Rat Surprises after all the Christmas deliveries. 'Mum?' he called again.

No one answered. Boo gulped. 'Mr Bigpaws? Mrs Bigpaws? Woof? Woof woof?'

Silence.

The popcorn scent was so thick he could almost see it.

Boo padded across the shop and poked his nose around the door into the kitchen. And then he stopped.

There was Mr Bigpaws, strangely still. Mrs Bigpaws stood like a statue beside him. There was Mum, her paws stuck to the paddle she used for stirring the ice cream, her eyes desperate and

pleading. Their coats glistened weirdly in the lantern light. Why don't they move? wondered Boo.

The stink of popcorn and strawberry jam filled the room.

'Mum?' he whispered again.

There was the big kitchen table. There was the big wooden ice-cream vat, still half full of the last batch of the Best Ice Cream in the Universes. And there was …

Woof woof woof,
Woof woof woof,
Woof woof woof woof woof

SLEEPY WHISKERS BOOK
OF CHRISTMAS CAROLS

2

The Revenge of the Greedle

Boo felt his breath leave his body. The creature by the vats was like nothing he had ever seen before!

It was short. Its body was mostly mouth with teeth like needles; a black gaping hole waiting to be filled. Its belly sagged between stumpy frog-like legs. Its skin was red and shiny, and even though it had no fur it wore no clothes at all.

Tiny eyes stared at him with intelligence and cunning. 'Ah, the young ice-cream maker!' Its voice was sugary, like it had eaten a dozen cream buns and a box of fudge. 'Good afternoon! I am the Greedle.' The creature bowed.

The butcher, the baker,
The nice popcorn shaker.
None is as sweet
As a good ice-cream maker!
Go on, my Zurm! Get him!'

'No!' screamed Boo.

But it was too late. Something slithered across his back. Something big and slimy, oozing coldness wherever it touched his skin and fur.

The coldness smelt like strawberry jam.

He couldn't move. He couldn't even twitch his nose. His paws were glued to the floor. He struggled, just as the thing slithered in front of him.

It looked like a gigantic worm, long and much too white, with a blunt head and an ooze of strawberry-smelling slime weeping from its tail. That's what had glued him up, Boo realised desperately, as the giant worm's vacant eyes stared down at him. He tried to move his paws, his mouth, even a whisker.

The needle-fanged thing laughed. Its teeth were pearl coloured inside the blood-red mouth. It sounded genuinely amused.

The little puppy cannot move?

Ah, dear Zurm, I do approve.

Now pick him up and —

Its shiny red forehead creased into a frown. 'It can be hard to find a rhyme under pressure. *Remove* rhymes, but how do I fit it in? *So* pick him up and *now* remove? And we are going to remove you, you know.'

The horrible creature turned to the giant worm.

Now off you go, my darling Zurm,

And spread your glue, so cold and firm.

And when it coats this silly town,

They'll rue the greed that's my renown.

'Not one of my best poems,' the Greedle admitted.

14

But I have a tiny worry,
And I'm really in a hurry.

I can't risk anyone escaping and alerting a Hero.

'Glurk glurk gluuuuuurk …' breathed the Zurm obediently. Its voice was slimy too.

'No!' Boo'd meant it to be a growl. But it was just a croak, the only sound his strawberry-jammed-up jaws could make.

The Greedle looked at him in surprise.

So the little puppy can still speak
Even though it's just a squeak.
That's very good! But it's no use.
You really should —

The Greedle frowned again. 'It's just so *hard* making superb poetry on an expedition like this. Mostly, you know, I leave all this killing-whole-villages stuff to my bogeys. Which leaves me free for all the *good* things in life: poetry and perfume — my favourite is popcorn, such a lovely scent, don't you think? And food. Lovely, lovely food. But this little expedition is … special.' The monster grinned at him. Its fangs glinted. A drop of drool trickled down its tummy.

Revenge you see is very sweet,
Just like something yum to eat
For years ago, when I was small,
I crept up to an ice-cream stall.
Ah, small puppy, what delight,
I fell in love there at first sight,
All that ice cream, creamy white.
All I wanted was one bite …
And I was really so polite …
The fanged face lost it's grin.
But I had no coins with me

So you see I had to be
All alone and so hungry …

'It was ice cream that started it all,' hissed the creature. 'Ice cream that first made me *so* hungry! Determined that every good thing to eat in the universe would be mine! Mine! The revenge of the Greedle.'

I'm going to die, thought Boo. The Greedle's tiny eyes crinkled as it smiled. It was a smile that could freeze a universe.

'No, little puppykins.' The Greedle almost sounded friendly. 'You're not going to die. Not here. Not now. Everyone else in this silly little town will die, though, as soon as my Zurm oozes out and strawberry-jams them up — forever.

Their thirst will grow
All nice and slow.
And then they'll freeze,
Amid the snow.

A perfect Christmas present. Well perfect for me, anyway. Maybe not quite so perfect for them.'

'What do you want? What have you done to us?' Boo's squeak sounded like fingernails scraping on a blackboard.

'Guess,' said the Greedle gleefully. 'What's the one thing this silly little town has got that might interest the most powerful creature in the universes, hmmm? The statue of the World's Biggest Bone at the town hall? I don't think so. A nice puppy collar?' The

Greedle's eyes grew soft and dreamy. 'No, there's only one thing worth having in this place. One thing worth crossing the universes for.' It wrapped its tiny hands around the ice cream vat and began to drool.

'Ice cream?!' squeaked Boo. 'You just want some ice cream?'

'Not *some* ice cream!' cried the Greedle. '*The* ice cream. The Best Ice Cream in the Universes.

The Greedle's tiny steely eyes grew soft once more as they gazed down at the creamy mixture. 'When you are the most powerful creature in the universes you deserve the best! The best food in the universes!'

The Greedle's drool dripped onto the floor. 'The best pizzas, oooh yummmmm, with lots of bubbling cheese and a thick fat crust! The best potato chips, so crisp people can hear them crackle from the next universe when I bite into them. And *now* I have the best ice cream—and the ice-cream maker too! Mine *forever*!' The Greedle's smile grew wider again.

Only one thing can stop my scheme,
My ice cream ever after dream.
Only a dashing true Hero,
Can turn my plans into zero.
And so you see I really must,
Turn all bystanders into dust,
So no Hero will ever know,
What took place here among the snow …
'Hurry!' it hissed at the Zurm.
The sooner you strawberry-jam
The sooner you and I can scram!

18

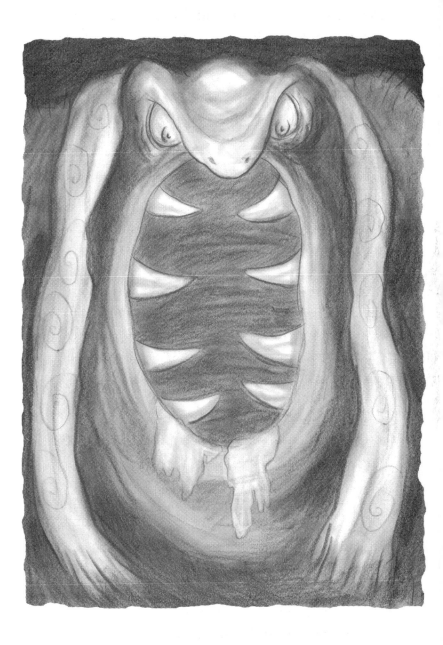

'Gluuurrrk!' The giant Zurm began to ooze out the door.

'No!' croaked Boo again. He had to do something!

But what? He couldn't use his jaws to bite. He couldn't even give a proper howl to call for help or warn everyone to get away.

He glanced over at Mum. But she was as unmoving as the Bigpaws. Only her big brown eyes gazed at him helplessly.

We need a Hero! he thought. That's how you got a Hero when things went bad — you put out a howl for a Hero!

But there were no Heroes in the ice-cream shop. There was no Hero in all of Sleepy Whiskers.

Except for you, said a whisper in Boo's mind. *YOU have to save the town now.*

But I can't, thought Boo. I'm not a Hero! He looked frantically at Mum. Mum could deal with everything! Curdled ice cream, rat fights in the larder.

But even Mum couldn't help them now.

Move, said the whisper in his mind. *YOU help them, Boo. MOVE.*

Behind him he could hear a long soft sluuuushhh as the Zurm oozed down the stairs. A vision of what would happen hovered in front of him ... Spot, glued to the floor, her Frisbee in her mouth, her eyes wide and desperate as she slowly starved. Old Ms Shaggy, strawberry-jammed solid as she spooned out ice cream for her nephews ...

The ice cream, thought Boo frantically. The Greedle wants our ice cream!

And suddenly he knew what he could do.

Try Fido's for all your Christmas needs!
Tiny bones and pigs' ears for the
Christmas tree, boiled poodle puddings
and doggie chocs a speciality.
Try our pre-chewed slippers too! You'll be
grr-grr-grr-grrrrinning!
At Fido's!

* * *

FROM THE SLEEPY WHISKERS GAZETTE

3

An Unexpected Hero

His jaws were too gummed up to move more than a whisker. His paws were stuck to the floor. Even his tail was glued solid.

But one thing could still move.

Maybe.

'Stop.' Boo tried to make the word sound as bold as he could. But he still sounded like a squeaky puppy toy.

The Greedle glanced back at him. Its tiny arms held the vat of ice cream lovingly. 'Stop?' it enquired. 'Now you know, you can't just say "stop". The correct thing to say is "Stop, or I'll" ...' It giggled. One small hand stroked the ice-cream vat.

But you see it's really true,
There is nothing *you can do.*

'Yes there is,' croaked Boo. 'Call off your worm! Just take the ice cream and go away. Or else I'll ...'

'Or else you'll what?' smiled the Greedle.

'This!' squeaked Boo, hoping desperately that he

could manage what he planned to do. He couldn't lift his leg more than a few centimetres. But maybe ... maybe ...

Boo took aim.

Yes, he could!

'Nooooooo!' It was impossible that so small a creature could groan so loudly. The Greedle stared at the yellow drop slowly melting a hole in the ice cream. 'The Best Ice Cream in the Universes!' it shrieked. 'You've polluted it!'

'And there's more where that came from!'

Boo hoped desperately that he was right. That drop had taken all his strength. If only he hadn't widdled on Ms Shaggy's gatepost he might have had more pressure! But it was too late for regrets now.

The Greedle stared at him in horror. Mum and the Bigpaws gazed at him too, with growing hope in their eyes.

'Call back your Zurm or I'll squirt the biggest puddle you ever saw! It'll be Frozen Widdle Ice Cream! You don't want to eat Widdle Ice Cream, do you?'

The Greedle's tiny eyes were bright and unwinking. 'Oh, I have no time for puppy foolishness!' it screeched. 'Do you know how many creatures I control, you silly little dog? Have you any idea of my true power? Obviously not. Without that ice cream, my Christmas dinner will be *ruined*, you little *brat*! There isn't time to make another batch.'

The Greedle grimaced wildly, its face falling into bulges. 'It looks like I'll have to leave Sleepy Whiskers without destroying it. But don't think *you're* off scott free, nasty puppy! Zurm!' The sudden yell echoed through the building.

'Glurk sqlurk?' The long slurring voice sounded as though it came from the other side of the street.

'Return!'

'Glurk!!'

The slithering sound grew louder once again. The smell of strawberry jam grew stronger. Boo heard the Zurm ooze across the icy road, then up the steps, through the shop and into the kitchen.

Boo tried not to shiver at the sight of it.

'Good Zurm,' said the Greedle gently. 'Roaches!' it added, in a sudden yell. 'Come here now!'

'Pick pick pick pick pick!' Something chattered in the tiniest voice Boo had ever heard. He stared in horror as a hundred little cockroaches scuttled into the kitchen.

'Take the ice cream,' ordered the Greedle.

The leader of the Roaches gazed up at the Greedle adoringly. 'Pick pick pick pick pick

pick pick pick??!' it chirruped.

The Greedle smiled. 'Very well,' it said indulgently. 'Just one little bite of wolf. Because it's Christmas.

Just one taste,
Of werewolf paste,
Then we'll make haste …

'*Aaaahhh!*' screamed Boo — it was as much of a scream as his glued-up jaws could make — as dozens of tiny fangs pierced his ankle. 'Stop it! Leave me alone! Leave us all alone! Or I'll widdle again!'

'Enough!' cried the Greedle sharply. 'Off with you, Roaches! And take my precious ice cream with you!'

Boo watched helplessly as the Roaches pulled their fangs out of his flesh. Half of them scuttled to the ice-cream vat. They surrounded it, lifting together. The vat slid out the hallway door, and vanished down the corridor.

The Greedle waited till the vat had vanished, then nodded to the rest of the Roaches. 'Now take the ice-cream maker. Carefully! We don't want to bruise her.'

'What! You can't take Mum!' Boo gazed in despair as the remaining Roaches surrounded his mum, and began to carry her down the hallway.

'Mum!' cried Boo. '*Mum!*'

But there was no answer.

The Greedle laughed. It was a happy sound. You would almost think it was the laughter of a whole happy family around the Christmas table — if you couldn't see the malice in the Greedle's small eyes, or the dripping hunger of its mouth. 'You can't even widdle in the ice cream now. I've got it safe. And the ice-cream maker too!'

Now there's nothing you can do!
I've got the ice cream, and Mum too!
Revenge can only be complete,
When only I have things to eat!

'I was going to take you as well,' the Greedle added conversationally. 'But I think, oh yes, I really *do* think you are just too much trouble. The Best Ice Cream in the Universes at last! And all for me. Only me! Forever!'

'Mum'll never make ice cream for you!' yelled Boo.

'No? Well, we shall see. At least I have one oh-so-delicious vat of the Best Ice Cream in the Universes to eat while I *persuade* her. Oh, that will be so much fun! I do like … persuading … people. Now, is there anything else?' The Greedle paused, as if it was thinking.

Ah yes, there is just one thing more.
Before I head out of your door …

'What?' panted Boo.

'Woofy Christmas, little puppy!' And the Greedle was gone.

Young pups should always remember that it is very bad manners indeed to widdle indoors uninvited, or where a Top Dog has already been. It's almost as bad as doing THAT on a rug.

DAME KARA VAN'S GUIDE TO WEREWOLF WIDDLE ETIQUETTE

4

Saved by Rat Surprise

Spot arrived half an hour later, scampering up the stairs and sticking her nose around the door of the shop.

Half an hour of standing, glued to the floor, desperate and terrified.

Where had the Greedle taken Mum? How long was he going to have to stand like this? Would the strawberry jam ever dissolve, or would he and the Bigpaws stay like this forever?

'Boo?' whispered Spot. Suddenly she howled. 'Mummy! Dad!'

She ran towards them, nudging them with her nose, then turned to Boo. 'What's wrong with you! Why can't you move?' she cried.

'We've been strawberry-jammed,' Boo whispered frantically. 'There's no time to explain now! Spot, hurry! You have to find a way to dissolve the jam.'

Spot looked bewildered. 'But how?'

'Try water,' said Boo desperately. 'There are

buckets under the sink. Hurry, Spot!'

Spot nodded. She pushed open the cupboard door, grabbed the bucket handle in her mouth, stood up on her hind legs then nudged the tap on. She picked the bucket up in her mouth again, then stopped.

Boo tried to control his impatience. 'You can't throw it in wolf form! You'll have to Change.'

Spot nodded. 'Shut your eyes!'

'This is no time to be modest —' Boo began, then shut his eyes hurriedly. 'They're shut! Now hurry!' At least Spot was good at Changing, he thought thankfully. She was the best Changer in the class. Not like him.

There was a muffled sound from across the room. Then Spot's voice said, 'You can open your eyes now!'

She was wearing one of Mum's aprons to cover her embarrassing bits, Boo realised. Spot lifted the bucket and …

'Urrrrkkk!'

The water was cold, and wet, almost as bad as a (yeurgh!) *bath*. And it wasn't going to work, thought Boo dismally, trying to lift his front paw. Of course something as simple as water wouldn't dissolve the strawberry jam. Maybe nothing would ever dissolve it! Maybe he and the Bigpaws were stuck like this forever and …

He tried to think. He HAD to think! What made jam come unstuck?

And then he had it!

'Essence of rat!' he whispered hoarsely. 'The big jar in the cupboard!'

Mum made essence of rat by salting the fresh rats and leaving them till they melted into lovely stinky juice. It made the frozen Rat Surprises extra surprising. But essence of rat also dissolved everything if you used too much — even the mixing bowl.

'Only one tablespoon to a bucket of water!' he added hastily.

Spot nodded. Boo watched her measure out the essence into another bucket of water. The familiar stench filled the room. It made him think of Mum, carefully adding a single drop to the Surprise mixture. Mum …

'Are you sure you want to try this?' asked Spot nervously, as the bucket began to bubble and turn purple.

'Yes!'

Spot threw the water over him.

It wasn't so bad this time. He was already wet, already cold. And suddenly …

One toe wriggled. His paw lifted off the ground, and then another …

'Free your parents!' shouted Boo. He raced down the hallway and out the back door. Where had the Greedle gone with Mum? He was sure he could run faster than that flabby creature — even faster than the Zurm or the Roaches. He lifted his nose and sniffed. He was the best tracker in class, everybody said so!

But there was nothing. No strange scent at all, except a lingering smell of popcorn and strawberry jam from the shop.

They have to have left a scent trail! thought Boo frantically. He put his nose to the icy ground and sniffed all over. A faint scent of flying-pig droppings, an even fainter scent of flowers under the snow, waiting to come to life. Up in the empty sky the stars twinkled like hundreds and thousands on an ice-cream cone.

But there was no scent of the Greedle. No scent of Zurm, or strawberry jam either. No vampire cockroaches.

There was no scent or sign of Mum at all.

It was impossible, thought Boo. Everything left some scent trail behind! And he knew his mum's smell as well as he did the scent of his own bum! Suddenly he remembered that horrid, gentle voice. 'The most powerful creature in the universes', the Greedle had said.

Maybe the most powerful creature in the universes could vanish! It had come out of nowhere. Maybe it had disappeared there too!

It was impossible, he thought. Things like that didn't just happen.

But then horrors didn't suddenly appear in ice-cream shops either, and carry away your mum.

If only he hadn't been so stupid! If only he'd kept threatening to widdle in the ice cream until the Greedle freed Mum and the Bigpaws. He was dumb! Dumb! Dumb! Just a cute little puppy, like the Greedle had said! Useless!

He'd never see Mum again.

Boo sat on the icy ground. He lifted up his nose, and howled.

Guinea Pig Delight

Ingredients:

1 guinea pig

Snip off whiskers. Serve hot or cold with salad.

From The Sleepy Whiskers Preschool Cookbook

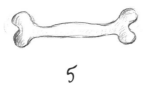

5

The Werewolf General

'Boo?'

Boo turned. It was Mr Bigpaws. The big wolf looked dazed. His wet fur clung to his body. He shivered in the cold night air.

'I … I'm sorry —' Boo began.

'It's not your fault,' said Mr Bigpaws hoarsely.

'But it is! That thing was after our ice cream! If Mum and I hadn't made the Best Ice Cream in the Universes the Greedle would never have come here.'

'Boo, that thing was evil! No one else is responsible for what evil things do to other people. Besides, you saved us all! We'd all have died, glued up, frozen and starving, without you.'

Boo choked back a sob. 'I tried to smell where it's taken Mum. But they've just gone! Vanished!'

'We'll do everything we can to track them down,' promised Mr Bigpaws. 'Every wolf in Sleepy Whiskers will be out sniffing the ground tonight.

We're putting out a Howl too. A Hero should be here soon to take charge of everything. The Hero will know what to do.' The big wolf hesitated. 'But, Boo — I've heard of evil creatures like that before. The rumours say they don't come like normal people, on paws or feet or tortoise trains. They say they can travel between the universes ...'

'The Greedle said it was the most powerful creature in the universes,' whispered Boo. 'I ... I didn't even think other universes really existed!'

Mr Bigpaws nodded. 'I'm sorry, Boo. We may never find your mother. Don't give up yet,' he added hurriedly. 'Maybe the Hero will know some way to find your mum, even if she's been taken to another universe.' Even as the Mayor spoke Boo heard the Howl go out from the hill behind the town, a cry from werewolf to werewolf that would travel across the world.

Suddenly Boo couldn't handle any more. He crouched down and put his paws over his nose. 'I failed. I failed Mum ...' His voice died away.

'You didn't fail,' said Mr Bigpaws. Boo peered up through his paws. There were tears on the big wolf's face. 'I've never seen anyone as brave as you, Boo. You saved us all.'

Boo shook his head. He couldn't speak.

'Come on, Boojum, boy,' said Mr Bigpaws gently. 'You can't stay here.'

'Yes I can!'

'All right, you can. I think you can handle

anything, Boo.' Boo was shocked to hear genuine admiration in the Mayor's voice. 'But you shouldn't *have* to stay here. Werewolves stick together. Please, Boo. Come home with us.'

Boo whined. But what choice did he have? He was too tired to think. Too cold, too scared to even try to think. Boo got to his feet and limped after Mr Bigpaws.

⋇ ⋇ ⋇

The Bigpaws' house smelt of chewed bones and old rugs and puppies who weren't quite house-trained. One side looked out onto the park, with the creek running through it and trees to lift your leg on and a wide flat oval to play Chase the Stick and Catch the Rat. The other side looked out onto the marketplace, with its Hot Rat stalls and the shops selling new collars or human pants or dresses. You could even see the Best Ice-Cream Shop in the Universes from here. Boo didn't look that way often. It hurt too much.

There had been no sign of Mum since Christmas Eve, two days ago. No smell of her either.

It had been a strange Christmas, watching everyone being happy. The Bigpaws had been as tactful as they could. But how could there be a proper Christmas without Mum? Without the smell of ice cream, and the rats hanging up to dry before they were turned into Surprises?

But everyone was kind. Too kind, thought Boo, as he lay with his nose tucked into his bum on the big squashy sofa in the living room. He wished they'd

yell at him, say the words that echoed in his head.

Why didn't you *think*, Boo? Demand that the Greedle free them all before it took the ice cream? Then Mum would be safe, and he'd be back home, and everything would be as it always had been, as it should be, warm and happy.

'Boo?' Mrs Bigpaws came into the room. 'Someone to see you.'

Boo lifted his head off his paws as old Ms Shaggy trotted in behind her. She was in werewolf form today. Her fur was as grey as her human hair.

'How are you, Boo?' Ms Shaggy dropped the package she was carrying and gave him a quick nuzzle.

Boo wrinkled his nose. 'All right.'

'We're all so proud of you. I brought you a chicken neck. I know how much you like my chicken necks.'

'Thank you, Ms Shaggy.'

'It's been rotting in the garden for a whole week,' added Ms Shaggy, a bit desperately. 'I dug it up specially for you.'

'Thank you, Ms Shaggy,' said Boo again. He should feel something, he thought. But everything inside him was empty, as though the Greedle had taken all his warmth.

'You know, we all care a lot about you, Boo,' said Ms Shaggy. 'And your mother, too. If there is ever anything I can do to help, anything at all, just give me a howl.'

'Thank you, Ms Shaggy,' Boo repeated.

Ms Shaggy hesitated, as though she'd like to say more. But what was there to say?

Boo watched her pad out of the room. His head drooped onto his paws again. He should be doing something, he knew. Hunting for the scent again. Searching for clues. But it was as though the Greedle had frozen half his life.

How could things change so quickly? If only he could shut his eyes and then when he opened them again be back in the ice-cream shop. The vat would be churning a new batch of Crunchy Cockroach Supreme and …

'Boo? You have another visitor.'

Boo looked up. A big silver-haired werewolf stood next to Mr Bigpaws. One of the visitor's eyes was covered with a patch, but the other was the most piercing blue that Boo had ever seen. The stranger was carrying a rolled-up poster in his mouth. As Boo watched he dropped it by the sofa, then limped into the room after Mr Bigpaws, tactfully not widdling his mark on the doorpost, even though he was obviously a very Top Dog indeed.

There was something strange about this werewolf's legs, thought Boo. Then he realised. One leg was made of wood, with hinges at the paw and knee.

Clink, clunk went the wooden paw on the floor.

'Boojum Bark?' enquired the newcomer.

Boo stood up. Something about this visitor made you want to stand up straight.

'Woof!' he said politely.

The newcomer stared down his long silver-grey nose at him. 'Woof,' he said at last. 'So this is Boojum Bark.'

'Yes, sir,' said Mr Bigpaws. 'Boo, you remember we sent out a Howl for a Hero?'

Boo nodded.

'Well here he is! This is the Werewolf General! The great Silver Fang himself!' There was awe in the Mayor's voice.

'Sir!' Boo stood even straighter and tried to straighten his tail to attention too. 'I … I thought Silver Fang was just a character in a story!' he blurted out.

The Werewolf General smiled, showing long yellow fangs. 'The stories they tell about me are true', he said. 'Mostly, anyhow.'

A Hero, thought Boo. A real live Hero in the Bigpaws' living room! 'I've never met a Hero before.'

'A retired Hero,' growled the Werewolf General. He tapped his wooden leg on the floor. 'I don't do much Heroing these days. Seem to spend most of my time arguing on committees. But this case brought me out of retirement. The Interuniversal Council of Heroes asked me to come and see you. It's a nice place you have here,' he added to Mr Bigpaws.

Boo looked round at the puppy-chewed sofa, the paw prints on the window where Spot had chased a fly last night, the bone half-hidden under the mat.

The Werewolf General's grey whiskers twitched as

he smiled. 'It's a home,' he said simply. 'That's one thing that Heroes don't get time for, mostly. Homes.' The big wolf's muzzle was scarred and his ears were a bit tattered too. But he was still the biggest, strongest-looking werewolf Boo had ever seen.

'Sit down, Boojum. Or do you prefer Boo?' said the Werewolf General, sitting on his haunches himself. 'Oh, thank you,' he said to Mr Bigpaws, as Spot padded in and offered him a bowl of water with a bit of Mrs Bigpaws's freshly squeezed frog juice.

'Boo,' replied Boo politely.

'I'll leave you two to talk,' said Mr Bigpaws tactfully. He shepherded Spot from the room. The Werewolf General lapped for a second, then looked up at Boo again, his long tongue dripping. 'Well, young pup,' he said. 'I have to congratulate you.'

'Me?' said Boo. 'But ... but, sir, it was all my fault! If I'd just thought a bit more quickly ...' He stopped, his throat choked up again.

'Boo.' The Werewolf General's voice was gentler now. 'What you did was amazing. Not one werewolf in a million could have come up with a plan like that. Mr Bigpaws didn't, did he?'

Boo shook his head. 'No, sir.'

'And he's the Mayor — and with a lot more experience than you! Even Mrs Bigpaws didn't find a way to get free — and a mother wolf can be the most ferocious creature in the universes when her pups are threatened. You're a Hero, Boo.'

'Me?' squeaked Boo.

The Werewolf General looked at him seriously. 'Yes, you. Perhaps you're even a real Hero. Not someone who just does something heroic once. But someone who is a deep-down Hero. You have the potential to be a professional Hero, boy. You never suspected it?'

Boo shook his head numbly. Him? A Hero? Impossible! Heroes were ... strong. And brave. He wasn't either of those. He was cute! He had a curly tail! The only things he was good at were leaving droppings and making ice cream. And smelling very accurately. Heroes had names like Mighty Claws or Sparkle Fang. Not Boojum Bark.

The Werewolf General sat back and scratched a flea. 'You saved the town. Without you the Greedle would have had the whole town frozen. In years to come, people would have found the crumbled ruins of Sleepy Whiskers and wondered who must have lived here. Everything would have been gone.'

'Sir,' said Boo. 'Who ... I mean what is the Greedle? Do you know how it got here? Do you ...' He gulped. 'Do you know where my mum might be?'

The Werewolf General scratched another itch near his ear. 'Are you sure you want to know, Boo?'

'Of course!'

The Werewolf General smiled, showing his long fangs. 'Most people don't, you know. Most people want to think the universes are nice safe places always, that tomorrow will always be like today. Do you want to know what's really Out There, young Boo?'

Boo gulped. 'Yes.'

'Then I'll tell you,' said the Werewolf General.

(Disgusting!) Baths

Hard as it is for many wolves to accept, a (dreadful!) bath once a week can really add to the lustrousness of your coat. It's even better than a good roll in a cow pat.
I know you'll get the creeps just thinking about it, young pups. But a regular (imagine!) bath can be worth it.

FROM LADY WAGGIE SPLUNKETT'S ADVICE
TO YOUNG WEREWOLVES

6

Wormholes through Universes

'How much do you know about Heroes, Boo?' asked the Werewolf General, settling down onto the Bigpaws' mat and scratching his ear with his hind leg.

'Not much,' admitted Boo, sitting on his haunches next to him. 'Mum read me a book about you, though,' he added shyly.

'I see,' said the Werewolf General. 'Well then. Do you know what a bogey is?'

'Someone who picks his nose a lot?'

'No. A bogey is a creature from the Ghastly Otherwhen. The Ghastly Otherwhen is another universe. The Greedle rules the Ghastly Otherwhen. It has the ability to tame other creatures, like the Zurms and the Roaches, and make them do its bidding. Bogeys invade other universes to find things for the Greedle. Food mostly.'

'Woooof!' said Boo slowly. Boo had hardly considered other towns, much less other universes.

The Werewolf General grinned. His fangs really did sparkle, even in the winter light from the window. 'Why do you think your shop was called the best one in the *universes*?'

'I never really thought about it,' said Boo.

'Most universes are okay, though different from ours. In some of them people don't turn into wolves at all. They just stay in human form.'

'Weird,' said Boo.

'There's a Phaery World, too, where no one grows more than thirty centimetres high and everyone has wings.'

'Like butterflies?' asked Boo. He and the other pups in the gang sometimes played a game of lying very still and snapping butterflies when they tried to land on their noses.

The Werewolf General seemed to read his thoughts. 'If you try snapping a phaery you'll regret it.' He grinned. 'I used to snap butterflies too when I was a pup. No, most of the other universes are pretty much like ours. But the Ghastly Otherwhen is … different.

'Everything from the Ghastly Otherwhen is bad. Or we think so. We don't know really what it's like. No one has ever managed to go there — or come back to tell us about it if they have. But if the Greedle controls it — well, it must be bad.'

'But how did the Greedle get *here*?' demanded Boo. You can't just get a tortoise train from another universe, he thought.

'The Zurms dig wormholes between the universes. In fact, all the connections between universes are because of the Greedle's Zurms. We'd never even have known about each other if not for them.'

Boo stared. 'Wormholes?' Wormy Ripple was the fourth most popular flavour in the ice-cream shop.

'Most worms chew through dirt. The Zurms chew holes through the fabric of reality and …' The Werewolf General saw Boo's blank look. He stood up, shoving his wooden leg a bit awkwardly till it was in line with his other three. 'Come on,' he said. 'I'll show you.'

'Show me a wormhole? Where?'

The Werewolf General's fangs glinted as he grinned. 'Guess.'

⋇ ⋇ ⋇

Pad, pad, clink, clunk. Pad, pad, clink, clunk. The Werewolf General limped his way up the street to the Best Ice-Cream Shop in the Universes.

The snow had melted into puddles now. Pups chased balls of Christmas wrapping paper along the footpath. The Werewolf General stood back to let a tortoise train pass, then climbed the steps up to the shop and pushed open the door with his nose. He sniffed deeply, then lifted his leg.

He glanced at Boo. 'May I?' he asked politely.

'What? Oh, of course.' Boo blushed. Imagine a Top Dog like the Werewolf General asking if he could widdle on the doorpost!

'Woof! Good scents in here! Is that Dog Biscuit Sorbet I can smell?'

Boo nodded. The shop felt so cold. Not just winter cold, but empty cold, like all their happy life had vanished.

'And Rat Surprises.' The Werewolf General looked back from the menu. 'Why do you call them Rat Surprises?'

'Well, it's a surprise for the rats,' Boo managed.

'I see.' The Werewolf General bit back a smile. 'Where are your bedrooms? Through here?'

'Our what?'

The Werewolf General just looked at him down his long grey-fuzzed nose. Boo gulped. 'This way, sir. Mum's is the first room, and mine's the next.' And a mess, he thought. But there was no Mum around to tell him to bury his bones now.

He led the way down the corridor.

Mum's room was just as she had left it: the frilly bedspread, Mum's collars neatly hanging on hooks by her mirror, the pig's ear she'd been chewing on the bedside table …

The Werewolf General sat back on his haunches. 'Right, this is a test. What place is every pup scared of? Where does every pup know, deep in their hearts, that evil lurks?'

'Grrr …' Suddenly Boo understood. 'Woof! Under the bed?'

'Exactly. All of us know instinctively that the dark place under the bed is something to be scared of. But most adults just won't admit it.' The Werewolf General shook his head. 'I don't know if the Greedle gets its Zurms to put their tunnel entrances under beds because it's a traditionally scary place, or we feel they're scary because we know that things like tunnels might be there. But every time a Zurm tunnels between the universes the hole comes out …'

Boo stared at Mum's neat bedspread, with its pattern of bones and butterflies. '… under a bed.'

The Werewolf General nodded. 'Yours or your mother's, in this case. Well, Boo? Are you brave enough to look?'

'Y … y… yes. I mean, grrr!!' Boo crept over to Mum's bed, and stuck his nose under the bedspread. It was dark under there, but there was still enough light to see.

Nothing.

He drew back. 'There's nothing there.'

The Werewolf General raised a shaggy grey eyebrow. 'Are you sure?'

'Yes, of ...' Boo hesitated. Was he sure? True, there was no great gaping hole there, big enough to fit a vat of ice cream, a Zurm, the Greedle, Mum and the Roaches. But there'd been a sort of smell ... an almost popcorn smell ...

He crept forward again, and sniffed. 'There *is* something there,' he growled, puzzled. 'The scent of popcorn is stronger here. But I can't see anything!'

'Good dog.' The Werewolf General calmly scratched a flea behind his left ear. 'Now work it out.'

'Um ... could it be an invisible hole?'

'No such thing as invisible holes. A hole is a hole.'

'Then ...' Suddenly Boo understood. 'It's shut! That's why I couldn't smell it till I put my nose under the bed! That's why I couldn't smell where they'd taken Mum!'

'Correct. So how do you open a hole between the universes?'

Boo sat down on his haunches too, and tried to think.

Grrr! Grrr! How did you open a wormhole? There wasn't a handle, or he'd have seen it. Maybe it was a word or phrase, like 'Abracadabra' or 'Open Sesame'. But surely he'd have heard the Greedle say something as it vanished down the hallway. His werewolf ears could pick up even a whisper. A hidden lever?

And then he had it.

'I think I know the secret,' he said slowly.

'Yes?'

'The secret is … there is no secret!'

Boo felt the Werewolf General's eyes on him as he padded across the chilly floor, then crouched and crawled under the bed. He lay there, waiting.

Nothing happened.

For a moment he was sure he'd got it wrong. Then suddenly the floor beneath him began to drop.

He could smell dirt, popcorn and damp, and …

'Stop!' barked the Werewolf General.

'But …' began Boo.

'Come back! Heel, Boo! Heel!'

Boo leapt back up to the bedroom floor. He glanced behind him. The floor had returned to its normal level now.

'What … what happened? Is it magic?'

The Werewolf General grinned, showing all his fangs. 'Heroes don't need magic! You worked out how to do it, that's all.'

'But don't you see what this means!' cried Boo. 'We can go and get Mum back!'

The Werewolf General raised one shaggy eyebrow again. 'You and me, eh? The two of us trot down the wormhole to the Ghastly Otherwhen — a place no Hero has ever managed to escape from — bring your Mum back and have a nice bowl of dead-cow juice at the Bigpaws'? Is that what you're thinking?'

'Sort of,' admitted Boo.

'We wouldn't stand a chance. I'm sorry, boy, but you just have to face it. There is no way to rescue your mother — none at all. Not from the Ghastly Otherwhen.'

'But — but couldn't we get other Heroes? Lots of Heroes together? Surely we can come up with some sort of plan?'

The Werewolf General laughed, a little sadly. 'I was like you once, boy. Eager to get out and save the universes! Well, I saved some people. And others ...' He gave a furry shrug. 'Let's not talk about those. No, boy, forget the past. Grieve for your mother, howl for her on the mountain top. But don't ever think you'll be able to bring her back, no matter how great a Hero you become.'

'Hero!' Boo gulped. 'Me?'

The Werewolf General grinned. 'Come on back to the Bigpaws'. It's time you learnt how to be a Hero properly.'

SCHOOL FOR HEROES
ENTRANCE EXAM

A ghoul attacks a supermarket when you're out shopping. Do you:

a. take a photo with your mobile phone to show everyone at home;

b. send a text message to a friend so she can come and see the show;

c. sneak a packet of potato crisps when no one's looking, or

d. attack the ghoul with a box of Yummy Flakes, tie it up with plaited canned spaghetti, call the police and sweep up the mess?

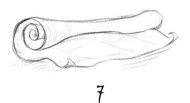

7

A school for Heroes

It was warm back at the Bigpaws'. Mr and Mrs Bigpaws still seemed awed at having a genuine Hero in their home. Spot shyly brought Boo and the Werewolf General a couple of plates of crackly dried pigs' ears, then left them alone in the living room.

The Werewolf General lay down on the mat in front of the fire and stretched out his forelegs, both the real and the wooden one, in the manner of a wolf about to settle in for a long story.

'I was like you once, young pup,' he growled softly. 'An ordinary werewolf living in a village pretty much like Sleepy Whiskers. Life was good — chasing wild boar … or sometimes they'd chase us. Sitting on the crags and howling at the full moon. The normal teenage things.

'And then the Horrorlump arrived out of the Ghastly Otherwhen.' The Werewolf General shook his silvery grey-furred head. 'It had been sent by the

Greedle, of course. The Greedle must have wanted your ice cream very badly to have come to get it. Usually it only sends its minions.'

'What did the Greedle want in your village?'

'Honey,' said the Werewolf General crisply. 'The bees gather the nectar in the Razorwood trees, and there's no other honey like it in the universes. So the Greedle sent the Horrorlump to get it — and to take the bees and destroy our village, because the Greedle likes destroying things almost as much as it loves keeping the best food in the universes for itself. And it has always wanted to be sure that no one's coming after it later, too.

'Horrorlumps don't stick their prey together with slime. They cut them into pieces and eat them with barbecue sauce.'

'That bit was in the book,' barked Boo eagerly. 'The one that Mum read me. Didn't you Howl so loud and so high that all the snow fell down in an avalanche and buried the Horrorlump and —'

'And then I was a Hero. But what the book wouldn't have told you, is that then I went to Hero School.'

'What's that?' asked Boo.

The Werewolf General reached over and grabbed a rolled-up poster he'd dropped when he first entered the room. 'The School for Heroes is the hard work you need to do to become a real Hero. The part most people don't want to think about. See?' he said.

Boo stared at it. It had 'School for Heroes' written

at the top and showed a handsome human about to punch an evil bogey. Boo could tell it was evil because it was snarling and its fangs were dripping blood. Words were exploding all around the Hero's fist. Boo spelt them out slowly. 'Wham! Bam! Pow! What do they mean, sir?'

'They're Hero techniques. Wham! Bam! Pow! is a form of martial arts that Heroes have to study. Just like you're going to do.'

'Me?' squeaked Boo. 'But I've already been to school! I was there for two whole years! I'm full up with education! I can read. I can even write. Well, sort of,' he added honestly. 'I dribble a bit when I hold the pen in my mouth and the paper gets all squishy.'

'Just shut up and listen,' growled the Werewolf General. 'The School for Heroes isn't an ordinary school.'

'Where is it? Is it over near Werewolf City?'

'It's in another universe.'

'Another universe! How do you get there?'

'Stop yapping! Your mouth is robbing your ears!'

Boo's tail drooped between his legs.

The General continued. 'Anyone can use the Zurm tunnels once they know they are there. That's how we Heroes can get to other universes to fight the bogeys. It's how you get to the School for Heroes, too.

'The School for Heroes is on a mountain ...' The Werewolf General smiled. '... A slightly unusual mountain. It's called Rest in Pieces.'

'Rest in Pieces? Woof,' apologised Boo quickly. 'I didn't mean to interrupt.'

'It's an old Hero saying. "Old Heroes never die. They just rest in pieces".' The Werewolf General tapped his wooden paw against the floor. 'When you know you've fought your last bogey you retire to Rest in Pieces. Oh, you can go home, of course. But there'll be no one to share the memories with. How can folks at home know what it's like to face a valley full of bogeys, with only a teaspoon and your wits?'

Boo's jaw dropped open. 'You mean you can?'

'Ha! I did it once. Just make sure it's a sharp teaspoon — and even sharper wits. But that's another story. Most retired Heroes are content to play Biff! Bam! Bingo!, while they yarn about old times, or race their wheelchairs down the mountainside. But some of them have set up a school — the School for Heroes — to teach young Heroes how to do it.

'Not just anyone can go to the School for Heroes. You have to be recommended by a practising Hero. And you have to have done something heroic to be accepted, too. Like you did.'

'But I just widdled in some ice cream!'

The Werewolf General smiled. 'And when I defeated the Woozlelump in the universe of Pingle I just bashed a teaspoon with a lump of granite till it was as sharp as a dagger. It's not just what you do, Boo. It's having the presence of mind to do it, and the courage to do your best, no matter what you're facing. That's what makes a Hero.'

'So if I go to the School for Heroes,' said Boo slowly, 'I'll learn how to use things like teaspoons to defeat bogeys too? And I'll meet other Heroes — lots of Heroes — who might help me rescue Mum?'

'No! Stop wagging your tail like that, boy. I'm serious. You have to give up any idea of rescuing your mother! No one — repeat, no one — can get into the Ghastly Otherwhen and survive. But yes, you'll learn Hero skills. And I hope you make other Hero friends. Heroes need friends. Look, boy, our universe needs another Hero. We've had two bogey attacks already and the Greedle came here in person in the last one. I hope you go to Hero School because I'm getting old, not for the faint hope you might be able to rescue your mother.'

Boo hardly heard him. 'Of course I'll go!' he barked. For the first time since he'd seen the Greedle, Boo's tail felt like it could wag forever. 'When do I start?'

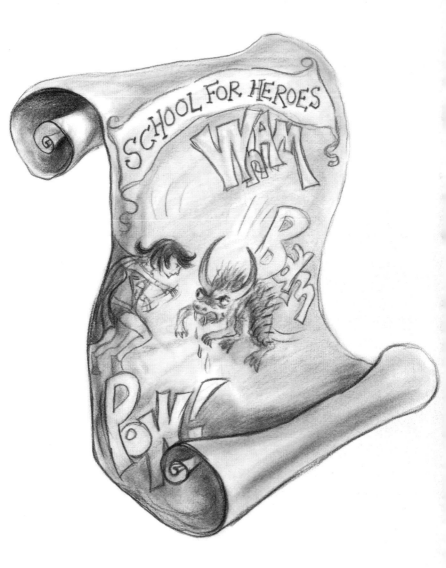

SCHOOL FOR HEROES
RULE #2

You may think that because you're at
the School for Heroes you don't have to worry
about dumb school rules and teachers
who don't understand you.
Think again.
That's life, kid. Get used to it.

8

Underpants, Toilets and Weird Humans

It turned out going to Hero School wasn't quite as easy as all that.

'First of all,' growled the Werewolf General, as the two of them went for a walk and a sniff along the creek bank, 'you have to learn to Change.'

Boo stared at him. 'Change! Changing's okay for girls — they get to wear pink dresses and stuff like that. You can't get your teeth into anything when you've Changed!'

The Werewolf General sniffed a tree stump, then raised a shaggy eyebrow. '*Can* you Change yet?'

'Of course!' said Boo. The Werewolf General stared at him. 'Well, sort of,' he added. 'Why do I have to?' He was growing more confident with the Werewolf General now.

The Werewolf General lifted his leg on the stump,

then grinned. 'Partly because it's hard to hold a pen with paws, even when you're a Hero. But there's another reason, too. Come on. Let's see how good you really are.'

Boo bit his lip. He hated Changing. But if that's what he had to do to learn how to rescue Mum, then he'd do it.

'Okay,' he said shortly. He badly wanted a widdle, but it would be bad manners to widdle where the Werewolf General had. He compromised with a few drops on a small stone nearby.

The Werewolf General casually lifted his leg on the stone, too. 'Go on then. Change.'

Boo took a deep breath. He'd done it a couple of times, he told himself. He could do it again.

One … two … three … PLUNG!

It felt like a backwards sneeze, like climbing into a box that was too big, then expanding to fit it. It felt like …

'Bluurk,' said Boo, as he fell over.

'Hmmm. You need a bit of practice.'

Boo scrambled to his feet again — his two much too big feet — and tried to keep his balance. 'Can I Change back now?'

'No.'

'But, sir, why?'

The Werewolf General grinned. 'What do you see when you look in the mirror, boy?'

'A wolf!' said Boo promptly.

The Werewolf General said nothing.

Boo sighed. 'A puppy.'

'What sort of puppy?'

'A cute little puppy with a curly tail,' admitted Boo. 'But I won't always be like that!' he added hopefully.

'Now, look in the pool. Can you see your reflection now you're in human shape?'

Boo flapped his feet across the ground to the creek, and peered down.

'Grfff!'

'Exactly,' said the Werewolf General with satisfaction. 'No werewolf — or puppy either — looks *cute* when they've Changed! We're big! We're tough! And even at your age we're very, very hairy!'

'Y—y—y—yes,' said Boo, starting to shiver. There was just so much bare skin when you'd Changed, in spite of the hairy bits! He stared at his reflection again. Was that really him? That water looked good too. He was thirsty! He bent down further ...

'Don't try to lap!'

Splosh! The warning came too late. Boo sat up in the pool and brushed dead leaves out of the furry bit on top of his head. 'Lesson number two,' said the Werewolf General. 'Drink from cups when you're in human shape — or make a cup out of your hands. They don't lap from pools. Or doggie bowls either.'

Boo pulled out a tadpole that was trying to swim up his nostrils. He stared at it. Normally he'd have chomped it down. But wriggling tadpoles just didn't seem as tempting in human form. He began to struggle out of the pool. 'Human shape is *dumb*!' he complained.

'True.' The Werewolf General carelessly lifted his leg and left a few drops to mark the nearest tree. 'Why do you think I stay in wolf form most of the time, too? No, trust me on this, young pup, er, boy. If you turn up at Hero School looking cute and fluffy no one will take you seriously. They'll want to pat your head, not teach you to Wham! Bam! Pow! But you don't have to stay in human shape there forever.'

Boo brightened, then frowned. Even his lips felt weird in human shape. 'I don't?'

'Of course not! Just for a day or two, till they get to know you. Then when you Change back to puppy form, they'll still see the big hairy Hero you *can* be, if you want to be.'

Boo flexed his muscles — but carefully, in case he fell down again.

'By the way,' added the Werewolf General, 'you'll need to wear clothes to school as well. At least while you're in human form.'

'Clothes! But I always wear my collar —'

'Pants. Shirt. Shoes,' barked the Werewolf General crisply. 'Trust me, Boo. The other students at the School for Heroes will not be impressed with a kid who wanders round in just a collar.'

'But I —'

'Do you want to go to this school or not?' barked the Werewolf General.

'I …' Boo subsided. 'Yes, sir.'

'Then you'll learn to wear clothes. And Change. And eat with a knife and fork. And not lift your leg on doorposts either,' he added. 'Even in werewolf form.'

'What?' Boo tried to prick up his ears, then realised he couldn't. 'Where do humans widdle then?'

The Werewolf General gave a big doggie grin. 'They do their weeing in things called toilets, in rooms they call bathrooms. Then the toilets wash away the smell! You'll have to practise using your hands to help you widdle, too. Humans can't widdle without hands.'

'Crazy!' said Boo. He tried to scratch his ear with his foot and discovered he couldn't. He picked himself up off the ground.

'Just remember, young Boo, don't under any circumstances lift your leg on a doorpost at school.'

'I won't.' Boo shook his head. But even that didn't feel right in human form. How did kids at the School for Heroes know what everyone else was thinking and feeling if they couldn't smell each other's wee? How could they tell who was Top Dog?

The Werewolf General looked at him kindly. 'I know it's hard, young pup. It was hard for me too. But you're a Hero. You'll manage.'

'Woof,' said Boo sadly. 'I mean, yes, sir.'

'Right. Now let's get you some "walking on two feet" practice.'

✳ ✳ ✳

So Boo practised. He jogged up and down the creek in human form every day. And even though the first few days he fell down more than he jogged, he kept on going.

He practised holding a pen in his fingers and his teeth, for the time he'd be able to go back to wolf shape. (The secret, he discovered, was not to think about Rat Surprises or poodle pancakes so he didn't dribble down the pen.)

He did fifty push ups, then a hundred, then two hundred every day, to make his muscles more heroic. And every night he ran for hours across the hills. Okay, he was in wolf form then, but it still made him fitter. And somehow the darkness and the solitude made things easier. He missed Mum most when other people were there, but she wasn't. And every time he pushed his body up another hill he could think, I'm doing this for Mum! Everyone was kind. None of the Bigpaws family snickered as he tottered about on two legs, gradually getting surer on his feet.

Even the puppies didn't giggle when he came to dinner wearing a shirt and pants, or tried to eat his rat casserole or poodle pasta with a knife and fork while they slobbered from their bowls.

At least, thought Boo, as he sat in his room, trying to work out how to turn *then* push a door handle (the Werewolf General had given him one to practise on) I'll be able to come home at night.

Home. The Bigpaws's home. Would it ever seem like his?

Only one more day to go …

Someone gave a short bark outside the door. 'Woof!' called Boo. Mr Bigpaws pushed the door open with his nose. (Why do humans make doors so *complicated*? wondered Boo.)

Mr Bigpaws dropped the package from his mouth. 'For you,' he said.

At least hands are useful for unwrapping things, Boo decided, pulling off the fancy cat-perfumed pink wrapping paper.

'It's … it's a shirt!' he said, staring.

It was the most wonderful shirt he'd ever seen, totally unlike the plain blue T-shirt that the Werewolf General had given him. It was a deep blue silk with purple embroidery. Someone must have spent days making this, thought Boo.

'Thank you —' he began, but Mr Bigpaws shook his head. 'It's from the Rover family,' he said. 'When you saved the town you saved them too.'

'But, but …' began Boo. How could he explain that he hadn't meant to save the Rovers especially? But he *would* have tried to save the Rovers if he'd thought about them, he realised suddenly. So maybe …

'Another present!' Spot bounded up the stairs and dropped the parcel at his feet. 'From Mr and Mrs Backscratcher!'

It was a pair of silk pants, as gorgeous as the shirt. 'Red, so they don't show the blood,' said Spot helpfully, sitting on her haunches and watching him with her tongue hanging out. 'I bet Heroes bleed all over the place.'

'Spot!' barked Mr Bigpaws. 'That is *not* a tactful thing to say!'

Boo stared at the trousers. 'Grrr-eat.'

'Well, Heroes do *Biff! Bam!*ming! don't they? So they have to get a bit bloody sometimes.' Spot sniffed the wrapping paper. 'Hey, want to play Tear the Paper with me?'

'No thanks,' said Boo politely. He wasn't sure he could chase paper in human shape yet.

The presents came all day after that. More human clothes: boots from Bandy Sam the collarmaker, socks, underpants …

Boo frowned at the underpants. Underpants made it impossible to sniff someone's bum properly. Even werewolves in human form never wore underpants; just a skirt or a leather kilt that could be pushed out of the way easily. Why wear clothes where no one could see them?

How could you know if someone was friendly if you couldn't sniff their bum? Especially if you only had human nostrils, which could hardly smell a dead cat right under their noses. Humans must push their clothes down when they want to smell each other's bums, Boo decided. Humans would have to push their pants down before they widdled or did *that*, too. Crazy! Humans must be pushing their clothes up and down all the time!

Nah, there had to be *some* way to sniff a human's bum, even with clothes on. Maybe if you pushed your nose up their leg … He'd just need to practise human-type bum-sniffing when he got to the School for Heroes.

The packages kept on coming. A wear-on-the-back-type school bag, not one for carrying in the mouth. Exercise books, notebooks, pens ... Boo gulped. It had been ages since he'd written anything. He hoped there wouldn't be too much writing stuff at school.

Lunch box, hat ...

'Everyone is so proud of you,' explained Mrs Bigpaws, as she padded up the stairs with the next present (a big box of dried rats, so he could have one every morning tea). 'They're proud of the way you chased away the Greedle. They're proud you're going to the School for Heroes, too. Our very own Hero, here in Sleepy Whiskers! Mr Bigpaws and I are so proud to have you here, Boo,' she added.

'Me too,' said Spot, poking her nose around the door. 'Hey,' she added, casually scratching her ear, 'if you see any hunks at school — werewolf-type hunks, I mean, could you sort of ask them home?'

'I'm probably going to be the only werewolf there,' growled Boo gloomily. 'That's why I have to practise Changing.'

Spot scratched her neck with her hind leg. 'The only werewolf! That's going to be so weird!'

'Yeah,' said Boo.

✷ ✷ ✷

It was hard to sleep that night, even in his favourite

position, with his nose pressed to his bum and his tail tucked round the other side.

It wasn't that he hadn't got used to his new basket at the Bigpaws'. It wasn't even the thought of a strange school tomorrow either. Much, anyway.

It was just … everything. Wondering.

Wondering about Mum, and what had happened, and where she was.

Every time someone came to the door he pricked up his ears, hoping it might be Mum, if somehow she'd managed to escape.

Every time he trotted through the marketplace he wondered if he might see her face in the crowd.

And every time he looked over at the Best Ice-Cream Shop in the Universes he hoped there'd be a light in the window.

Mum, come back through the wormhole …

But there never was.

Suddenly Boo scrambled out of his basket. There was something he had to do!

He slipped out of his bedroom and padded down the stairs. At least he was in werewolf form now, and could go quietly. Out the front door, and down the street, then up the mountain behind the town … his claws clicked against the rocky slopes. The scrubby trees stood like strange guardians outlined against the starry sky.

There was a rock on top of the mountain. It was big and flat. A hundred werewolves could sit there in the moonlight. But tonight there was only Boo.

Boo lifted up his head, and howled.

It was a howl for Mum. It wasn't a funeral howl, where everyone who had known a dead wolf all howled together. Mum wasn't dead. She wasn't!

But it still felt right to howl for her.

The sound flew across the valley. Maybe, just maybe, thought Boo, Mum might somehow hear its echoes, far off in the Ghastly Otherwhen, where the Greedle had her prisoner.

The moon floated across the sky, like a big scoop

of orange ice cream. But Boo kept on howling. It was only as it began to slide down to the horizon that he stopped.

His throat felt hoarse. He was tireder than he'd ever felt in his life before. But he'd done what he had to do.

Boo padded slowly down the mountain.

What was tomorrow going to bring? What sort of strange creatures would he find at the School for Heroes? Okay, there'd be humans. But humans were a bit like werewolves, except that they had never learnt to Change. The Werewolf General had said there'd be other creatures, too. Students came from all the universes — well, all but the Ghastly Otherwhen — to go to the School for Heroes.

What if one looked like a rat, and he ate it accidentally?

What if one came from a universe where they ate werewolves, and they ate him accidentally?

It was terrifying, he thought, as he crept wearily into his basket. But it was exciting, too. One day he'd be a real Hero like the Werewolf General. People would write books about him! Wolves would howl songs about him. Puppies would stare at him in the street. Maybe he'd even be head of the Council of Werewolves when he grew up, just like the Werewolf General …

No one would ever think he was cute again!

Boo fell asleep at last. And when he dreamt, he dreamt of Heroes.

Boo woke early, despite his late night. He padded out of his basket and poked his nose out the window.

Dawn was a pink glow on the horizon. The sky was turning blue instead of grey. Sleepy Whiskers was just waking up. Mr Brownear was hanging up spiced kittens to dry in his backyard. A tortoise train trudged down the street in the slush from the melted snow, bringing in a load of rugs from one of the mountain villages. A tiny pig flew from flower to flower in Mrs Bigpaws's garden, sticking its snout down to lick out the cold winter nectar, then it flapped lazily up to the old spaghetti tree.

It must have a nest up there, thought Boo. Maybe there'd be piglets in spring, too. Maybe Mrs Bigpaws would make piglet jam, just like Mum used to do.

Yum.

Boo blinked. He'd just thought about Mum, and it hadn't hurt! Well, it *had* hurt — but not the fang-wrenching pain of the last weeks. Somehow now he was sure he *would* rescue her. Somehow Mum was going to be safe!

It was time to Change. Boo took a deep breath and concentrated.

PLUNG!

The floor dropped down and the ceiling grew closer. The world lost most of its smell, too. Woof! thought Boo. He'd even kept his balance this time!

He reached for his clothes. Underpants first. That

always took a while. You had to be an athletic genius to manage underpants at first go, Boo decided. It was bad enough having to balance on two feet, without having to stand on only one leg and put the other in a hole at the same time. Humans probably had a 'getting into your underpants race' at their Olympic Games.

Now other pants on, shirt on, shoes on — grrr! Cow guts! He'd forgotten his socks again. Shoes off, socks on, shoes on again. Hat on, school bag — he'd even had a (yuck!) *bath* yesterday. The Werewolf General had told him that Two Foots had a (double yuck!) *bath* every night.

The (triple yuck!) *bath* had washed off just about all his smell, too. It was hard to recognise himself without his smell! But if a (noooooo!) *bath* was what it took to become a Hero — and find Mum — Boo would do it.

Boo looked at himself in the mirror. A cool-looking and slightly ferocious Hero looked back, wearing a blue silk shirt and red silk pants, with shaggy hair instead of furry puppy fuzz. I rock! thought Boo. Even if he still felt a bit unsteady on only half his usual legs.

The Werewolf General was right, he admitted to

himself. There was nothing 'cute' about this kid at all!

'Grrr!' he said to the kid in the mirror. 'Grrr-owl!' He grrred again as the reflection growled back.

It was funny, he thought. If the Greedle had never invaded Sleepy Whiskers he'd be going to deliver Poodlepops today, not going to learn to be a Hero.

But somewhere deep inside him, he realised, he *wanted* to go to the School for Heroes — and not just to learn how to rescue Mum.

Who am I really? he wondered. He'd been so sure a few weeks ago. Boojum Bark, delivery wolf and apprentice ice-cream maker. He'd spend his life making frozen Rat Surprises and Poodlepops, take over the shop one day and have pups of his own. An everyday sort of werewolf.

And now? Now he was going to be a Hero.

Somehow it felt … right. As long as he didn't fall flat on his face, anyway. Boo trudged his two feet down the stairs to breakfast.

The family were already perched on their cushions at the low kitchen table lapping up their breakfast. Spot sniffed and giggled. 'You smell like soap!'

Boo gave her his deepest growl. 'It's not funny!'

'No, of course it isn't,' said Mrs Bigpaws hurriedly. 'You smell very … smart, Boo dear. Here's your breakfast. Eat up. You've got a long day ahead of you.'

Boo looked at his plate. It was fried eggs and sheep's eyeballs. Normally he loved fried eggs and eyeballs. But this morning the eyeballs kept looking at him as though to say, 'We know what's going to happen today, even if you don't'.

Boo stabbed an eyeball awkwardly with his fork and gulped it down hurriedly. There! That stopped it looking at him anyway.

What was he so nervous about? The Werewolf General said he was a Hero!

Then why did he feel like a puppy who'd only just learnt to open its eyes? Why did his tummy feel like it was filled with beetles?

Stop it, he told himself. He could be trotting through Sleepy Whiskers now, on his way to deliver the first carton of Kittenlicious ice cream of the day. Instead, he was going to learn how to *Wham! Bam! Pow!*

I can do it! he told himself firmly. I can walk on two legs. I can use door handles.

But if he ate another eyeball he'd be sick.

Boo pushed his plate away. 'Um, thank you for breakfast,' he said.

'But, Boo,' began Mrs Bigpaws. 'You've hardly eaten anything! Have another eyeball!'

'No, really, thank you.' He picked up his school bag. 'I ... I'd better be off,' he muttered. He pushed open the door ... and gasped.

HERO SCHOOL EQUIPMENT

Please ensure that every student Hero brings:
1 Hero costume, washable, with their
name and universe on the label
12 Packets of Band-Aids
2 Coils of rope, for tying up bogeys
Lunch

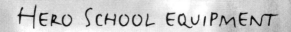

9

Footsteps down the Wormhole

The garden was full of werewolves. Wolves in human form, wolves in fur and collars. Old wolves, young wolves, the pups from the Chase-the-Ball pack. There was old Ms Shaggy in human form with her great-nephews, and all the customers of the Best Ice-Cream Shop in the Universes.

And there, out front, sat the Werewolf General, with all his medals gleaming on his collar.

Boo heard Mr Bigpaws come out behind him. He cleared his throat. 'Woof!' he called in his best Mayor-Making-a-Speech voice. 'Today we send off one of our own to the most exclusive school in all the universes! Boojum Bark, this is a proud day for Sleepy Whiskers! Now, you go and show them all what a werewolf Hero can do!'

The crowd cheered. 'Grrr! You show them, Boo!' called someone.

Old Ms Shaggy shuffled up and gave him a kiss on

the cheek. It's funny to feel lips on bare skin, thought Boo.

'Good luck, Boo,' she whispered.

Boo gulped. 'Er — woof!' he muttered. There was no way he could say any more.

The crowd parted as he marched towards the Best Ice-Cream Shop in the Universes. The Werewolf General limped up and began to pad by his side.

'Embarrassing, isn't it?' he muttered out of the side of his mouth, his wooden paw clunking on the paving. 'All part of being a Hero. You wait till they throw flowers. Or all the girls kiss you. Actually,' he added, 'that bit isn't too bad.'

The wolves in human shape were still clapping behind him, and the wolves were thudding their tails on the ground. Suddenly Boo felt better. New silk pants, new silk shirt, *and* walking with the Werewolf General.

Cool! He felt his mouth turning up into a grin. If he'd still had his tail he'd have wagged it. I'm going to show those kids at the School for Heroes, he decided. Look out, you lot! The werewolf is coming to the mountain!

Boo pushed open the door of the Best Ice-Cream Shop in the Universes. Even without his wolf nose he could tell its smells had changed. Mum's scent was fainter, and the smell of ice cream, too.

There was even a faint smell of mouse. Mice usually avoided werewolf homes. Mouse-on-toast was Boo's favourite afternoon snack.

But not this morning. His tummy squirmed at the thought.

The Werewolf General glanced at him sympathetically, but he didn't say anything.

Mum's room looked just the same. There was the drawing he'd given her on Mother's Day three years ago, and the squeaky toy he'd played with when he was a tiny puppy …

No, he couldn't think of Mum now. Concentrate, he told himself. This is the start of my Hero career!

Boo knelt down and lifted the bedspread. At least under the bed looked the same.

'Got your lunch?'

Boo held up his school bag and nodded. 'And my Band-Aids and rope.'

'Good,' barked the Werewolf General softly. 'And good luck. See you this afternoon.' He gave Boo a comforting nuzzle, his big damp nose cool on Boo's warm hand. 'Now, once you're down in the tunnel, turn right and head for the heat. You'll pass other tunnels down there. Ignore them. Oh, and as soon as you come out of the tunnel yell "Student approaching!" so that the tunnel guards know you're not a bogey.'

'What do they do to bogeys?'

The Werewolf General shrugged his furry shoulders.

'Depends who's on duty. Bildoon the Bold decapitates them with his false teeth. I saw Fearsome Fanny of Frogmore bash a bogey into submission with her hearing aid once. The older a Hero is the more ways they learn to attack bogeys.'

Boo gulped. 'Head for the heat. Yell "Student approaching!" Right. Um, how do I find my way back here?'

'That's easy. Every time you take a trip down a wormhole your next trip takes you back to where you came from. The only way to go somewhere else is to go with someone who came from there in the first place.'

'Why?'

'No one knows. Well, maybe the Greedle or the Zurms do. But they're not telling. Now, good luck.'

'Wh—what if I meet a bogey down there?'

The Werewolf General grinned, showing his long fangs. 'Run.'

Boo took a deep breath. 'I'm a Hero!' he reminded himself. Then he crawled under the bed.

The floor began to sink.

✳ ✳ ✳

Down, down, down. The world was darkness. Like falling through Crushed Cockroach chocolate ice cream, thought Boo, except it isn't quite as cold. And then the falling feeling stopped. His feet felt rock, even through his shoes.

Boo looked around. At first, all he could see was

darkness. Then slowly his eyes began to make out where he was.

The wormhole ceiling was twice as high as the top of his head. The walls looked like rock, but when he brushed them with his hand he found them cool and soft. He pushed and felt his fingers slide into …

Boo gulped. Nothingness, so cold he could feel his fingers freeze. He quickly pulled them out and blew on them to warm them up.

Now, which way to go? Turn right and follow the warmth, the Werewolf General had said.

If only he was in wolf shape! He couldn't smell any warmth at all. Just a faint scent of popcorn and strawberry jam and … Boo sniffed. Yes, there was one smell strong enough to sniff even in human form. Mouse droppings! But there couldn't be mice down here! What would they live on?

Boo shrugged. Some droppings must have fallen from under his mum's bed.

He suddenly realised there were more questions he should have asked. How long would it take him to get to the school? How would he know when he'd got there?

Boo gulped. It would all sort itself out. Maybe there'd be a big flashing sign saying: 'School for Heroes! This way ➤ ➤ Welcome!'

Get real, Boo told himself. How hard is it to follow the warmth? Concentrate!

Yes! He could feel it now, even in human form. A faint breath of heat coming from … that way.

Now, walk …

Boo walked.

The tunnel floor was surprisingly smooth and brown, like a well-made Rat Surprise. It sloped downhill to begin with, then sharply upwards.

Now he was getting used to it, even his human-shaped nose could pick up other smells as well as popcorn and strawberry jam. Strange scents he'd never smelt before. Other bogeys? he wondered. Or other universes? He sniffed again, hoping there might be a faint trace of Mum's scent too.

But there wasn't.

But there was the smell of mouse, even stronger now. Maybe the mice are down here, thought Boo, not up in the shop at all. But why would mice live in a wormhole, where there were no crumbs to eat?

Nah, it couldn't be mice. Maybe some bogeys smelt like mice, he decided. Giant bogey mice with fangs … Stop it, he told himself. Maybe wormholes always smell of mouse as well as strawberry jam.

Boo sighed and kept walking. At least he was getting more practice walking like a human.

He was pretty sure he was going the right way. The tunnel was getting hotter, and hotter still. A new smell melded with the scents of mouse and mouldiness. Almost the smell of fire, like the time Mum had burnt a batch of ice-cream cones.

Was someone cooking something?

How far did this tunnel go? He still couldn't see any sign of light from the other end. What if he was late for school? What happened to unpunctual Heroes? What if —

Suddenly he stopped and listened. Someone else was in the tunnel. He was sure of it.

Someone ... or some*thing*!

The Greedle!

Except ... this didn't smell like the Greedle.

What was it? If only he had his wolf nose! He strained to hear instead.

Squeak! Pitter patter, pitter patter ...

There *was* something in the tunnel!

What had the Werewolf General told him? If he met a bogey he was to run.

Boo listened again. Yes, it was still there. *Pitter patter, pitter patter ...*

He should run *now*! If he started running now he might get to the school before the bogey caught him.

But ... what if this *wasn't* a bogey? What if it was another kid going to Hero School? He'd look like a coward scampering from a bogey! He'd be a coward!

Just wait and see, Boo decided cautiously. If it looks like a bogey I'll run. Except ... how will I be able to tell a kid from another universe from a bogey?

He bit his lip. If it tries to rip my head off, he decided, it's probably a bogey. And if it says, 'Hi, what class are you in?' it probably isn't.

Which isn't much help.

Pitter patter, pitter patter … the sound was closer now.

At least, he thought, it sounds like a very *small* bogey. But maybe they're the worst. Maybe small bogeys pierce your skull with their long hollow fingers and suck out your brains and …

Stop thinking like that! he told himself. You're a Hero! Or you will be. Just keep walking. Don't run.

Pitter patter, pitter patter …

Well, maybe walk a little faster …

Sweat poured down his neck. The heat was intense now. The burning smell was even stronger, like the time the barbecued rats had all caught fire. Even the rock beneath his shoes was hot.

And either his eyes had adjusted to the dimness, or there was more light in the tunnel. Boo looked back, then squinted ahead. Aha! It was lighter ahead than behind! A strange red flickering light. He was nearly there!

Just a little further and he would see what was following him, even if he couldn't smell it. Boo stepped up his pace. He was steady enough on his two feet now to stride along.

The weird red light grew brighter, and brighter still. It was so bright it hurt his eyes. Boo stopped and looked behind.

Nothing.

'Squeak!'

Boo looked down.

A mouse stared up at him. 'Squeak!' it said.

A mouse! Boo glared. An ordinary mouse-sized mouse! Not even a bogey mouse. He'd been scared of a plain old mouse. How dare a mouse invade his hero's tunnel!

'Shoo,' he said.

The mouse twitched its whiskers. But otherwise it didn't move.

'Look,' said Boo, 'if you don't head back the way you came right now, I'm going to chomp you up for morning tea. Or morning mouse. Get it?'

'Squeak,' said the mouse. It still didn't move.

Boo sighed. He didn't like hurting things — apart from bogeys, he reminded himself. But he wasn't going to make his first appearance at the School for Heroes with a mouse scampering after him.

I'll just have to catch it and frighten it a bit, he decided. How hard could it be to catch a mouse in human form? If a wolf could catch a rat before it was turned into a Surprise, then even a human could catch a mouse.

Boo bent down slowly. The mouse stood there as his hand came nearer, then darted away just as he grabbed.

Missed it!

Why were human hands so clumsy? Teeth were better. You could really grab with teeth.

Boo lunged again. The mouse jumped. It ran up his arm, squeaked at him triumphantly, then jumped up onto his head. How dare it! Boo snatched at his hair frantically, just as the mouse jumped down onto his shoulder.

Grrr. He wasn't going to let a mouse get the better of him! But there was no way these clumsy hands could grab a mouse.

There was only one thing for it, Boo decided. He'd have to Change. Just for a few seconds, just time enough for his fangs to grab the mouse.

PLUNG!

Ah! Four legs instead of two! That was better! And real teeth! The tunnel seemed larger. The smells were richer, deeper. Yes, there it was, right by his nose!

Snap!

'What the —?' Boo struggled frantically. Something had grabbed him! Held him! He couldn't move!

Was it another of the creatures of the Ghastly Otherwhen? Or ... or ...

Or just his school clothes, Boo realised suddenly. He was trapped inside his school clothes!

Grr! Cat guts! He'd forgotten about his clothes when he Changed. Now, how to get out of them ... undo the buttons, that'd be a start.

Boo stopped. There was no way his paws could undo the buttons. He'd have to Change back to human form, then undo the buttons, then ...

Wriggle, wriggle, pat, pat, pat ...

Boo froze. It was the mouse. Wriggling up his hind leg and ... and, yes! The cheek of it! Running along his back!

I'm a Hero! he thought. How dare that mouse

treat me like this?!

Maybe he could sort of edge his feet out of his clothes. Ah, that was it.

The mouse was standing on his head now. Boo smiled to himself. He knew what to do.

One. Two. Three. Woof!

Boo opened his mouth, flicked his head sideways and snapped his jaws.

'Missed you!' he snarled.

'Squeak, squeak, squeakity squeak!' protested the mouse. It scampered desperately down the tunnel towards the flickering red light.

'Come back, you miserable mouse!' roared Boo. 'Woof! Woof woof woof!' He galloped after the mouse, his paws pounding on the tunnel floor, dragging his clothes along with him. No mouse was going to outrun him!

Suddenly the light was even brighter, a red glow all around him. But his nose was nearly touching the mouse now!

'Got you!' he growled, as his jaws closed round the furry softness.

'Squeak!'

'Aha, you varmint!' A wooden walking stick thwacked Boo on his furry nose. 'Thought you'd escape Mervin the Magnificent, did you!' *Thwack! Thwack! Thwark!*

'Leave off, Mervin! That bogey's mine!' Suddenly something looped around Boo's throat. Something pink and fuzzy, he realised, tearing at it before it choked him.

'Oh no it's not! Finders keepers!'

Thwack! Thwack!

'Ow!' yelped Boo, still pulling at the pink stuff. It's wool, he thought. Someone had captured him with pink wool!

'Nonsense! You guard the wormhole Tuesdays and Thursdays! This is on Monday!'

'It is not! I remember Monday! We had roast tentacles for lunch on Monday.'

'That was *last* Monday, you senile old —'

'Senile! Old! I'll show you old!'

Boo gazed up at his attackers. They were arguing so hard now they were leaving him alone. The first was an elderly gorilla in a red cape, wrinkles and wheelchair, waving a walking stick. The other was an even older human woman, with a mass of too-red hair, a red sparkly dress hanging on her withered body, and a walking frame. She steadied herself on it with one hand while the other held the pink knitting that had captured him.

It looked like it was going to be a beanie.

Cat guts! What had he forgotten to say? 'Student approaching!' he yelled.

'Squeak!' The mouse tried to wriggle free when his jaws opened. Boo snapped them shut again.

'Squeak!' said the mouse reproachfully.

'What?' The gorilla stared at Boo, its hand around its ear. 'Speak up, puppy dog! What did you say?'

'He said "Student approaching",' shouted the old woman disgustedly. 'Blasted students. Haven't had a good bogey to bash for months. Come on,' she said to Mervin the Magnificent. 'There's Biff! Bam! Bingo! up in the dining room this morning. Bet I can Biff! Bam! you senseless in half an hour. And there're tentacle scones for morning tea, too. We can keep an eye on the wormhole from the tea-room window.'

Suddenly the wool vanished from around Boo's throat.

'Th—thank you …' he began.

But the ancient Heroes and their wheelchair and walking frame were already creaking away.

Boo blinked, finally free to stare around, the mouse dangling from his mouth. He had never dreamt that the school would be like this!

The wormhole had come out in a hollow surrounded by cliffs, deep in the heart of a hard sparkling mountain of black crystals rimmed with yellow. The sky above was red; even the light around Boo seemed tinged with flames, a deep pulsating fire. Thin grey smoke filled the air, with tiny threads of black and yellow. And below …

He gulped, making the mouse bob up and down in his jaws.

'Squeak!' protested the mouse. But Boo just stared down.

Down, down, into a pit where the world swirled and bubbled, red and vicious. What is this place? thought Boo frantically.

Blub, blub, blub went the molten rock below. The ground shivered in a tiny earthquake, then grew still.

And then he realised. He was in a volcano.

Boo gulped again. He'd come to the wrong universe! Who'd put a school in a volcano?!

Heroes, he thought. What could be more heroic than a volcano as a school?

Something flickered past his nose. It was a bat with shiny black wings and red sparks for eyes.

'Squeak.' The mouse wriggled again, trying to get free.

'Tuff luckff, mouff,' said Boo. He stared around again, trying to make out shapes in the smoke. There was the deeper black of a cave entrance, and paths, too, leading up through the cliffs. A sign on one of them said, 'Danger! Wheelchairs crossing!' High up on the cliff was another sign: 'Rest in Pieces'.

So he *was* in the right place! But where was the school?

'Hey!' It was a girl's voice. 'Some *thing's* come through the wormhole!'

'It's pretty small, whatever it is.'

'It doesn't *look* like a bogey. *Much* too small and dumb-looking!' said the first girl's voice. 'And what's that in his mouth?'

They must be students too, thought Boo in relief. They'll know where I should go!

Suddenly Boo realised what they saw. Not the tough werewolf Hero he and the Werewolf General had planned, dressed in red and blue silk, striding out of the wormhole. Instead, he was a small, ruffled puppy, crouched among a tangle of wrinkled shirt and pants.

With a mouse in his mouth.

'*Errrrrrk!*' It was the first girl's voice. 'A mouse! A mouse!'

He had arrived.

NOTE TO ALL PARENTS

The Hero School is for all races from all universes. (Except, of course, the Ghastly Otherwhen). Unfortunately, this means that in their home worlds some of our students might regard other students as dinner. Parents are politely requested to make sure that all school lunches are:
a. wriggling as little as possible; and
b. do not resemble any of your child's school mates, even covered in tomato sauce.
A special warning to all vampires:
'I forgot my lunch' is no excuse for trying to suck up to your teacher.
Thank you for your cooperation.

signed Dr Mussells, Principal

P.S. Please remind all students to give way to wheelchairs. A wheelchair at 250 kilometres an hour is no joke. Neither are retired Heroes.

10

Why You Don't Sniff a Princess's Bum

'Shut up, Princess.' The second girl's voice was softer. 'You're supposed to be a Hero. Heroes aren't afraid of mice.'

'*Huh*,' said the first girl. 'I can beat you at Heroing *any* day, Yesterday. Big slithering things with fangs — no worries. I just don't like mice.' She peered down at Boo. 'I'm *not* very fond of puppies either. Especially *smelly* ones.'

'I think he's cute,' said the girl called Yesterday. 'Look at his curly tail!'

Cute! Boo's mouth opened in his best warning growl.

'Squeak!' yelled the mouse. It leapt to the ground and scurried back up the wormhole.

Boo hardly noticed it go.

'Er, woof!' he growled, in what he hoped was a

good deep Hero voice, as he hurriedly began to shake himself free of his clothes. 'I'm not a dog.'

'Oh, *yeah?*' said the girl — Princess, that was her name. 'Four paws, lots of fur. You're a woof-woof.'

'Princess! Don't be mean!' said the girl called Yesterday.

Boo tore the last tangle of shirt off his fur and looked at the girls. Both were about his age. Yesterday was tall, and skinny as an ice-block stick, and sort of brown. She wore a drab brown dress down to her knees, made of some strange leather and roughly trimmed with a knife. She had long brown hair and brown skin, too, as if she spent a lot of time in the sun. Her feet were bare, and so tough looking she didn't even seem to be uncomfortable on the hot ground.

But Princess! She was … gold and glowing. Boo decided she was the most glorious girl he'd ever seen!

She was the most heroic girl he'd ever seen, too. Even her hair was heroic! It was the same rich yellow colour as old Ms Shaggy's fangs, and her eyes were as green as one of the dead slugs Mrs Bigpaws kept in the fridge as a special treat for the pups.

Princess was dressed in the most sensible human clothes Boo had ever seen, too: just a wisp of silky pink skirt and a pretty pink top that left her tummy bare. There was a small crown on her head.

Cool, he thought, wagging his tail hopefully. It'd be easy to sniff her bum in clothes like that. Then he'd really know what she thought about him! He padded forwards, dragging his pants behind him. He shoved his nose up her leg and …

'*Eeeerk!*' said Princess again. Suddenly Boo felt one of her sparkly pink sandals kick him in the chest. Hard. '*What* in the Otherwhen do you *think* you're doing?'

'Um, sniffing your bum?' said Boo, trying to untangle himself from his pants again.

'Sniffing my bum! My actual *bum*! How dare you?! Do you know who I *am*? My dad would have you beheaded for that!'

'Cool it, Princess,' said Yesterday. 'No one here's impressed that your dad is King of Puke.'

'That's *Pewké*, pronounced "Pookay", you peasant,' said Princess, tossing her heroic golden hair. 'And I don't like dirty little puppies sniffing my bum.

Especially when they've just swallowed a mouse.'

'No, I didn't. It escaped,' said Boo.

'You know, he looks more like a wolf to me,' said Yesterday, looking at him critically. 'Look at his jaw, and the shape of his ears. A wolf puppy, anyhow. Anyhow, dogs and wolves always sniff bums. It's how they tell if you're friendly or not.'

'Oh, right. *Nice.* As though I'm going to be friendly after having my bum sniffed!' Even with her face all screwed up in distaste Boo had never seen anyone as gorgeous as Princess. 'And I'm *Princess* Princess, remember? Princess Princess Sunbeam Caresse von Pewké, to be precise.' Princess Princess fluffed her heroic hair. 'Dad knew I'd be coming to the School for Heroes one day. So he made sure *everyone* still called me "Princess" even with the dumb school rule.

'I think Princess is a great name! And I only smell bums when I can't smell your widdle.' Boo sat back on his haunches. 'If you'd like to do a widdle I could smell that instead,' he added helpfully.

'How *dare* you?! That's it. I've had *enough* ...' began Princess Princess.

'Shhh. I mean shhh, Princess Princess.' Yesterday looked as if she was going to smile, but didn't quite know how to. 'He's new here, remember?' She held out a hand. It was long and thin and brownish too, with calluses along the fingers. 'Hi. I'm Yesterday.'

Boo sat on his haunches and held out a paw. 'I'm Boo.'

Princess Princess snickered. 'Hey, it's like the joke. You know, about Boo.'

Yesterday frowned. 'Boo who?' she asked.

'There's no need to cry!' said Princess Princess triumphantly, just as a bell began to peal somewhere deep inside the black cliffs around them.

'Ha, ha,' said Boo. He put his paw down and stood up, his tail between his legs, and tried to give a doggie grin.

'We'd better get a move on or we'll be late for class,' said Princess Princess. 'I'm top of every class, you know. Bogey recognition, *Wham! Bam! Pow! Zoom!*ing ...'

'And modesty,' said Yesterday softly.

105

Princess Princess frowned. '*What* did you say?'

'Oh, totally,' said Yesterday.

Princess Princess shrugged. 'I don't know what the teachers are *thinking* of, letting a *dog* in here.' She smiled suddenly. Princess Princess's smile was like a sunrise, thought Boo, poetic for the first time in his life. Or a sunrise with pearly white teeth anyway.

'Of *course*! You must be a new guard-dog!' said Princess Princess. 'Sit, boy! Sit!'

Boo sat before he'd realised it. Sweat was beginning to drip down his fur. That volcano was hot! 'Um ... no, I'm not a guard-dog,' he said. 'I'm a Hero. Or I'm going to be one, anyhow.'

'*What?*'Princess Princess's laughter wasn't like a tinkling stream. But Boo decided that tinkling streams would sound a lot better if they sounded like Princess Princess. 'Don't be *ridiculous*. Woof-woofs can't be Heroes. Even if they can talk. Three-headed Bulgoonians, yes. Vampire turtles, sure. But *not* little puppies! Yesterday, take Boo-Hoo here down to the kennels. It doesn't matter if you're late for assembly — no one ever notices *you*,' she added, striding off.

Boo watched her go, then turned back to Yesterday. She was regarding him curiously, her big brown eyes wide. Her dress smelt strange, Boo decided, like some animal he couldn't quite recognise. He would have liked to sniff her closer, but was afraid she'd be as angry as Princess Princess had been. 'I know you're not a dog,' she assured him. 'You really are a new student, aren't you?'

'Yes,' admitted Boo. He peered down at the bubbling magma again, then around at the black cliffs and the even blacker entrance to the wormhole. There was a strange ledge of rock above it, he realised, shaped just like a bed. 'I'm a werewolf actually. Um, where is the school?'

'Here, of course.' Yesterday gestured at a big dark cave further along the cliff. 'That's the entrance over there.'

'In a *volcano*?'

Yesterday shrugged. 'I think the heat is good for the old Heroes' arthritis. Plus it's, well, sort of heroic, I suppose, living in a volcano.'

'But isn't it dangerous being in a volcano?'

'Only when it burps,' said Yesterday. 'I think that's where the Hero bit comes in,' she added dryly.

Another bell clanged deep in the cliffs, its shrill tone overpowering even the *glug, glug, glug* of the magma. 'Come on.' Yesterday began to hurry across the hot black rock towards the cave entrance. 'You'd better see Dr Mussells.'

'Who's he?'

Yesterday didn't break her stride. 'The Principal. Didn't you know?'

Boo shook his head as he scurried after her, leaving his tangled clothes at the wormhole entrance. The smoke from the lava tore at his nostrils, and his paws already felt like they were about to become werewolf kebabs. But if Yesterday's bare feet could take it, he was sure his paws could too.

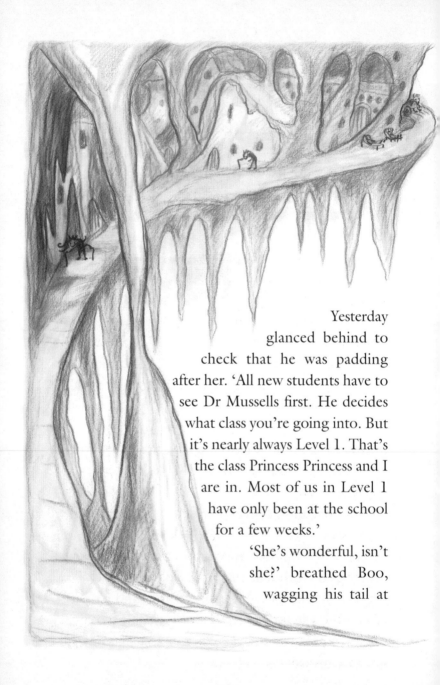

Yesterday
glanced behind to
check that he was padding
after her. 'All new students have to
see Dr Mussells first. He decides
what class you're going into. But
it's nearly always Level 1. That's
the class Princess Princess and I
are in. Most of us in Level 1
have only been at the school
for a few weeks.'

'She's wonderful, isn't
she?' breathed Boo,
wagging his tail at

the memory of Princess Princess's yellow hair.

'Princess Prinny?' Yesterday sighed. 'I suppose so. By the way, watch out for wheelchairs. There aren't any speed limits at Rest in Pieces.'

'How fast can a wheelchair go?'

'Fast,' said Yesterday. 'Especially when it's being driven by a Hero. The retirement village is up there,' she added, gesturing up through the smoke to where the cliffs loomed above them. 'Heroes like to have a good view of everything that might be happening, like a bogey invasion. The school is all down on this level.'

'Do … do you really think it's okay my being here? Being a werewolf I mean.'

A smile hovered at the edges of Yesterday's mouth but didn't quite make it. 'You wait till you meet Dr Mussells,' was all she said.

Boo trotted at her side. It was all too much to take in — the bubbling molten rock, the choking smoke, the smells of rock and strangers …

'Aaaaaaghhhh!' yelped Boo.

Yesterday peered down into the pit hidden under what looked like a normal stretch of black rock. 'Are you all right?' she asked politely.

'Woof! I mean, yes.' At least the pit had a soft layer of ash at the bottom. Boo shook the ash off his fur, embarrassed again. He ought to have smelt the pit coming. But at least he'd been in wolf form. If he'd fallen down the pit in Two-Foot form he could have broken one of his legs. 'Um, are there lots of these?' he asked cautiously.

'Pit traps? A few. They're to make us think where we're putting our feet. Or maybe just so the oldies watching up in the tea room can have a good giggle. Come on, I'll help you up.' She bent down and grabbed hold of his collar.

'No, I'm too heavy ...' began Boo, then stopped as he felt himself firmly hauled back onto the path.

'I'm stronger than I look,' said Yesterday. She still hasn't smiled, thought Boo. Does she ever smile?

'Um, should we do something about that?' Boo nodded towards the now open pit trap.

Yesterday shrugged. 'No need. One of the *Aaaagh!*ers will cover it up again. Till someone else falls into it.'

'Ughers?' enquired Boo cautiously.

Yesterday shook her head. '*Aaaagh!*ers. *Zoom!*ers teach us how to *Zoom!*. *Wham! Bam! Pow!*ers teach us about —'

'*Wham! Bam! Pow!*,' finished Boo.

'You've got it. And *Aaaagh!*ers teach us about things that make you go *Aaaagh!* Mostly by leaving traps for us to learn not to fall into. Come on,' she added. 'Dr Mussells's office is just through that cave there.'

'The one under the big long rock that looks like a black banana?'

'That's it,' said Yesterday. 'I'd better run or I'll be late for assembly. See you later!'

DOES YOUR CHILD SHOW HERO POTENTIAL?

The School for Heroes will turn YOUR CHILD
into a guaranteed Hero! suitable for all species.
classes with bite for vampires

subjects you can really get your teeth
into for werewolves

extra help for zombies to pull
themselves together

achieve true lift-off for phaeries!

Go to www.schoolforheroes.org today!

11

Doom! Doom!

Boo padded along the hot stone floor of the corridor. Wisps of yellow smoke oozed from the walls. A bat flickered by. Boo shivered. Despite the heat he felt cold … cold and alone.

He wished Yesterday were still with him. The School for Heroes was so much bigger than he had expected. He'd passed a dozen empty caves already, with round windows carved into the black baked rock, looking out onto the smoky air outside. Some of them had swords on the walls, or battle-axes. But none of them looked like a Principal's office.

Maybe he'd gone the wrong way.

Another bat flickered past, its red eyes vivid against the black of the walls. Boo turned to watch it go, just as a door opened, and an elderly chicken came out. It towered over him, its feathers grey and tatty-looking, and its red comb gnarled and straggly. Only its claws looked sharp and savage. It carried a laptop under one wing.

'Um, excuse me,' he barked politely, trying to look like he'd never chased a chicken in his life. 'I'm looking for …'

The chicken gazed down at him wildly. '*Clawk! Clawk! Clawk! Clawk! Clawk!* I see doom! Doom!' it clucked. 'There'll be crying and lamentation and utter defeat! Escape, if you can! Doom! *Doom!*'

'Er, I'm looking for the Principal's office,' said Boo, not sure whether he should be running for his life or if the chicken had just gone gaga.

'Principal's office?' The chicken peered down her beak at him vaguely as a few grey feathers fluttered to the ground. 'Do we have a Principal's office? Ah yes, I remember now. It's the second door on the left.'

'Um, thank you.'

The chicken strutted off down the corridor leaving wisps of feathers behind her.

At least he knew where he was going now. Boo took a deep breath and tried to cock his tail up at a jaunty angle as another bat flickered through the smoke.

This was it!

✼ ✼ ✼

'Hello, down there!'

Boo peered up as the headmaster swung down towards him. Dr Mussells's biceps rippled under his lilac silk shirt. His teeth gleamed white.

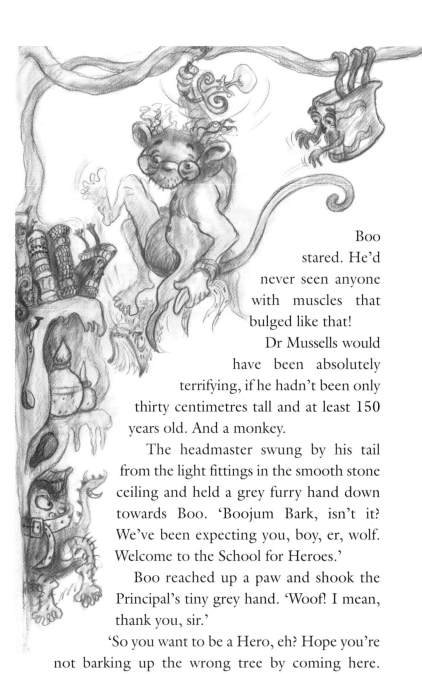

Boo stared. He'd never seen anyone with muscles that bulged like that!

Dr Mussells would have been absolutely terrifying, if he hadn't been only thirty centimetres tall and at least 150 years old. And a monkey.

The headmaster swung by his tail from the light fittings in the smooth stone ceiling and held a grey furry hand down towards Boo. 'Boojum Bark, isn't it? We've been expecting you, boy, er, wolf. Welcome to the School for Heroes.'

Boo reached up a paw and shook the Principal's tiny grey hand. 'Woof! I mean, thank you, sir.'

'So you want to be a Hero, eh? Hope you're not barking up the wrong tree by coming here.

He-he-he.' Dr Mussells let go of the light fitting and jumped down onto his desk. 'Get it? Barking up the wrong tree! But I've had a good report on you from the Werewolf General. You show great potential, I gather. Good man, er, wolf, your Werewolf General.'

The Principal leapt onto his chair and leafed through the documents on his desk. 'Gave the Greedle a gutful, did you? Impressive, very impressive. Shows guts. Guts — gutful — get it?'

'Um, I didn't really give it a gutful of anything much,' admitted Boo. 'I just threatened to widdle in the ice cream —'

'Exactly. Real heroic drama there,' said Dr Mussells, reaching under his desk. 'Make a good mini-series. Always useful for a Hero to star in a mini-series. Makes a good break from fighting bogeys. Like a banana?'

'Um, thank you, sir.' Boo stretched his jaws around the banana. 'Sir, I'm not sure I am a Hero, really,' he admitted.

Dr Mussells shrugged his tiny furry shoulders. 'Well, if you're not a Hero this is the place to find out. But the Werewolf General is rarely wrong. Except the time he thought that skeleton bogey was just a tasty bone. Lost his leg to that one … Now, you'll start off in Class 1.'

Boo put the banana down. 'Sir,' he said. 'What I really want is to rescue my mother! The Greedle took her, and …'

Dr Mussells began to peel another banana with

one furry hand. 'Hold it right there, Boojum. Students often have particular causes they want to fight for. They want to save their world from giant squid, or warm it during an ice age, or rescue a princess from a tower. I'm always amazed how many princesses are dumb enough to get trapped in towers. And I have to tell them all what I'm telling you now.'

'What's that?' asked Boo.

Dr Mussells swallowed his banana in one gulp. 'You'll have to wait. A beginner Hero isn't even much good at rescuing a princess — likely you'd get her halfway down the tower and drop her. Then all you'd get would be a bit of a squash. Get it? A squashed princess. A bit of a squash. He-he-he.'

'Ha-ha, sir,' said Boo. 'So, when *can* I start hunting for my mother?'

Dr Mussells grabbed another banana with his foot, threw it up into the air, caught it with his other foot, tossed it to his hands and began to peel it. 'If she's in the Ghastly Otherwhen? Never, if you have any sense. But if you still want to, well, Heroes can choose their own assignments when they reach Level 4. You'll start as a Level 1, like everyone else. You need to complete your first bogey assignment to get to Level 2.'

'When will I get to Level 4, sir?' Boo asked urgently.

'Can't tell you. Some Heroes never make it past Level 2. Good for frightening off mutant earwigs and not much more. But I'll tell you this, lad. No Hero has ever managed to get into the Ghastly Otherwhen

— or out of it, anyway. If your mother is there she's gone for good. Accept it and move on,' said Dr Mussells flatly, throwing the banana peel into the air. The peel circled the room twice, then landed in the bin by his feet. 'By the time you are in Level 4 hopefully you'll have given up all ideas of tackling the Ghastly Otherwhen.'

'No, I won't, sir,' barked Boo firmly.

'We'll see.' Dr Mussells took a bite of his banana. 'By the time you've tackled a few Insane Monster Silverfish and learnt how to stop a giant pus hole from erupting you may think differently.' He shook his tiny furry head. 'Wish I knew how the Greedle gets pus to erupt like that. Now, off you go. Assembly is in three minutes. Turn right and follow your cute little furry nose. Any other questions?'

Boo did his best to ignore the 'cute' word. 'Um, I met a giant chicken a few minutes ago. She was yelling out, "Doom, doom". I wondered if there was a problem.'

'Doom?' Dr Mussells screwed up his furry face. Then his expression cleared. 'Ah, that will be Miss Cassandra. She's our Finder.'

'What's that?' asked Boo.

'She Finds the bogeys for us. You'll study with her when you get to Level 2. *If* you get to Level 2. All Heroes have to learn a bit of Finding. How can you defeat a bogey if you don't know it's there? Of course, mobile phones have made a great difference, but the Greedle mostly sends out its bogeys to places with no communications towers. No, nothing beats a good crystal ball or a set of entrails when it comes to locating a bogey.'

'But the doom?' asked Boo hesitantly.

'Probably just the likely netball results for next weekend. Staff versus the Old Students.' Dr Mussells shook his head sadly. 'I'm afraid the team is going to be sadly defeated.'

'Which one?'

'Does it matter? Anything else?'

'No, sir,' said Boo.

'Good boy, I mean, wolf. Have another banana. Don't wolf it down all at once. Get it? He-he-he.'

'Ha-ha. Thank you, sir,' said Boo. He took the second banana in his teeth, added the first one and headed out the door.

RULE 164

If a Hero saves a kingdom, the king traditionally has to give half of it to the Hero, plus his daughter's hand in marriage. Heroes can find this embarrassing if they are a girl, already have a wife, or just don't like the look of the princess — or the kingdom. Luckily there aren't many kings around these days, as good manners means you have to accept any princess you're offered. And a true Hero is always well mannered.

THE HEROES' RULE BOOK

12

A Wee Problem

Boo had just hidden the bananas in a small hole in the corridor's stone walls when suddenly he knew …

He needed a widdle.

It wasn't a simple full bladder. The first thing a wolf did in a new place was to wee on the doorposts — as long as a Top Wolf hadn't widdled on them first — just to mark out a tiny bit of territory that was his. In the last half-hour he had seen more new things than he'd ever come across in his life — and he hadn't widdled on a single one of them!

If only things didn't smell quite so strange. It wasn't just the scent of the heat, smoke and molten rock. There were so many other smells too. Strange chicken stinks, strange gorilla and monkey stinks, strange people stinks … and even stranger 'not quite people' stinks. The scent of lots of different lunches, and the scent of school bags and shoes …

He *had* to have a widdle!

But not on a doorpost. The Werewolf General had been very clear about that. All right, so he *hadn't* managed to stay in human form! And he'd forgotten to yell 'Student approaching!' But at least he wouldn't lift his leg on a doorpost. He had to find a … what were they called? A bathroom! That was it. Then he could have a nice enormous widdle and … and maybe then the urge to widdle a few drops on the next door post wouldn't be quite so strong.

There had to be a bathroom somewhere, he decided. Even Heroes have to wee. He lifted up his nose and sniffed.

Hot rock, hot smoky air. But no smell of fresh widdle, or even old fading widdle. Nothing! Boo sat back, puzzled. Surely a werewolf would be able to smell where a whole school full of Heroes is widdling?

So where were all the student Heroes widdling? Maybe … maybe when you were a proper Hero you learnt not to widdle at all. But then you'd burst. And the Werewolf General widdled, and he was a Hero.

No, he just needed to sniff some more.

Boo lifted his nose up again. Yes, there was something now. Not a wee smell exactly. But a concentrated people smell — a *lots of people smell*.

That must be the bathroom! At last!

Boo trotted down the corridor, and followed his nose into a small passage. The rocky ceiling was lower here, and there were no windows either. But the smell of people was even stronger.

Boo frowned. It still didn't smell like widdle.

There was a door at the end of the passage. It was even narrower than the corridor, and the room inside was dark, too. Maybe the bathroom was up there. Boo padded inside and up three stairs.

The smell of people grew stronger. It still wasn't a toilet smell. Maybe, he thought, Hero wee doesn't smell like ordinary werewolf wee.

It was really urgent now. He wished wolves could cross their legs like humans could. But one of the first things a pup learnt at Changing class was never to Change with a full bladder. Not if you wanted dry legs.

He looked around desperately. All he could see was an empty floor, with a shiny rock wall on three sides, and a long curtain on the other. Was this really a bathroom? Where were those toilet things?

He should have asked the Werewolf General exactly what toilets looked like.

It had to be a bathroom, decided Boo desperately. What else could a bare room like this be?

Do all Two-Foots have black curtains in their bathrooms? Boo wondered.

He couldn't wait any longer. He had to widdle now! Toilet or no toilet. But at least it was private in here. No Heroes could see him widdle and get offended. Now to find something to lift his leg against. That thing would do, he thought — a stand of some kind, over by the far curtain.

Boo padded over and lifted his leg. Ahhh! he thought, as the puddle grew on the floor. That's

better! How had he managed to hold on so long?
Another two minutes and he would have burst —

The long black curtain rose.

Boo stared, his leg still raised.

Two hundred curious faces stared back from the
giant cavern of an auditorium. Human faces, furry
faces, faces with fangs or blue flaming hair.

'Ahem.' It was Dr Mussells, who had suddenly
appeared at the other end of the stage. Boo watched,
horrified, as the Principal knuckled towards him and
peered down at the puddle.

'You appear to have a wee problem,' said Dr
Mussells. 'Wee problem? Get it? He-he-he.'

Someone giggled in the audience. And then the laughter started. It boomed around the giant cave, louder even than the *glop* of lava from outside.

Boo lowered his leg.

'I think perhaps you need a wee mop too,' said Dr Mussells gently. 'Wee mop. Get it? Jones the Janitor will give you one. But it can wait till after assembly, lad. Now if you'd like to sit down — in the audience this time — I'll get on with the announcements.'

Boo slunk off the stage. His life as a Hero was not going well.

A bird in the hand is better
than a hand in the bird ...
especially if the bird is a vulture.

OLD HERO SAYING

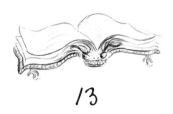

13

A Mate named Mug

One classroom: a round cave with smooth stone walls and a high grey ceiling, and a faint stench of rock and burning.

Eleven desks of dark, charred-looking wood.

Two bats, fluttering around the ceiling.

Ten kids, mostly human shaped, though one had green skin and three eyes, one looked like a furry lump of fungus, and another looked like a small ferocious pink bird. But even the bird only had two feet, as well as two tiny hands on the end of each wing.

One teacher, who might have been human 500 years before. She wore tight purple lycra, a necklace of small daggers, a wrinkled face like a half-empty balloon and a frown. Or maybe she only *looks* like she's 500 years dead, thought Boo.

Was she a *Zoom!*er or a *Wham! Bam! Pow!*er or an *Aaaagh!*er? Or something else? wondered Boo warily, trying to stop his tail drooping between his legs.

It had taken ages to mop up the widdle, and then to find Jones the Janitor (who had two legs, one hand and a patch over his eye and a belt full of the sharpest screwdrivers Boo had ever seen) again to give the mop and bucket back. By the time he'd finished that *and* gone back for his bag *and* fetched the bananas Dr Mussells had given him, everyone else was in their classes.

Twenty-three eyes, all staring at him.

Boo gulped. He was a Hero, wasn't he? Then he needed to behave like one.

'Woof! I mean, hi!' he barked, forcing his tail to stand up straight — or as straight as a naturally curly tail could go.

'It's that dumb puppy-dog *again*.' It was Princess Princess's voice. 'The one that widdled in assembly. I *told* Yesterday to take him to the kennels, Ms Snott.'

Ms Snott raised an eyebrow, though the rest of her wrinkles stayed where they were. 'Quiet, you bits of decomposing slug vomit,' she ordered the giggling class. 'Yesterday is not your servant, Princess,' she added calmly, her lips barely moving. 'Even if you are a hereditary hero princess. There are no servants on Rest in Pieces. I've told you that before.'

'Well, excuse *me*. 'And it's *Princess Princess*, by the way.'

'Nor will any of you bits of stray donkey slime use royal titles here. The only titles at the School for

Heroes are the ones you earn. Which means that if I want to call you a nasty piece of slimy earwax, I will.' The small black eyes stared expressionlessly at Boo. 'We've been expecting you. Sit down.' She gestured at the only vacant seat.

Boo could see why the seat was vacant. It shared a desk with the giant lump of fungus. Though the blob didn't smell like a simple fungus, thought Boo. There was something else under the green fuzz. But none of it looked fierce or heroic.

'But he's a *dog*!' protested Princess Princess.

'Werewolf,' said Ms Snott and Boo together.

'What?!' Princess Princess stared at him. 'Werewolves are strong and ferocious!'

Boo grinned, showing his fangs.

Princess Princess looked at him critically. 'Maybe a were-puppy,' she decided.

Boo's grin vanished. He tried even harder to keep his tail up. 'I can go on two feet too,' he offered.

Ms Snott started to nick bits of what looked like tentacle from between her teeth with one of her daggers. 'Two feet?'

'I can Change so I look human.' I should have Changed on the way here, he told himself, as the class kept staring at him. But there'd been too much new stuff going on to think about it.

'Oh, *sure*,' said Princess Princess.

'No, I can. Really.'

The tip of Boo's tail began to wag. Surely Princess Princess would be impressed by him as a human. Muscles, fangs, lots of shaggy black hair in just the right places ... what more could a Princess Heroine want?

He concentrated.

PLUNG!

The desk grew smaller. The ceiling grew closer. The room's smells grew much fainter and less interesting. Boo stretched out to his full height and turned to Princess Princess, grinning.

'Aaaagh!' screamed Princess Princess.

Boo blinked. What was wrong with her? Had she seen another pit trap? Or maybe a bogey had invaded! He'd save her! He glanced around the room, ready to attack. No traps to be seen. No strawberry-jam-oozing bogeys either. And why was everyone staring at him like that?

'He's … he's *naked*!' cried Princess Princess.

'Here. You take this.' It was the lump of fungus in the next desk. A few flies buzzed round his head. He handed Boo a textbook. *The Nasty Book of Nasties*, the cover read. *And 1001 fun things to do about them.*

Boo stared at the book. 'Um, I don't think I can read this now …'

'Not *read* it, Boojum.' Ms Snott's voice still seemed expressionless. Or was there just the faintest hint of a smile in it? 'I think Mug means for you to hold it.'

'Yeah,' said the lump of fungus, helpfully. 'You hold it like this!' The fungus made a vague gesture over its lower fuzzy front. 'But you be careful,' the fungus added. 'Books is Heroes too!'

'Oh,' said Boo. How could books be Heroes? He grabbed *The Nasty Book of Nasties* and held it over his private bits. 'Thank you,' he said to the fungus. 'Woof!' he added, as the book suddenly wrapped his legs in a leather lassoo.

'A word of warning, Bark,' said Ms Snott. 'You'll find that the books at this school are about some pretty heroic subjects. And that means the books need to be heroic too. And now,' Ms Snott added,

'I think perhaps you'd better go and get some clothes. And then the rest of you bits of pus-filled toe-jam can get on with the lesson.'

'A bogey ate my homework' is no excuse
for failing to hand in homework
on the due date. At the school for Heroes,
bogeys ARE your homework.

THE SCHOOL FOR HEROES RULE #1

14

Ms Snott and Dr Hogg

Boo felt like mud. Not even mud. Goose droppings. Green, *sloppy* goose droppings, the sort that were so loose they didn't even smell any good.

Cat guts! How could he have been so dumb? You have to stay in human form till they get used to you, the Werewolf General had told him. Wear clothes, the Werewolf General had said. Use a bathroom. So what did he do? He went mouse-hunting as a werewolf, widdled on stage in front of a large audience, and ended up naked in the middle of a classroom.

He hadn't even been able to sniff out a bathroom!

From now on I'll stay in human form, he decided. All the time, too! Soon everyone will forget that Boojum Bark was ever a fluffy puppy widdling in the school hall. I'll be the most heroic Hero they ever saw!

The stench of the volcano filled his nostrils now that he was outside again. Down below the school the magma went *glop, glop, glop.*

What would happen if the ledge collapsed? Boo wondered. Would the School for Heroes go toppling down into the boiling rock? Or was there some kind of magic holding everything together?

No, he reminded himself. Not magic. The School for Heroes wasn't about magic. It was about perfectly ordinary skills. Ha! thought Boo. As though anything about the School for Heroes could be ordinary.

A bat peered at him briefly, then flapped down into the lava pit. It seemed to be hunting sparks.

His clothes were still at the entrance to the wormhole where he'd stepped out of them. He picked them up and looked at them sadly. They had looked so fine when he'd left home. Now they were wrinkled, and covered in fine white ash. He must have torn them when he was struggling with the mouse, too. They also smelt of mouse.

But they were all he had to wear. Boo pulled them on, brushed off the ash as well as he could, and stepped out of the wormhole again.

It was funny, he thought, as he began to walk back along the smoky ledge, carefully avoiding the now covered-up pit trap. The tiny earthquakes from the volcano felt a bit like Sleepy Whiskers had, when the Zurm was digging the wormhole. But he was being silly. This was the one place in the universes where you didn't have to be scared of bogeys. He was just feeling hypersensitive, because everything was so strange and new.

'Doom! Doom!'

Boo stared. It was the chicken again, the weird Finding teacher. (Well, weirder, he decided.) Miss Cassandra, that was it.

Her tiny chicken eyes rolled as she stared at him. 'Flee! Flee!' she clucked.

Boo shook his head. 'I don't have any fleas. I used Mrs Bigpaws's flea powder this morning.'

Miss Cassandra's eyes stopped rolling for a moment. She looked down her beak at him, annoyed. 'Not *that* sort of flea. "Flee" as in run! Escape! Hide!'

'Oh. Why?' asked Boo cautiously.

Miss Cassandra's tiny black eyes blinked at him. 'Why? Why what? Or was it who?' She blinked again. 'Ah yes, I remember. I had a vision. A werewolf puppy and a hundred bogeys, and danger to the entire school! Doom! Doom! Flee!'

For a moment Boo felt like running for the wormhole and never coming back to the School for Heroes again. And then his werewolf stubbornness took over.

'No!' he said.

'What?!'

'I'm staying here. I don't care if I'm not a real Hero. I don't care if there's doom and all that stuff either. Just as long as I can learn enough Hero stuff to rescue my mum and keep Sleepy Whiskers safe!'

Miss Cassandra stared at him. 'Er, exactly who are you again?' she asked, her voice quavering a little.

'I'm Boojum Bark.' It was time to show a bit of courage here, decided Boo. He stuck his chest out.

'Hero and werewolf!'

Miss Cassandra flapped her wings, sending tiny puffs of feathers spiralling down towards the bubbling lava. 'You're not Hamad the Heroic?'

'No.'

'Or Gladys the Glamourpuss?'

'No!'

'Oh. Sorry about that. Clawk! Clawk! Clawk! Clawk! Clawk!' Miss Cassandra turned her back on him and strutted up one of the paths in the cliff.

⋇　⋇　⋇

Boo plodded back to the classroom and sat down as inconspicuously as he could next to the lump of fungus. Now that he was closer he could see the features behind the fuzz. Green skin, hollow black eyes and *lots* of flies. Boo stared. And were those *stitches* around his neck and fingers?

'Right, you putrid scraps of rotten scrambled eggs,' said Ms Snott, her lips hardly moving, or her wrinkles either.

'Why does she keep insulting the class like that?' Boo whispered to his neighbour.

'Her always do that.' The lump of fungus's idea of a whisper was a softer rumble. But not much softer. 'Her says it gets us used to insults in case bogeys try to make us angry by saying mean stuff. I think she talking to you now …'

'I *said*,' repeated Ms Snott, 'perhaps you'll tell this mob of quivering jellies a bit about yourself, Boojum.

What heroic act did you perform to make you a student Hero? Stand up!'

Boo stood. His smart new clothes were wrinkled, and there was a rip in the pants, just where you didn't want a rip to be. That blasted mouse! He dropped his hands over the tear and hoped no one noticed. 'I ... um ... what sort of bit?'

'Not the bit that you're trying to hide behind your hand,' muttered Princess Princess, just loud enough for everyone to hear. A ripple of laughter ran through the classroom.

'Now, now,' said Ms Snott. 'Well, Boojum?'

'Well ...' To Boo's embarrassment his voice turned into a squeak. He tried again. 'Well, I'm a werewolf.'

'Were-*puppy*,' muttered Princess Princess.

'And ... and I scared off the Greedle and its Zurms when they tried to invade my village ...'

Suddenly the class went silent. Real silence, of the not-even-a-wriggle or a yawn-down-the-back type.

'Ah, yes,' said Ms Snott. Even she looked respectful now, though her wrinkles still didn't move. 'I heard about that.'

'That was you? How did you do it?' It was Yesterday. Boo hadn't noticed that her desk was on the other side of Princess Princess's. 'No Hero has ever fought the Greedle in person. Not and won,' she added.

'Well, I, er ... I didn't exactly fight it. I sort of widdled in its ice cream so it decided to take it and run ...'

The silence shattered into laughter.

'Some Hero!' snorted Princess Princess. 'You pee-ed it off! Hey, everyone, he's a Pong Fu Hero! Or should that be Kung Poo!'

'It worked, didn't it, Princess Priss?' Yesterday's voice was soft, but somehow the class quietened at her words.

'Exactly,' said Ms Snott. Her voice was still expressionless. But Boo was learning to listen for the emotion behind her words now. 'Brains beat muscles once again. Continue, Boo.'

'And the Werewolf General — he's our world's big Hero — he said I was a Hero too. So I had to come here. And I said yes because,' he gulped, 'if I really learn how to do this Hero stuff properly I can rescue my mum and ...'

'Oh, *yawn*! Another I-must-rescue-my-family loser. BORING!' It was Princess Princess again. But she can't mean it, thought Boo. She's just ... um ... she's just ... he tried frantically to think of a nice reason for Princess Princess to be so nasty.

'Thank you, Boo. You may sit down. Just out of curiosity, your royal lowness, Princess — stand up girl! — why did *you* come to Hero School?' The ancient teacher still showed no expression as she gazed at the princess.

'Me?' Princess Princess sounded surprised. 'Because I look totally *cool* in Hero costumes, of course. And because our royal family is *naturally* heroic so of course we get to come to the school whenever we want to. My grandfather tricked three wicked gnomes out of their treasure. And my aunt gave a *dragon* indigestion.'

'But what did *you* do, Princess?' asked Ms Snott quietly.

Princess Princess looked at her defiantly. 'I'm the best student Wham! Bam! Pow!er in the school, even though I've only been here two weeks! *And* I'm the best Zoom!er, too!'

'So you've never actually fought a bogey?'

'What's *that* got to do with anything?' Princess

Princess spun lightly on one foot and punched the other into the air. 'I'm obviously heroic! And my dad says that only a Hero is good enough to marry me, and the School for Heroes is the best place to meet one. A Hero *prince* at least, of course. Or a king. Or even a small-time emperor,' she added. 'My dad's King of ...'

'Thank you, Princess,' said Ms Snott. Even her eyebrow was still now. 'And now you mangy mucous-guzzlers can all turn to page sixty-three of *The Nasty Book of Nasties*, and if it bites you there are bandages in the cupboard. Today we are studying the Spotted or Green-Fanged Mumbler, one of the lesser but smellier bogeys from the Ghastly Otherwhen. Now, can any of you think how you might recognise a Green-Fanged Mumbler?'

The lump of fungus put up his hand. 'Him got name tag?'

'Good answer. But not quite. Any other of you black-toed, ear-wax munchers got any ideas?'

Boo put up his hand with the others. He had a feeling it was going to be a long, long time till lunch.

☀ ☀ ☀

It was.

Boo's head ached halfway through the first lesson ... and human heads were bigger than wolf heads so there was more to ache. He *hated* being in human form. And having to wiggle his fingers to write instead of holding a pen in his jaws was even worse. How was anyone supposed to remember all the bogeys? Or what worlds they came from?

But the rest of the class seemed to manage. Especially Princess Princess. She appeared to know *The Nasty Book of Nasties* by heart.

And what does it matter? he wondered. Surely all a Hero had to do was wait till something started eating people or freezing them to make chess pieces like the Grubberlubby. And then you knew they were evil — or at least had been made a servant of evil by the Greedle — without having to count their tentacles, or remember which monster had blue fangs and which one had cockroaches living in its belly button.

But what if …

Boo's hand was in the air before he realised it. Uh-oh, he thought. This isn't the time to make myself conspicuous. He slunk his hand down again, but it was too late.

'Yes, Boo?' asked Ms Snott, showing as much emotion as a strawberry ice cream.

'Um … what about the bogeys who don't look like monsters?' he asked. 'They won't be in the book, will they?'

'Duh,' said Princess Princess. 'There are another *twelve* volumes, you know.'

'Yes, but … but what if a particular bogey isn't in those either?'

'Of *course* they are —' began Princess Princess.

'Any creature might be evil, if it's been taken over by the Greedle,' cut in Yesterday. 'That's what Boo meant, wasn't it, Boo?'

Boo nodded.

Ms Snott fixed him with her black stare. 'You want to know how to recognise a bogey again?'

'Yes,' said Boo.

Ms Snott smiled, though it took a while for her wrinkles to move into what were evidently new positions. 'You want a way to be absolutely sure if you're safe or in danger?'

'Yes, please,' said Boo.

'There isn't one,' said Ms Snott flatly. 'Class dismissed.' She hobbled from the room, leaving a scent of lycra and talcum power behind her.

Boo stood up to go out, but the blob of fungus stopped him. 'She go. But we stay.' The blob of fungus grabbed a can of fly-spray from under his desk, gave his flies a quick squirt, then sneezed. Boo watched in horror as one of his long green teeth fell out.

'There's another class before lunch,' said Yesterday, leaning down and picking the fungus's tooth up from among the still-twitching flies as though nothing unusual had happened. 'I ... I'm really sorry about your mum, Boo,' she added, handing the tooth back.

'Thanks,' began Boo. He fought back the pang that sliced through him whenever he thought of Mum, then stared as the blob of fungus casually plopped his tooth back into his mouth. 'Um, why ...' he began.

Yesterday shook her head warningly. 'Shhh. Mr Hogg is coming. He teaches *Zoom!*ing. He's an old pig.'

'Is he strict?' Boo whispered back.

'No, he *is* a pig,' hissed Yesterday, just as Mr Hogg trotted through the door.

The new teacher was small and pink. He wore a flamboyant pink suit with a hole in the trousers for his curly tail, and an extraordinary pair of glasses on his nose.

Mr Hogg sat back and stared at the class over his glasses. 'A new student, I see!' Boo had expected him to grunt, but instead the pig's voice was high and unexpectedly musical. 'Stand up, young man!'

Boo stood.

'And what is your name?' demanded Mr Hogg.

'Boo, sir,' said Boo. 'I mean Boojum Bark.'

Mr Hogg smiled, showing neat piggy teeth, so white and even that Boo suspected they were false. 'I suppose you are thinking, Bark, how you had roast pork for dinner last week?'

Boo gulped. 'How did you know, sir?'

Mr Hogg sighed. 'Because for some reason every student has roast pork the week before their first class with me.' Suddenly the beady eyes twinkled. 'But not pork like me!'

'Wha—what?' Boo blinked. He was tied up — tight — with thick red ropes! And he hadn't even seen Mr Hogg move.

Mr Hogg buffed one tiny trotter against his fluffy pink scarf. 'You are thinking: "Ha, wrinkled old pig, how did he do it? *Did* he do it?" It is quite simple. You just *Zoom!* into Otherspace while your victim

145

stays stationary, remembering to pick up your choice of rope, string, barbed wire or dried cow gut, pause for afternoon tea — if you've remembered to take your picnic basket to Otherspace with you — brush off the chocolate cake crumbs, then *Zoom!* out of Otherspace and re-enter your ordinary world at the point from which you left and tie up the bogey tight as you can.'

'Um, simple,' croaked Boo.

'Don't croak, lad. It's not becoming. You're a wolf, not a frog,' said Mr Hogg. 'And *do* something about those pants. Red is just not your colour. As I was saying —'

All at once Boo was free, nor was there any sign of the ropes that had tied him.

'Er … how did you do that?' he asked.

'Just good heroic science, my boy! And totally normal Hero skills!'

Suddenly Boo realised the wrinkled little piggy eyes were twinkling at him. 'Now,' said Mr Hogg, 'I'll show you how to do it.'

* * *

It was no use. No matter how hard Boo concentrated he couldn't even get into Otherspace, much less *Zoom!* about it. Luckily the rest of the class seemed to find it hard too, though not as difficult as it was for him.

All except Princess Princess. When it was her turn to come to the front of the class she turned a somersault right by Mr Hogg's table — and suddenly Mr Hogg's pink trotters were tied up with his pink scarf.

'Excellent!' cried Mr Hogg. 'You can untie me, girl, thank you. Now, shall we try it again with the rest of you? Bark, out here again …'

At last the bell rang for lunchtime. Boo was starving — he was used to a quick lap of ice cream whenever he wanted it, or at least a frozen lizard. He hadn't even dared to snap one of the flies that buzzed around the lump of fungus in case Princess Princess saw him at it — not that flies tasted as good in human form as they did to a wolf.

His head felt stuffed with too many facts. He didn't want to know all this, he just wanted to know about the Ghastly Otherwhen and how to find Mum. But it was just beginning to dawn on him that he really was being trained to be a Hero here — a full-time Hero, not just a kid who'd *Zoom!* in, grab Mum, then go back to being an ice-cream delivery wolf.

Did he really want to be a full-time, proper Hero? Worse — did he even have a chance of being one?

It had seemed so easy back in Sleepy Whiskers: go to school and learn a bit of heroing. It had never occurred to him that he mightn't be any good at it.

Everyone here seemed so much better at being a Hero than he did.

Boo pulled his lunch box out of his bag, then walked out of the classroom, down the corridor, and out the entrance again. The black cliffs loomed above. The yellow crystals glinted in the red volcano light. Below him the magma swirled and bubbled, sending up another cloud of steam.

But there was no sign of any other students.

Boo sighed and stared around. Maybe they had vanished. Maybe vanishing was one of the secret Hero tricks that he hadn't learnt yet. No, he could hear voices coming from somewhere in the smoke …

Maybe they'd all gone invisible.

If only someone friendly was around! Even that nice girl Yesterday had disappeared. If only …

'Hi. Remember me? Me Mug,' said a voice above him. Boo looked up. It was the giant lump of fungus.

He looked exactly like the Rat Surprise that Boo had accidentally left under the table for two weeks. Except this kid was two metres tall, which Rat Surprises usually weren't. But at least he looked friendly. Or Boo supposed he did, under the fungus.

'Of course I remember you.' How could anyone forget sitting next to a giant lump of fungus? thought Boo. 'But I don't think you're a mug at all,' he added, trying to be friendly too. 'Some of your answers were really good.' Not that any of them answered the questions, thought Boo. In fact, he wasn't even sure his neighbour had heard the questions, much less understood them. But he was glad he'd been kind when the … thing … smiled. Green crumbly teeth gleamed inside the fuzz.

'No, it's just me *name* is Mug.' Mug batted away a few flies then peered down at Boo, dribbling slightly. Boo moved his sandwich out of range. 'Me had something me meant to ask you. But can't remember. Me forget head if not sewn on.'

'Sewn on?' asked Boo.

Mug grinned. His teeth were fuzzy too. 'Me zombie,' he rumbled. 'From Zombie Island. You not guess?'

'No,' said Boo. 'I've never met a zombie before. Is everyone in your universe a zombie?'

'No. Not till they dies. Zombies nice peoples,' Mug assured him. 'It good life on Zombie Island when you dead. Well, us likes it anyhow, so we go dead real soon. We likes dogs, too. Also wolfses. Even before you

149

dead. Long as you remember, don't chew eyeballs if find it lying about. Me always losing eyeballs.'

'I promise I won't chew any eyeballs,' Boo assured him.

Mug grinned again. 'Me remember what me wanted to ask now! You have friend here?'

'Me? No,' said Boo, startled.

'You want friend?'

'Well, yes,' said Boo cautiously. How could you say no to a question like that?

'Good!' Mug took out another can of fly-spray from a pocket hidden among his fungus fuzz, squirted it at the flies, then sneezed again. This time an eye fell out. 'Me want friend too! Me had friend once,' he added, putting the can of fly-spray back in his pocket and the eye back in his eye socket. 'But you wanna friend who blow out goobies when him sneeze, chews him's toenails and blows up toilets when him farts?'

'No,' said Boo.

'Him not either,' rumbled Mug sadly. Then he beamed. 'But me no longer blow goobies everywhere!'

'Um, good,' said Boo weakly. He gave Mug's bum a cautious sniff, hoping he wouldn't notice. It smelt a bit like one of Ms Shaggy's rotten chicken necks, even with his limited human nostrils. But it also smelt friendly, and unexpectedly kind.

'Me got handkerchief!' Mug held up a large ball of what looked like pure congealed snot. 'Me fart now *before* me gets to toilet. Me not chew toenails. Me civilised!' said Mug proudly. 'Me have you for friend now!' He peered down at Boo's lunch. 'What you got for lunch?'

'Rat sandwich.'

'Hot lake!'

'I think you mean "damn",' said Boo.

'That too. Me got zombie spaghetti and dead-slug quiche. You wanna swap?'

'Zombie spaghetti?'

'It delicious,' Mug assured him. 'Just make sure swallow hard or it wriggle back up.'

'Um … could I swap a rat sandwich for the dead-slug quiche?' Boo loved snail quiche, and the snails were usually pretty dead by the time they'd been quiched. He figured that dead-slug quiche should be much the same, but without the crunchy bits. Maybe having Mug for a mate wasn't going to be quite as bad as he had thought.

'Don't worry if quiche slither a bit as it go down. It zombie quiche. Just chew extra. Slugs no good at slugging up out of your tummy again. Hey,' rumbled Mug. 'You like to borrow my spare pants?'

Boo glanced down at his pants. They still weren't hiding the bits pants were most importantly designed to cover.

'Yes, please,' he said.

* * *

The pants were too long, and smelt of zombie and fly-spray, and his bum looked like it sagged almost to the floor. But it was better than having his rude bits poking out in class.

And now he knew where the toilet was as well. The water steamed a bit when you flushed it. That was why he hadn't been able to smell all the Hero widdle, he realised. The water flushed it all away.

'We go sit by skinning pool,' said Mug, after he'd shown Boo how to wash his hands afterwards and how *not* to drink from the toilet bowl. 'That where other kids have lunches.' He began to trudge out the door then down the corridor.

Boo stuffed his torn silk pants down behind the dirty towel basket and scurried to keep up. He still hadn't quite got the hang of walking fast on only two feet. 'Don't you mean swimming pool?'

'Nup. This pool boiling water. All water hot in volcano. You swim in that and all your skin come off. So it skinning pool. Come on. Pool over there.'

Boo followed him out of the big school's entrance, a black mouth in the even blacker cliffs, then across the ledge above the lava pit to what looked like a big fallen boulder. There was a narrow passage there, Boo realised, between the boulder and the cliffs, just wide enough for Mug's bulky shoulders to slip through, that he hadn't noticed in all the smoke and ash.

'How come you're at the School for Heroes?' Boo asked, as he followed Mug into the crevice.

Mug beamed back at him. 'Giant Slugs attack our island. But me got secret weapon.'

'What is it?'

'It secret! But Giant Slugs taste good,' added Mug happily. 'We got enough slug now for years! Slug stew, slug pancakes, chocolate slug cake, slug pavlova, slug and chips. My mum make best slug and chips, even better than zombie spaghetti. Zombie spaghetti more useful, though. Hey, watch out. Trap just there … where you want to sit?'

Boo stared. The ledge was wider here: like a flat rocky oval. The same black cliffs loomed above them, and the lava pit spat and bubbled. But on this ledge a big pool of water gleamed like a silver mirror edged with rounded boulders. A pair of ancient Vikings paddled a longship through the steam. All around, students from what looked like dozens of universes were sprawled on the rocks, chatting and eating their lunches, and casually avoiding the odd spear cast by the Vikings.

Boo looked at the water longingly. He'd love a swim, though he wasn't sure he could dog paddle as a human. But even as he looked another wisp of yellow steam drifted up from the surface.

'Let's sit over there,' said Boo, pointing at a group sitting on the highest boulder of all, right next to the pool.

Mug stared. 'But they girls!'

'Yes,' said Boo. He had noticed the golden gleam of Princess Princess's hair as soon as they'd come through the arch. It's as yellow as two-day-old widdle, he thought admiringly. She was sitting with Yesterday and another girl from their class. He headed over without waiting to see if Mug followed.

'Er, hi,' he said. 'Mind if we sit here?'

'So *then* the prince said to Dad, I think she's the most beautiful princess I've ever ... It's the Pong Fu champion. Were you speaking to me?' asked Princess coolly, casually grabbing one of the flying spears and throwing it back to the Heroes in the longship.

'Um, yes,' said Boo, as the spear thudded into the side of the ship. One of the wrinkled Vikings gave a salute of approval.

'No dogs allowed,' said Princess Princess. 'Hey, I just thought of a joke. What's got four legs, barks and goes tick tock?'

'I don't know,' said Boo.

'A *watch*-dog!'

'Ha-ha,' said Boo, trying to smile.

'Don't be mean,' said Yesterday. 'Sit down.' The

scales on her rough leather tunic gleamed a little in the damp from the steam.

Boo sat down next to her. The rock was warm on his bum, but not uncomfortably so. Even in his human form he could smell the pool below, like a kitchen kettle that had been boiling too long. Mug lowered himself next to him. Boo hoped no zombie bits fell into the pool below. He supposed even zombies didn't like their bits boiled.

'This is T'ai T'ai,' said Yesterday. The three-eyed, green-skinned girl Boo had seen in class nodded to him. She was sharpening her claws with a nailfile. 'And you know Princess Princess Sunbeam Caresse of Pewké.'

'I've never heard of Pewké,' said Boo, trying to sound as though he sat on a warm boulder in a volcano talking to a gorgeous princess every day of his life.

'Oh, it's just a small universe. But very select,' said Princess Princess.

'What that mean?' rumbled Mug.

'No dogs except on a lead,' said Princess Princess. 'And no zombies, either. My mum would go *ballistic* if she found a bit of zombie in the castle.' Her lunch box had a gold crown on the top, Boo noticed. Her sandwiches even had the crusts cut off.

'Aren't you eating?' Boo asked Yesterday. She was the only one without a lunch box in her lap.

Yesterday shrugged. Her shoulders looked so thin they were almost sharp. 'I forgot my lunch.'

'Ha,' said Princess Princess. 'Yesterday *always* forgets her lunch. She's anorexic. That's someone who refuses to eat,' she added, as Mug's mouth opened to ask, 'What that?' again.

Yesterday flushed. 'I am not.'

'Then how come you never bring any lunch?'

Yesterday shrugged again.

'Um, would you like a bit of mine?' Boo offered Yesterday his lunch box.

'Are you sure?'

'Sure I'm sure. It's rat sandwich,' he added generously. 'There's plenty.'

'Or slug quiche,' rumbled Mug. 'I got zombie spaghetti too. It stop wriggling now. I think it having nap.'

'Well, er …' began Yesterday.

'I've got a couple of bananas, as well,' offered Boo. 'Dr Mussells gave them to me.'

'He must really like you,' said Yesterday. 'He hardly ever gives anyone his bananas.'

'What if he doesn't like you?'

For a moment Yesterday looked like she might smile. But she didn't. 'You don't want to know.'

She took one of the bananas and began to peel it. Her fingers were so slender they almost seemed transparent.

How can Yesterday be a Hero? wondered Boo, watching her eat the banana hungrily. She doesn't seem strong enough to chase a mouse, much less a monster. Then he forgot about her and watched

Princess Princess instead.

Princess Princess even ate beautifully. Her teeth were as white as poodle bones that had been bleached in the sun. And her lips were as red as a rat steak …

'What are *you* goggling at?' demanded Princess Princess.

'Oh, nothing.' Boo looked down at his slug quiche instead. Bits of it were wriggling slightly, but Boo hardly noticed.

Princess Princess sighed. 'I suppose you live with your nasty aunt and uncle.'

Boo looked puzzled. 'Um. No. I live with the Mayor and his family. And they're really nice.'

Princess Princess snorted. 'Can't you do *anything* right? The "I'm a poor orphan who's going to save

his family" is *supposed* to have a mean aunt and uncle who make him live on scraps.'

'They don't make me live on scraps at all. We had baked corgi last night and —'

'I *so* didn't need to know that,' said Princess Princess. 'We had our usual banquet at the palace. Roast swan, roast goose, roast venison, potatoes, carrots, asparagus, artichokes, pumpkin, green salad, tomato salad, rice salad, hot bread rolls, apple pie, peach pie, pavlova, six sorts of jellies, lemon pudding, date custard and ginger sponge. Oh, and ice cream. What did you have for dinner, Yesterday?'

Yesterday, who was staring at Princess with an open mouth, shut it and shrugged her thin shoulders. 'Can't remember,' she said shortly.

'See?' said Princess Princess. 'I *said* she was anorexic. Hey, what's the difference between a werewolf and a flea?'

'We're bigger?'

'No! Werewolves have fleas but fleas don't have werewolves!' Princess Princess threw her scraps out into the pool. The water bubbled around them for a moment, then they blackened and sank. 'I'm going to hang-glide above the lava. Mickey the Magnificent is giving me lessons. It's *dangerous*, of course, but that's what being a Hero is all about. Anyone else coming?'

Boo felt his mouth hang open. 'But ... but you could burn yourself!'

'Not if you know what you're doing,' said Princess Princess airily. 'It's just a matter of making sure the updraught is strong enough to keep you above the lava.'

'Um … I'll just watch,' said Boo.

Princess Princess snickered. 'I *said* you were a watchdog!'

Boo watched her go. There had to be some way to make Princess Princess like him, he thought wistfully. Maybe if he stayed in human form long enough she'd forget she'd ever seen him as a puppy. The Werewolf General had said he'd only need to stay in human form for a couple of days, but Boo had a feeling it would take longer than that to get Princess Princess to forget she'd seen him lift his leg on the school stage.

And there was one other thing that would really impress Princess Princess too.

Learn to be a Hero.

I need to make a list, he thought glumly, ducking as a spear whistled over his head and the water steamed and bubbled below him.

* *Become the biggest Hero in the whole School for Heroes.*
* *Find Mum and rescue her.*
* *Make Princess Princess like me.*

Now he just had to figure out how to do it.

The first thing every Hero has to remember is to Wham!, THEN Bam!, THEN Pow!.
A Bam! Pow! Wham! just doesn't have the same effect at all.

Ms Punch — Helpful Hints for Heroes' Homework

15

Wham! Bam! Pow!

He just had to figure out how to do it, thought Boo, staring at the rubber bogey hanging from the rope that dangled from the giant gymnasium cave's ceiling.

'Right,' said Ms Punch, wafting above the class. 'This is an Insane Jellyfish ...'

Boo had been startled to find that one of the teachers was a ghost. Ms Punch had been killed during the 'Horrible Ghastly Otherwhen Skeletons with Special Nasty Features' invasion on her home world a hundred years before, when the Greedle decided that her people made the best sponge cake in the universes. As Ms Punch said, being a ghost for a hundred years gave her *plenty* of time to work out what she'd done wrong — and to make sure none of her Hero students made the same mistake.

And she'd never really liked sponge cake anyhow.

Mug's hand went up. 'It not jellyfish, Miss. It lump of rubber.'

Ms Punch sighed. The gust sent parts of her drifting across the room. 'There's always one,' she muttered to herself. 'Pull yourself together, Punch. Very well,' she said more loudly as her wisps came back into one shape again. 'Let us *pretend* that this is an Insane Jellyfish. Now, can any of you tell me a jellyfish's weak spot?'

Princess Princess's hand shot into the air. 'Vibration, Ms Punch! If you Wham! Bam! a jellyfish there and there they begin to wobble and can't stop.'

Ms Punch gave a ghostly smile. 'Excellent. Perhaps you would like to demonstrate?'

'Of course, Ms Punch!' Princess Princess swaggered out to the front of the class in her high-heeled sandals. 'This is how you do it,' she said. One perfect heel went Wham! One dainty hand went Bam! And then she somersaulted, kicking hard with both feet as she turned over.

Pow! The jellyfish was wobbling so hard the entire room was filled with vibration.

'Superb as always! Now, Yesterday! Your turn!' called Ms Punch, wafting above them.

Yesterday stood in front of the monster till it had stopped wobbling.

Wham! Bam! Pow!

It had none of the elegance of Princess Princess's Wham!s. The jellyfish didn't wobble much, either. But Ms Punch just nodded. 'Passable,' she said. 'Not enough vibration to destroy it, but you'll give it a nasty headache. You, boy, what's your name? The zombie in the corner.'

Mug shook his head. 'Me Mug. No need to *Wham! Bam!* thingie, Miss. Me got secret weapon.'

'Oh, deary me …' muttered Ms Punch, fading in and out. 'Look, my dear young zombie, you *all* have your own Hero skills. But my job is to teach you the Hero basics of *Wham! Bam! Pow!*'

'Oh,' said Mug. He stood in thought for a moment. 'No worries.' He stomped over to the jellyfish.

Wham! Mug hit the jellyfish such a solid blow his arm fell off.

Mug bent down and picked up his arm, then swung it hard against the jellyfish.

Bam!

The jellyfish shuddered.

'Hmm. Not exactly traditional,' said Ms Punch, floating through the wall and back again. 'But it did the job. Now you, boy.' She nodded at Boo. 'What's your Hero skill?'

'Widdling!' giggled Princess Princess. 'Kung Poo!'

Ms Punch raised a ghostly eyebrow. 'Perhaps a traditional approach would be more effective!'

Boo gulped. He walked stiffly up to the jellyfish then put his hands up in what he hoped was the correct Wham! position.

Wham!

The jellyfish swung wildly. Whap! It thudded back into him.

'The idea is for *you* to knock *it* out,' said Ms Punch, drifting above Boo as he picked himself up. 'Not the other way around. Can you see your mistake now?'

'Your boo-boo!' gurgled Princess Princess. 'Hey, get it? Boo's boo-boo. That's what we should call him! Boo-boo! Boo-boo does Kung Poo!'

'Try again,' said Ms Punch kindly.

Boo aimed his leg. How had Princess Princess done it? He kicked out as hard as he could.

Bam!

And the world went black.

✳ ✳ ✳

The world was green and black. It stank too.

Had the Greedle's bogeys attacked again? He *knew* those vibrations felt strange … Boo sat up fast and bumped his head on something soft and furry.

Mug.

Mug's green face looked down at him in concern. 'How many fingers me holding up?' he asked.

'Four,' said Boo.

'Really?' Mug looked at his hand in amazement. 'So that what four look like. Me thought me had five. Me must have dropped fingers somewhere. You okay?' he added.

'I … I think so,' said Boo. 'What happened?'

'Jellyfish *Wham! Bam! Pow!* you,' said Mug helpfully.

'But I was supposed to *Wham! Bam! Pow!* it!'

Mug shrugged. He'd sewn his arm back on, Boo realised, or someone had. The blue thread stood out against Mug's green fuzz. 'Maybe jellyfish flip-flopped you then.'

Boo tried to stand up. His legs felt wobbly, like the jellyfish.

No, he thought, *not* the jellyfish. He never wanted to think about jellyfish again. What sort of Hero was he? He couldn't even *Wham! Bam! Pow!* a lump of plastic.

'Ah, you're up again. Can't keep a good Hero down, eh?' Ms Punch floated back into the gymnasium cavern, her ghostly feet drifting through the stone floor like a pillowcase dragged by a puppy.

'Yes, Miss. Sorry, Miss,' muttered Boo.

Ms Punch's ghostly white eyes stared at him knowingly. 'Feeling bad, eh, Bark? Feel like you're a slug, not a Hero?'

'Something like that,' muttered Boo.

'Don't let it worry you,' said Ms Punch. 'Some Heroes just aren't cut out for *Wham! Bam! Pow!* Stick to your speciality. What is your speciality anyway?'

'I'm not sure,' said Boo. 'Widdling maybe. And biting.'

Ms Punch stared. 'Widdling? You mean you really do that, er, Kung Poo?'

'I'm a werewolf,' Boo explained.

Ms Punch's face cleared. 'That explains why you're so clumsy with your hands. Look, Bark, are you sure you wouldn't be more comfortable as a wolf in *Wham! Bam! Pow!* class?'

'Yes, Miss. I mean no, Miss.' Boo wished his head didn't ache. Everyone would think he was even less of a Hero if he went back to being a cute furry puppy. Especially Princess Princess! 'I mean I really want to be a human-shaped Hero,' he added.

'Hmmm.' Ms Punch floated above him, peering down thoughtfully. But all she said was, 'The rest of the class are in the library. It's manifesting down past the oval at the moment. Too far away for you to join them — the bell will be going in a few seconds. You're probably feeling a bit too fragile to cope with the library in any case. The books are being especially heroic today — they've been Wham!ing and Bam!ing all over the library. Get a good night's sleep and we'll see you tomorrow.'

'Yes, Miss,' said Boo miserably, as once again the bell pealed deep inside the volcano, making his head ache even more.

'Me glad you okay,' said Mug as the echoes died away. 'Get friend then lose friend all in same day — that bad.'

'Yes,' said Boo weakly. 'It would be.'

'Hey, is Boo all right?'

For a wonderful moment Boo thought it was Princess Princess. But it was only Yesterday.

'I'm feeling fine,' said Boo, not quite truthfully. 'Just dumb.'

Yesterday gave an almost smile. It looked nice, thought Boo ... not brilliantly, heroically beautiful like Princess Princess's smile. But nice. Boo wondered what Yesterday would look like if she smiled properly.

'Don't worry,' she said. 'We all do dumb things sometimes.'

'Not Princess Princess,' said Boo. 'She's perfect.'

Yesterday's smile faded a bit. 'Yes, Princess Pea is always perfect,' she said. 'Do you want a hand to get to the wormhole?'

'No,' said Boo. 'I'm okay.'

And he was. Sort of.

'Come on,' said Yesterday. 'Mug and I will go with you, just in case.'

They walked out of the gym, down the black stone corridor, and out onto the ledge. The wormhole was a black smudge in the blackness of the cliff. One by one students were lining up to walk into it.

It was Princess Princess's turn at the entrance now. Boo watched her stride inside, under the fossilised bed. He imagined her stepping out into a grand ballroom in a castle somewhere. But no, the entrance in her universe would be under a bed too, wouldn't it? He bet Princess had the most heroic bedroom in

the universes, with swords on the wall, and diamond battle-axes embroidered on the blanket …

The three of them got into line. Yesterday reached the entrance first. 'See you tomorrow, Boo,' she said.

'Yeah. See you,' said Boo glumly.

Mug was next. 'Bye,' he said. He hesitated. 'Me glad me have friend,' he added, holding out a fuzzy hand.

Boo shook it. He'd expected it to be all squishy, like the fungus-covered Rat Surprise. But instead it felt muscular under the fuzz. 'I'm glad you're my friend too,' he said, and was surprised to realise that he meant it.

Boo began to walk down the wormhole. After a few seconds he looked back. But it was impossible to make out anything in the redness that was the door to Hero School.

Boo turned back and began to walk again. He was pooped! But there was so much to think about too. Did he really want to be a Hero? Did Princess Princess really hate him or was she just pretending, the way girls sometimes did? What would Princess Princess wear tomorrow?

Could any first day at any school anywhere possibly have been *any* worse?

'I really made a mess of it!' cried Boo. 'Nothing, nothing, *nothing* could be worse than today!'

'Squeak!'

Boo looked up. The mouse was perched on a tiny ledge of rock above him.

Suddenly he felt something dribble down his nose and drip, drip, drip into his mouth.

The mouse had wee-ed on him.

RAT AND BANANA ICE CREAM

Ingredients:
1 dead rat, squashed, or 1 teaspoon essence of
rat (make sure it doesn't dissolve the spoon)
half a cup of cream
2 mashed bananas
juice of two lemons
half a cup of castor sugar

Method:
Mash everything together well. Pour into a
plastic container and cover with a lid. Place
in freezer. Take container out every half-hour
for three hours, mash contents, then put back
in the freezer. Eat within three days.

PS If you leave out the rat you have plain
banana ice cream.

THE BEST ICE-CREAM RECIPE BOOK
IN THE UNIVERSES

16

The Kung Poo Hero Returns

He still hadn't caught the mouse when he reached the end of the wormhole.

The Werewolf General was waiting for him up in Mum's bedroom. Boo was glad to see he was still in wolf shape. He'd had enough of humans for a while.

'Well,' asked the Werewolf General, 'how did it go?'

'Um, okay, sir,' lied Boo, crawling out from under the bed and standing up unsteadily. It felt strange to be back in the cold of a Sleepy Whiskers winter after the heat of the volcano.

The Werewolf General smiled. 'That bad? I remember my first day. I chased a guinea pig right round the school hall. And then I caught it.'

'What was wrong with that, sir?'

'The guinea pig was the Principal. She had me tied up in knots before I could blink. Don't suppose she's still there?'

'I don't think so, sir. The Principal now is a

monkey. And one of my teachers is a pig. Not a guinea pig. A real pig — he tied *me* up in knots. But it's okay really …'

'Hmm. Don't worry, Boo. It'll get better,' growled the Werewolf General gently.

'Yes, sir. Thank you, sir,' said Boo. 'Um … there hasn't been any sign of Mum, has there?'

'No, Boo.' The Werewolf General looked down his nose at him sympathetically. 'I would have told you if there had been.'

'Oh. Well, I just wondered,' said Boo.

At least I can Change now, he thought, and relax. He shut his eyes and concentrated.

PLUNG!

The world steadied itself on four paws instead of two feet. He could smell old ice cream and the fresh kitten pie the Werewolf General must have had for lunch.

Boo stepped out of his shirt and borrowed pants and tossed them into his bag, then picked up the handle in his teeth and trotted out of the ice-cream shop and down the chilly path. It still gave him a pang to have to leave the shop. He wondered what the Werewolf General would think if he asked if he could come home? Surely he'd be okay by himself. He was supposed to be a Hero, wasn't he?

But Mr and Mrs Bigpaws might be hurt. And they'd been so kind … and he had to admit that it was nice to come back to a house full of pups and good cooking smells. And it was just slightly terrifying to think of sleeping in a room next to a wormhole, even with the Werewolf General in town to keep an eye on it.

Mr Bigpaws was in the kitchen with Spot when Boo pushed through the doggie door. Boo sniffed. 'Woof! What's for dinner?'

'Chicken salad,' said Mr Bigpaws, using his teeth to arrange the chicken heads on a platter among the lettuce and tomatoes. 'How was the School for Heroes?'

'Oh, fine,' said Boo.

'I thought it would be,' said Mr Bigpaws proudly. 'We werewolves make the best Heroes in the universes.'

'I bet you're the best student they ever had,' Spot said excitedly. 'You'll have to tell us everything over dinner!'

Boo gulped. 'Oh, sure.' He slunk off to his bedroom, hoping no one would notice his tail between his legs.

A stitch in time saves you losing
your fingers on the way home.

OLD ZOMBIE SAYING

17

Midnight at the school for Heroes

His basket was too hot. Of course it's too hot, thought Boo. His basket was bouncing on bubbles of molten rock. Soon his whiskers would burst into flame and then his tail ...

Boo knew he was dreaming. But that didn't help. There was no escape in dreams.

Suddenly the volcano vanished.

The world was black, and colder than the freezer in the Best Ice-Cream Shop in the Universes. Even the smells were frozen in this land of night.

But he could see. There were frozen things hanging in the darkness — hams and legs of lamb, a dead deer, and giant fish. There were massive cakes, oozing cream, all frozen too, and bags of strange berries glistening with frost. And there among the food was Mum, trapped in a giant block of ice, her mouth open in a frozen silent scream. And all around the frozen world was … nothing. Just cold and dark and pain …

Boo opened his eyes. He shivered. He felt cold. Colder than he had ever been, despite the snuggly blanket and cushions in his basket.

He snuggled back down, but he couldn't sleep. Was Mum really frozen somewhere in the Ghastly Otherwhen? What was the Ghastly Otherwhen like? One thing was for sure. Unless he learnt to be a proper Hero he'd have no chance at all of ever saving her.

But could he really become a Hero?

He couldn't even *Wham! Bam! Pow!* properly. But he'd learn! And … and maybe Princess Princess would come with him and help rescue Mum, too.

Boo had a sudden vision of himself and Princess Princess striding through the Ghastly Otherwhen together. Princess Princess's Hero clothes would flutter in the wind and he'd be in human shape, but half a metre taller than he was now and even more muscly …

No more widdling this time. He'd *Wham! Bam! Pow!* any bogey that came along! Woof! And he'd *Zoom!* the Greedle till *it* widdled in terror! Princess Princess would watch wide-eyed and then she'd say …

Boo sighed and scratched his ear with his front paw. It was no use. He couldn't go back to sleep. And he couldn't imagine Princess Princess looking at him all wide-eyed and admiring.

Not yet, anyhow.

He had to face it. He was a long way from being the sort of Hero who could invade the Ghastly Otherwhen. But he wasn't going to stop trying! Boo rolled over onto his back with his paws in the air and tried to sleep again. But something niggled at him. His pants!

Boo sat up in bed and scratched his other ear with his hind leg. How could he have forgotten his pants? He'd promised to give Mug back his spare pair in the morning — and there was no way he was going to spend another day smelling of green fungus.

He had to get his pants back now, wash and mend them, then iron them fresh for school tomorrow. Boo hesitated. Would the wormhole take him back to school even in the middle of the night? He shrugged. He just had to hope it would.

Boo crept out of bed and padded down the stairs, then bounded swiftly over the slushy ground to the ice-cream shop and stepped inside. The shop's dark was no problem for a werewolf — Boo could see with his nose even better than his eyes.

He padded into Mum's bedroom, feeling the familiar pang as he smelt her scent, then crawled on his tummy under the bed. The floor sank below him. Suddenly he was in the wormhole again.

No smell of mouse this time. Either he'd scared it away or it was asleep. Boo scampered along the wormhole floor. It was easier going on four legs than two.

Ah, there was the reddish light of the volcano. He could smell it, too, a bit like someone was burning a tin of flea powder. He'd needed his thick winter coat back in Sleepy Whiskers, but once again he felt like shedding half his fur.

And suddenly he was there.

'Student approaching!' he called.

No one answered. Boo peered out. A skinny tiger with bald patches on its fur and a patch over one eye snored in a heap by the wormhole. Boo bent down and yelled in its ear, 'Student approaching!'

'What?! Who?! How?!' The tiger leapt shakily to its feet. 'Don't worry,' it growled, unsheathing its claws. 'I'll save you!'

'I don't need saving. I just came to get my trousers.'

The ancient tiger stared at him grumpily. 'What did you wake me up for, then?' It settled back down onto the warm rock and in a second it was snoring again.

Boo gazed around. The school looked different at night. The smoke cloud had lifted, leaving wisps that seemed to cling to the dark rock in case they fell into the gurgling mass below. The cliffs were dark smudges against bright stars, each as red as if it was a spark from the volcano. The bare rock ledge glowed red in the light from the caldera. Even the bats had vanished.

A faint echo of music and creaking wheelchairs and walking frames sounded from further up the cliffs. Boo wondered if the old Heroes were dancing, or if there was some Hero skill they practised to music.

Glug, glug, glug, went the lava down in the crater like a giant pot of Mrs Bigpaws's cow's head in tomato sauce.

School smelt different at night, he thought. No smells of all the different students, no smells of lunches from fifty universes; just boiling rock, tiger fur, and the far-off whiff of talcum powder and denture gel.

Boo lifted his nose and sniffed again. No, there was someone else here! He could smell someone … or was it something? A familiar smell …

Yesterday, that was it. It was *her* smell. But there was something different about it tonight. Boo sat back on his haunches and pricked up his ears. What was Yesterday doing here? Maybe she'd stayed at school overnight ... or maybe she'd come back again to study in the library, or ... what *would* you come back to Hero School at night for? wondered Boo. Not many students had to collect their trousers!

Anyhow, this wasn't getting his pants. Boo trotted over the dark rock and around the cliff to the bathroom. Luckily the door was ajar, so he didn't have to Change to use the door handle. He'd had enough of being human shaped!

Boo wriggled his nose behind the paper-towel bin and pulled out the pants with his teeth. Now, to take them home and sort them out so he'd look hot for Princess Princess tomorrow. He'd even have another (spew!) *bath*.

It was only a matter of time before Princess Princess forgot that she'd first seen him with fur and paws, thought Boo, as he scampered back towards the wormhole entrance. Suddenly the scent he'd smelt before wafted across the rocks, clear even above the scent of burning rock.

Boo sat back on his haunches and let his pants drop to the hot rock. 'Woof!' he barked softly. 'Yesterday?'

No one answered. Boo called again. 'Yesterday? I know it's you! I can smell you.'

A shadow moved over by the rubbish bin. 'Boo? What are you doing here?'

'Just getting my pants.' Boo waited for her to giggle when she saw him in cute-puppy form again. But she didn't. 'What are *you* doing here?'

'Me? Oh, nothing.' Yesterday was wearing the same tatty tunic that she'd worn during the day. Her face looked whiter and thinner in the starlight. She was holding a big bulging bag.

Boo trotted over and sniffed the bag. It smelt like it was made from the same sort of leather as her tunic. 'Why are you at school in the middle of the night? And what's that?'

'It's none of your business,' she said sharply.

Boo thought about what she'd said. 'Well, no,' he agreed cautiously. 'But I'm curious.' He wondered if she'd object if he sniffed her bum to find out more. Probably, he thought. Humans were so weird about their bums.

Yesterday suddenly looked as if she might cry. 'Please, don't ask any questions! I'm tired and … and just go away! I'm going home now,' she added. 'Go on. You go first!'

'Well, all right,' said Boo, hurt. He padded off over the warm ledge, picked up his pants in his teeth again, then marched past the snoring tiger and into the wormhole. He could hear a faint slithering as Yesterday dragged the bag over the smooth stone to the wormhole's entrance. And then the noise vanished behind him, and there was just silence …

Boo trotted down the tunnel, his paws growing colder, his pants in his mouth. Why *had* Yesterday been hiding in the shadows of the School for Heroes? What was so secret? And if his nose wasn't mistaken — and wolf noses were never wrong — what had she been doing emptying the school rubbish bin into a big leather bag?

FOR SALE

One collar, never worn, usual hooks
for watch, wallet and mobile phone.

FROM THE SLEEPY WHISKERS GAZETTE

CLASSIFIED ADS

18

A Warrior Mouse

The mouse was sitting smack bang in the middle of the tunnel when Boo sank down through the wormhole the next morning, in human form again, muscles bulging heroically, his pants mended and everything washed (including himself) and ironed and perfect.

'Squeak!' The mouse peered up at him.

Boo peered down at it from his unsteady human height. 'If you wee on my clean clothes again, I'm going to have you for breakfast,' he said. 'Well, second breakfast anyway,' he added, remembering he was full of Mrs Bigpaws's pigeon pancakes.

The mouse wrinkled its tiny nose at him. 'Squeak!'

'Look,' said Boo. 'Mice are scared of werewolves. Remember? I'm big and ferocious. You're small and squeaky. Keep out of my way and I'll try to forget you're here. Okay?'

'Squeak!' The mouse jumped up onto his shoulder.

'That does it!' roared Boo. 'Got you!'

'Squeak!' The mouse peered up tremulously from Boo's fist.

'Right,' said Boo, staring down at it. No more squeaks, he thought. No more mouse widdle on his head or the smell of mouse droppings on his clothes. Just one chomp and the mouse would be gone.

'Squeak?'

He couldn't do it. The mouse was so small and so spunky — and suddenly he felt small too, and not at all spunky, a new kid on his way to a strange school through a strange tunnel.

Boo sighed and put the mouse down on the floor of the wormhole. 'Look,' he said. 'I'm sick of playing hide-and-squeak with a mouse. Just go away. Go find some cheese or find a place to hide like a normal mouse. Please?'

'Squeak?' The mouse ran up his trouser leg, squeezed out between his shirt buttons, then dived up into the pocket of Boo's shirt.

'That isn't what I meant,' said Boo.

'Squeak?' The mouse peered out, then snuggled down again.

Boo stared at his pocket. The mouse wasn't hiding. It looked like it had deliberately chosen to sit in his pocket.

Boo grinned. 'Do you want to go to the School for Heroes, too?'

He hadn't been serious. But the mouse poked its head up over the edge of his pocket again, and twitched its whiskers. 'Squeak,' it said determinedly.

'Does that mean you want to be a Hero?'

'Squeak,' agreed the mouse.

'Look,' said Boo. 'I hate to tell you this. But mice just aren't Heroes.' He stopped, suddenly remembering Princess's voice yesterday, saying, 'Dogs just can't be Heroes.'

If a werewolf could be a Hero, maybe a mouse could too? Nah, he thought, ridiculous. But if the mouse *really* wanted to be a Hero then he didn't have the heart to stop it trying.

'Look … just stay out of the way. No poking your head up in class or when anyone can see you. Any uncalled-for squeak out of you and I'll pick you up by the tail and throw you in the volcano. Understood?'

'Squeak!' It was a little muffled by the pocket, but it was clear enough.

'Okay,' said Boo. He picked up his school bag and began to walk down the wormhole to school.

LOST

school library. If anyone has seen where
it's manifesting at the moment please report
its whereabouts to the librarian.

DR MUSSELLS, PRINCIPAL

19

Bogey Secrets

So the days continued.

Boo learnt about the Top Ten Nasties in *The Nasty Book of Nasties*. He learnt to stay out of the library when the books were practising their Book Kan Doo.

He learnt to stay out of the way during wheelchair races, or during the oldies' spear practice. Some of the ancient Heroes refused to wear glasses, so their aim was a bit out. Or maybe old Heroes just had an ... *interesting* sense of humour.

He *almost* managed a ten-second Zoom! He discovered the *Aaaagh!*er pit next to the gymnasium, and the one just to the right of the assembly door, too, and used up half his Band-Aids. He also learnt never to share Mug's zombie spaghetti sandwiches (they wriggled round inside him all afternoon). And every afternoon when he came home after school, he went down to the creek just to practise a bit more, punching at the branches and trying to tie up the boulders in a *Zoom!*

If only determination was enough to make a Hero! But whatever happened, he'd know he'd done his best.

There had been no more warnings from Miss Cassandra. Boo had only glimpsed the giant chicken strutting far off down the corridors. Level 1s weren't eligible for Finding class. Some of the bogeys from the Ghastly Otherwhen were just too ghastly for beginning Heroes to even look at.

Boo was grateful. He had enough to cope with already without a giant chicken yelling 'Doom!' at him.

It was so hard doing stuff in human form. His brain didn't seem to work as well when it was perched up above two feet instead of down close to four. And he couldn't get used to managing hands and feet at the same time either.

If only he'd Changed more before trying to be a

Hero! Or if only he could go back to wolf form here …

He hadn't admitted to the Werewolf General that he hadn't started going to school in wolf form, as the Werewolf General had advised. The old Hero wouldn't understand! How could he explain he'd made such a fool of himself in wolf form? The whole of Hero School — not just Princess Princess — would giggle at him again as soon as they saw his cute puppy face.

No, he just had to stay looking human. Even when it was most difficult — like now.

It was *Wham! Bam! Pow!* class down in the big gymnasium cavern again this morning. Boo stared as Princess Princess neatly crushed a lump of lava with her foot. When he'd tried it all he'd got was a sore toe. She must be the most heroic student the School for Heroes had ever had, he thought glumly. If only he could be good at *something*. *Anything*, that Princess Princess would admire.

'Oh, Boo,' she'd say —

The bell rang, deep in the rock of the school. Boo abandoned his daydream and traipsed after the others across the gently steaming black rock to their classroom, carefully avoiding the two ancient heroic octopuses having a sword duel in the basketball court.

It was Ms Snott's class first. He settled down at his desk just as she arrived, her wrinkled face immobile as always.

'Good morning, Ms Snott,' the class chanted.

She was wearing bright green lycra today with two small daggers strapped to her ankles. 'Good morning, you horrible little band of garbage guzzlers. Today we are studying ...' she flicked the lights off and the screen lit up, 'the feeding habits of Zurms. Now, who can tell me all about Zurms? Yes, Princess?'

Ms Snott hadn't even looked to see Princess Princess's hand shoot up, beating Mug's green fungus paw. She just knew the first hand up would be Princess Princess's.

Princess Princess knew *everything*.

'The Giant Zurm or Strawberry-Jammer of Death is under the control of the Greedle,' parroted Princess Princess. 'It is the only known creature able to dig holes between universes. No one knows why it does this, as the matter dividing the universes is not thought to contain nutrition of any kind. Instead, Zurms coat their prey in strawberry jam excreted from their rear ends, then wait for the jam to harden and their prey to decompose inside. Then they suck out the sludge because Zurms don't have teeth.'

'Correct,' said Ms Snott, sounding as though today was the most boring day of the most boring year of her life. She started to trim her nails with one of the daggers. 'Can any of you pus-filled pimple-faces tell me how you can tell a Giant Flower Grub from a Zurm who is going to turn you into a giant Zurm strawberry-flavoured slime-shake?'

'Giant Slug good to eat too. Slug quiche, slug and chips. Specially when it won't stop wriggling ...'

offered Mug. 'Maybe Giant Grub taste different from giant worm.'

'Er, Giant Flower Slugs aren't in the textbook,' said Princess Princess.

'No, Princess,' said Ms Snott, calmly replacing her dagger. 'Most of life isn't in a textbook. The textbook is only about bogeys. Luckily one can go for days, sometimes, without meeting a bogey at all. The friendly Giant Flower Grub lives on the Pretty Nice Really Garden World. It eats the mould spores that attack the daffodils. If you wipe out the Giant Flower Slugs you wipe out the daffodils. Giant Flower Grubs are an endangered species — killing even one of them may mean that there aren't enough of the others to keep breeding more Giant Flower Grubs. So, if a Giant Flower Grub suddenly crawled up out of the lava …'

Automatically the class looked out through the small round stone-framed window at the lava bubbling below. But to Boo's relief no grub of any variety appeared.

'… how would you know what to do?'

Mug tried to raise his fungus paw but Princess Princess's hand sprang up again. 'I'd Wham! Bam! Pow! it anyway, till it was grub jelly,' she said. 'Just to make sure. Who cares about daffodils?'

'Quite a lot of people,' said Ms Snott, showing a hint of interest for the first time that day. 'I myself am very fond of daffodils. Especially toxic ones that can kill a bogey with one sniff. My mother has won the Best Poisoned Daffodil Award at the All Universes Flower and Toxin Show three times in a row ... but enough of that.

'The important thing is that a certain breed of wasp on the Pretty Nice Really Garden World feeds on daffodil nectar. If you wipe out the daffodils you wipe out the wasps. The wasp larvae feed on the poc-poc fly, which carries a disease deadly to the human inhabitants. So if you kill too many Giant Flower Slugs a lot of people on the Pretty Nice Really Garden World are going to die too.

'It's like the feral goats and feral cats in my own world,' continued Ms Snott. 'In their own environments the cats and goats play a valuable role. But when humans took them to new places the goats turned forests into deserts and the cats wiped out other species. So, can any of you putrid lumps of decomposing elephant vomit tell me one simple way to know when to *Wham! Bam! Pow!* goats, cats or Giant Grubs or when to leave them alone?'

Boo wished he could scratch his ear with his hind paw to help him think. Surely there was some heroic way to tell if something was an enemy or not?

Slowly, next to him, Yesterday put up her hand.

'Yes, Yesterday?' asked Ms Snott.

'I don't think there is a fast way. You'd have to study them till you worked out what was happening. But that would take ages.'

'Good answer,' said Ms Snott. 'Sometimes there *isn't* a quick answer. But what about the Giant Grub?

It's coming towards you ... close ... closer ... closer. You don't have time to study it. If it's a Zurm it will spread deadly strawberry jam all over your friends. But if you kill a Giant Flower Grub, people in a far-off universe may die instead. So what do you do?'

Yesterday's hand went up again. 'I'd stand in front of it. And if it started to ooze strawberry jam over me, I'd know it was a nasty one.'

'Correct,' said Ms Snott. 'Now, let us move on to —'

'Hey, wait a minute,' cried Princess Princess. 'That's *crazy*! You'd be risking your life.'

'Yes,' said Yesterday quietly. 'But isn't that what a Hero does?'

'Now *that*,' said Ms Snott, 'is the first *really* correct answer I have heard anyone in this class give. A Hero doesn't attack at all unless they are sure that what they're facing *is* an enemy. Now I think I'll go up to Rest in Pieces and have a cup of tea and a blueberry-and-tentacle muffin while the rest of you write out what I've said, oh, a thousand times. Or maybe I'll join the others in a nice game of Bogey Bowling. Yesterday, you may go and have an early lunch.'

Ms Snott limped calmly out of the classroom.

Princess Princess flung her gold pen onto her desk. 'It's not *fair*! You just lucked that answer. Now the rest of us have to waste our lunch hour writing down rubbish.'

Mug shrugged, making his fungus wobble. 'Me

197

thinks her name should be Princess Pea-brain …' he muttered.

'I'll help, if you like,' said Yesterday quietly.

Princess Princess brightened. 'Will you?' She tossed Yesterday her pen. 'Make sure you do them in my writing, won't you?' She strode out the door.

※ ※ ※

By the end of term, Class 1 were ready to do their first practical Hero exam.

'It's all a matter of *luck*,' Princess Princess explained to everyone at lunchtime, as the group sat with their lunch boxes on the boulders above the lava. The smoke clouds had parted again today, showing a glimpse of flickering red sky above.

Sometimes Boo wondered what was in the rest of this universe. Were there more volcanoes bubbling all around them?

But none of the students seemed to know, and he didn't like to ask the teachers. And it was a strict school rule that no one was allowed up the path to the retirement village. Some of the old Heroes were inclined to forget just who was a student, and who was a bogey. And no Hero who had battled the Fire-Breathing Bogeys of Bungus or the Belly-Popping Bogeys of Farrr Offf liked being disturbed, especially not during a game of Biff! Bam! Bingo!

'We have to wait till Miss Cassandra Finds some bogeys suitable for Level 1 Heroes breaking through to some universe or other from the Ghastly

Otherwhen,' continued Princess Princess. 'Sometimes Level 1s have to wait for *months* till the right sort of bogey comes along. We're not supposed to tackle really dangerous bogeys yet, of course. Just easy ones like poisonous Gurgle Bugs. Then when we beat the easy bogeys we become Level 2 Heroes.'

'What if we don't?' asked Boo.

Princess Princess took a neat bite from her chicken, lettuce, gold dust and tomato sandwich. 'You're *dead*, of course.'

'Oh,' said Boo.

'Unless you manage to escape the bogeys and get back here. Then you have to repeat Level 1 classes. Which would be *sooo* embarrassing you may as well be dead anyway,' added Princess Princess.

No one quite knew how Princess Princess knew things like that. Boo supposed she'd got the information from some of the Level 2s, who'd been through all this already. Even the Level 2s and 3s seemed to think Princess Princess was wonderful.

'I hope we get a mad robot,' said T'ai T'ai, polishing her claws on her tunic. 'I like the way they crunch when you pound them.'

'Me want *biiiigg* mutated fly,' said Mug. 'Me hate flies. Me have to squirt whole can of fly-spray every morning. Maggots do real bad things to hairstyle.'

Boo didn't say anything. His Wham! Bam! Pow!s was still clumsy, and a ten-second Zoom! wasn't going to get him very far with any bogey. He was sure he was going to fail his Level 2 test.

He was just as sure he had to try.

'Will we all get the same sort of bogey?' asked Yesterday. She'd forgotten her lunch today, too. In fact, she'd forgotten it every day since Boo had been at Hero School. He'd taken to asking Mrs Bigpaws to pack him a couple of bananas to give to her, because for some reason Yesterday didn't like rat sandwiches, or even corgi salad. But she loved bananas.

Princess Princess shook her head. 'Depends what turns up. I hope it's soon. It's going to be so *cool*! I've got a special costume all made up,' she added. 'It's cloth of gold with diamond spangles and new sandals with diamond heels as well.'

It's all right for her, Boo thought gloomily.

Princess Princess was the most brilliant Hero the school has ever had. *Everybody* said so. Why, she could tell you what was on page 578 of Volume 6 of *The Nasty Book of Nasties* AND Wham! Bam! Pow! a brick into the smallest fragments anyone had ever seen. The books in the library almost saluted when Princess Princess stalked past.

I'm not really a Hero, thought Boo dismally. The Hero act with the Greedle that had qualified him for entry was just luck. But if he was sent home he'd never be able to find Mum. He'd let down all of Sleepy Whiskers, too. They were so proud of having a home-grown Hero.

And besides, he realised, I have friends here now. Mug, and even Yesterday.

And if he left the School for Heroes he'd never see Princess Princess again!

AN INTRODUCTION TO THE SCHOOL FOR HEROES,
BY DR. V.B. MUSSELLS, PHD. DIP. BANANA

Heroes start at Level 1. A Level 1 Hero shows
promise, but has no real, useful Hero skills.
When a Level 1 Hero defeats their first bogey
they become a Level 2. Level 3s must defeat an
even more difficult foe to become Level 4s. Your
basic everyday professional Hero is usually a
Level 4, able to cope with a tsunami or an
Orge plague, and the most common creatures
of the Ghastly Otherwhen. Every challenge the
Hero survives gives them a higher rank.

The highest-ranked Hero in heroic history
was Wattalotta Mussells the Brave.
At Level 20, 'Lottie' disappeared into the
Ghastly Otherwhen. She may still be there,
preparing to overcome its ghastliness. Or maybe
the Ghastly Otherwhen is too much for even
a Level 20.

20

Exams and Bunny Bogeys

The news came that afternoon.

It was library class. Boo found library class difficult.

It wasn't that he didn't like books. He loved their smell. A good book smelt like a whole universe had been crammed within its pages. He even liked reading them, though books didn't taste as good when you had to turn the pages with fingers instead of licking them.

He also liked the librarian, Mrs Kerfuffle, who was small and round and could show you how to throw a book like a boomerang, so it knocked out any unsuspecting bogey *and* whirled back to your hand. (She was especially deadly with the dictionaries.)

No, the real problem was the library itself. But then the library was everyone's problem. Because when you had a ghost library, filled with the wisdom of a thousand dead Heroes, no one ever knew exactly where it would be.

Sometimes it was at one end of the corridor, sometimes at the other. Once, it decided to perch on the giant boulder that led to the skinning pool, and everyone had to climb up to it. Another time it hovered near the ceiling of Dr Mussells's office and Jones the Janitor (who was deadly with a well-thrown screwdriver) had to bring a rope and hook and they all had to help haul it down.

But when you got into the library it was pretty interesting, as long as it didn't decide to fly off while you were in it — and as long as you didn't go into it till the books had finished their morning dagger-throwing practice. And at least the books always returned to their places on the shelves just as soon as they were due, which made life easier for everybody — unless a student accidentally got in the books' way.

Today the library was floating a few inches above the lunch area. The books had been quarrelling among themselves all morning, but they were quieter now, the small ones doing push-ups together at one end of the library, and the big ones showing off their muscles by the doorway.

Boo had just chosen his books — a small and fairly friendly-looking history of the Ghastly Otherwhen and another called *101 Fun Projects with Cockroaches* — when Dr Mussells swung through the library door, his lilac silk shirt billowing. (Somehow ropes just appeared from the ceiling when Dr Mussells arrived. Boo supposed it was just part of being a monkey Hero.)

'Attention, Level 1!' he ordered, dangling by one hand from the door jamb and kicking one of the lurking books away with his foot. 'Miss Cassandra has just reported that there have been a couple of invasions of Level-1-type bogeys from the Ghastly Otherwhen.'

Princess Princess put up her hand. 'What creatures have invaded, sir?' she asked eagerly.

'A small mob of Icy Slithery Things in the Happy To Be Here Universe. It seems the Greedle is after Happy To Be Here's famous watermelon pizzas. And three Rabbits have invaded the World of Golden Grass. We're not sure what the Greedle wants with the World of Golden Grass,' Dr Mussells added, turning swiftly and punching a poetry book that was trying to practise skipping with his tail.

Boo brightened. 'Rabbit' was a nice bouncy word. Chasing Rabbits didn't sound too bad at all! Maybe Rabbits would be terrified by the mere smell of a werewolf and run away …

Suddenly Chapter 243 of Volume 1 of *The Nasty Book of Nasties* came back to him.

Rabbits

Rabbits are one of the Ghastly Otherwhen's most vicious small killers. Although Rabbits have no super powers, no one except a trained Hero is able to vanquish one.

Rabbits club their victims to death with their feet, which they use with deadly accuracy against anyone who tries to stop them, and then they eat them. Despite their small size, Rabbits eat almost all the time they are awake. One Rabbit on a diet can consume a small town in a week.

Hero rating: Level 1 and above.

Giant Rabbits: Just as vicious as ordinary Rabbits.
But bigger. Nastier, too.
Hero rating: Level 3 and above.
Vulnerable points: Please advise publisher if found.

Boo gulped. Maybe Rabbits wouldn't be as scared as he'd hoped. Please, he thought, let me get the Icy Slithery Things.

'Squeak,' said the mouse, peering out of Boo's pocket. Boo hastily shoved it out of sight.

Princess Princess's hand shot up again. 'Who gets to fight which bogeys, sir?'

'Miss Cassandra drew lots.' Dr Mussells smiled his blinding grin as he swung back and forth. 'Lots of adventure then. Get it? He-he-he! Now, T'ai T'ai the Bold, Fedor the Ferocious and Princess of Pewké will go out against the Icy Slithery Things. And Mug, Yesterday and Boojum Bark will fight the Rabbits. The rest of you will have to wait until more bogeys are sighted. Hopefully it won't be long before there's another invasion,' he added comfortingly. 'The Greedle always seems hungrier at this time of year!'

Boo gulped. He and Mug — the two most hopeless Heroes in the class! And Yesterday! Although at least Yesterday was better at Hero skills than him — and more intelligent than Mug. Even an elderly flea with flu would make a better Hero than him and Mug, he thought dismally.

They were doomed … he heard the echo of Miss Cassandra's words. Doom, doom …

It isn't fair, he thought. Without me, Yesterday and Mug would have a chance. They'd get a *real* Hero to complete their team. Maybe …

Suddenly Mr Hogg's pink face appeared at the door. 'Excuse me, Dr Mussells. A message from Miss Cassandra. The Icy Slithery Things have melted. An unexpected heatwave, I believe. The watermelon pizza is safe.'

'That's not *fair*!' Princess Princess stood up, her hands on her hips. 'I'm top of the class! I should have first go at getting up to Level 2! Dr Mussells, I *demand* that my group gets the Rabbits!'

'You demand?'

For the first time Boo saw Princess Princess embarrassed. 'Well, er, I mean … may I *please* go and hunt the Rabbits, sir?'

'Very well. You may join Mug, Yesterday and Boojum Bark.'

'*What*? That's not what I meant! I'm not going Rabbit-hunting with a zombie and a part-time woof-woof! Boo can't even Zoom! properly! And his Wham! Bam! Pow! is a joke. Count me out!'

Dr Mussells dropped down onto the library carpet, punched a stray thesaurus and looked at Princess Princess coolly. 'You either go with the others and try to pass your test or you leave the School for Heroes. Which is it to be?'

Princess Princess stared at him. 'You can't expel me! I'm a hereditary royal Hero! And the best student in the class!'

'Two choices,' said Dr Mussells, peering under a dictionary and coming up with a banana. 'Go hunt the bogey, or go home.'

Princess Princess stuck out her chin. 'You seem to forget I'm a princess.'

Dr Mussells ignored her. He seemed more interested in peeling his banana.

'I'm going to be the best Hero this school has ever seen. *Everyone* says so.'

Dr Mussells sniffed his banana, then offered it to the dictionary. The book took a small bite. 'You have three seconds to decide,' said Dr Mussells. 'Home or bogeys. One. Two ...'

Princess Princess glanced around the classroom, as though hoping her father's army was going to charge to her rescue.

The class avoided her gaze. Princess Princess sighed dramatically. 'Bogeys. But you wait till I'm a Level 20 Hero and put this in my memoirs. When do we go?' she added.

'Now,' said Dr Mussells, in between bites of his banana. 'The school minibus has logged the distress call, so it will find the way through the wormholes. It's ready to take you.'

⋇ ⋇ ⋇

The school minibus was parked by the gaping mouth of the wormhole, its tyres gently steaming on the hot rock. Boo stared at the bus curiously. It looked like an ordinary bus, apart from a few scorch marks on the sides and the bat perched on the windscreen wiper.

Princess Princess stepped into it first. She'd changed into her new Hero costume, two gold frills for a skirt and three frills for a top, with a lot of Princess Princess in between. Her sandals were gold too, with silver laces halfway up to her knees.

She still hadn't said anything to any of the others. She planted herself on the back seat, carefully spreading out her skirt so there was no room for anyone else.

Boo sat next to Mug. 'I wonder when the driver's coming,' he said, just as Yesterday slipped into the seat in front and the bus door slammed shut.

Suddenly the bus windows turned a steely grey.

'I don't think this bus has a driver,' said Yesterday softly. 'I think it's just going to …' a shiver ran through the bus, '… drive,' finished Yesterday as a sudden acceleration forced them back in their seats. The whole bus vibrated.

We must be heading through the wormhole, thought Boo. He had never imagined speed like this. It was as though he'd left his stomach and half his brain behind.

Suddenly the shivering stopped. The bus stopped too.

Boo stared out of the windows. They were clear glass again now, but all he could see was the sides of the wormhole. Where was the World of Golden Grass?

But, of course, he realised. Wormholes come out

under beds ... and the bus wouldn't fit under a bed. Not any bed he'd known. The World of Golden Grass must be above them.

Princess Princess leapt out first, flexing her muscles and looking around eagerly. The others followed her ... and suddenly the four of them were moving upwards. Boo ducked his head just before it hit the underside of a bed.

Or was it a bed? It was just a pile of hay, he realised, resting on a wooden platform raised on four poles. And the hay was in a tall, tepee-like tent. Its red and blue sides billowed slightly in the wind. Through the doorway he could see grassy gold hills rolling into the distance and puffy white clouds in a blue sky. The sun looked like a big fat cheese, almost the same colour as the grass.

So this was the World of Golden Grass.

It's ... pretty, thought Boo, as he followed Princess Princess outside. That was the perfect word for it. Pretty tents, all gathered in a circle around a big fireplace. A pretty garden, just beyond the tents, filled with pretty red flowers.

What did the Greedle want on a world like this?

He frowned. There was something ... odd ... about those flowers. They didn't smell like any flowers he knew. If only he was in wolf shape and could smell properly! He sniffed again.

Princess Princess looked at him crossly. 'Stop sniffing! You can at least *try* to act like a Hero. Hey, everyone, what do you call a flea that lives

in a dumb wolf's ear?'

No one answered.

'A *space* invader!'

'The flowers smell funny,' said Boo.

'They're not flowers,' said Yesterday grimly. She was wearing the same brown leather tunic she wore every day. He could tell by the pattern of the darns.

'What are they, then?' he asked.

'Bloodstained skulls.'

'How can you tell from this distance?' demanded Princess Princess .

'I've seen bloodstained skulls before.'

'*Where?*'

Yesterday shrugged. 'Come on,' she said, without answering the question. 'We'd better find these Rabbits.'

Mug stared around the circle of tents. 'Where all

the peoples?' he rumbled.

'Hiding from the Rabbits,' said Yesterday shortly.

'How do you know?' demanded Princess Princess.

Yesterday said nothing. There was a strange expression on her face. As Boo looked, she shut her eyes and concentrated.

Princess Princess stared at her impatiently. 'What are you *doing*?'

Yesterday kept her eyes shut. 'Finding the Rabbits.'

'Like that? But you're not a Finder! Only Finders can Find things like that! We haven't even had any Finding lessons yet.'

'That's how I passed the entrance test to the school,' said Yesterday shortly. 'I Found something.'

'What?' demanded Princess Princess.

Yesterday said nothing. Her eyes stayed shut.

'You're just trying to make yourself important,' said Princess Princess uncertainly. 'You can't actually Find. Real Finders are *extremely* rare and …'

'I … I have Found something.' Yesterday opened her eyes. She sounded puzzled. 'But it's not a Rabbit! It's long and brown and … and wriggling …'

'That just my lunch,' rumbled Mug. 'It a sausage.'

'But it's moving!'

'It a zombie sausage. Mum was out of zombie spaghetti this morning.'

'Oh. I see.'

'Ha! I *said* you couldn't Find anything,' began Princess Princess, as Yesterday closed her eyes again.

'Shhh,' said Boo, surprising himself with his

boldness. 'Let her try.'

'And let the Rabbits get away while we just *stand* here? I say we spread out and each climb a hill. Then we can see …'

'I've got them!' Yesterday opened her eyes. 'They're over that way.' She pointed. 'About three hills away. They're dozing after feeding last night. But there's a problem.'

Yes, thought Boo. We're on a strange world with ferocious bunnies and I'm so scared I want to widdle but I can't because I've got pants on and no toilet. But all he said was, 'What?'

'There are more than three of them,' said Yesterday flatly. 'I'm pretty sure that there are at least twenty.'

'That more than three?' rumbled Mug.

Yesterday nodded. 'And there's another thing.'

'What?' squeaked Boo.

'They're not ordinary Rabbits. They're Giant ones.'

Princess Princess stared. 'That's impossible! Miss Cassandra said there were only three ordinary Rabbits! The school wouldn't make a mistake like that! Send Level 1 Heroes out against a whole mob of Giant Rabbits! You're making this up.'

'Am I?' asked Yesterday coolly. 'You'll soon find out, won't you?' She began to walk in the direction she'd indicated.

'Stop!' cried Princess Princess. 'Look, if you're right, we have to go back! This … this isn't just an exercise at school! This is *real*! The four of us can't possibly fight a whole mob of Giant Rabbits.'

'I thought you were supposed to be this great Hero who could fight anything,' said Yesterday.

'*I* can, yes,' said Princess Princess. 'But not all by myself! The rest of you are useless! You're only just average at Wham! Bam! Pow! and you can't even Zoom! And Mug keeps losing bits of himself and Boo-Boo's hopeless. Don't you see?' Princess Princess's voice rose hysterically. 'We *have* to go back! The school can send out some Level 3s or 4s to deal with the Rabbits.'

Yesterday looked at Boo and Mug. 'What do you two think?'

Boo tried to decide. Part of him thought that Princess Princess was right. It was silly to try to fight bogeys that outclassed them. But somehow it felt wrong to leave …

'It's not that I'm *frightened* or anything,' added Princess Princess hastily. 'It's just not fair on you three.'

'Well, I think …' he began.

'Help me! Oh, please help me!' A small sheep-like creature scampered up the hill. Her face was like a normal human's, except for her silvery skin, and her fleece was pale gold.

Suddenly Boo had a vision of lamb chops, steaming on a golden platter, while the Greedle drooled. So that's what the Greedle wants from this world, he thought. That's why you've sent your

Rabbits here. To get your lamb chops — and have a nice feed themselves while they gather them.

'It's my little lamb!' The sheep woman was sobbing, the tears trickling into her golden wool. 'My little Darlene! She's only four years old!'

Yesterday put a thin brown hand on the sheep woman's woolly shoulder. 'You think she's run away?'

The sheep woman nodded, trying to catch her breath. 'She wanted to find her toy lambie. We all went down to shelter in the jail. It's reinforced concrete. It's the only place that's safe from the Rabbits. But we were in such a hurry Darlene forgot her lambie. You have to save her! You're Heroes, aren't you?' She looked a bit doubtfully at Boo and Mug, then more confidently at Princess.

Princess Princess punched a punch *Pow!* with her fist. 'I am. The others are pretty useless.'

'Oh.' The sheep woman glanced at Mug, Boo and Yesterday. Boo had a horrible feeling she agreed with Princess Princess's assessment. The sheep woman turned back to Princess Princess, her silver face pale and pleading.

'*You*'ll rescue her, won't you?'

'Well, actually, we have to go back to *school* —' began Princess Princess.

'We'll rescue your

lamb,' said Yesterday gently. She looked at the others. 'We all will, won't we?'

'Yes,' said Boo.

'Yes,' rumbled Mug.

'As if I have a choice,' muttered Princess Princess. She gave the woman a beaming smile. 'Of *course* we'll rescue your daughter! By the way,' she said casually, 'I'm Princess Princess Sunbeam Caresse of Pewké. Just in case you want to tell anyone who saved you all.'

The sheep woman bent her front legs in a sort of curtsey. 'Yes, Your Highness. Thank you, Your Highness ... it's just — you will hurry, won't you? The Rabbits might have her already.'

'The Rabbits are asleep,' said Yesterday quietly. 'Your little lamb is all right for the moment. Come on,' she said to the others. 'We need to hurry.'

Boo stared at the sheep woman as she ran back down the golden grassy hill. She looked so ordinary, in spite of her golden wool. Not anyone special.

It's funny, he thought. I fought the Greedle to save the people I knew, but now I'm going to fight to save someone I've never even met.

It felt like the rightest thing he'd ever done.

So this is what it's like to be a Hero, Boo thought. Then he ran to keep up with Yesterday and the others as they headed across the golden grass.

BUDGERIGARS

Once known as the most fearsome monster in the universes, budgerigars — or budgies as they are now known — shrank to their present small size while flying through an antimatter cloud in the Universe of Ork. Their beaks also shrank. No longer big enough to rip their prey limb from limb, budgies now eat birdseed, and make pleasant pets in cages.
Most of the time, anyway.

THE NASTY BOOK OF NASTIES, CHAPTER 6

21

The Attack of the Zombie Sausage

The tent village was behind them now, though Boo could still smell it faintly, even in human form, a smell of painted leather and death. The golden grass smelt dusty. There was another scent as well, a sweet, almost musky one that Boo had never smelt before. He supposed it was the scent of Rabbit.

In front of them a small stream sparkled between the rounded hills.

'Where are the Rabbits?' whispered Princess Princess. Her face was white. Maybe the sun's too hot for her, thought Boo. It was so lucky for them that she was with them. At least Yesterday and Mug had a chance with Princess Princess around.

Yesterday shut her eyes briefly. 'Still two hills over. Still asleep.'

Princess Princess bit her lip. 'Are you *sure* you can do this Finding stuff?'

'Yes,' said Yesterday quietly.

'Can you Find the little lamb?'

'She's playing with her toy lambie over there.' Yesterday nodded towards a small stone bridge further down the stream. 'She's safe for the moment.'

'Until the Rabbits come this way,' said Boo softly.

'Until they come this way,' agreed Yesterday.

'R—right.' Princess Princess's voice sounded strangely squeaky. She gulped and tried again. 'Right! We have to have a plan! Listen carefully. We creep up on the Rabbits and circle round them. Yesterday goes in front and Boo-Boo to the right and Mug to the left ...'

'No worries,' rumbled Mug. He frowned. 'Which way left?'

'We'll *show* you!' yelled Princess Princess. She forced her voice back to a whisper. 'And ... and I'll stay on this side of them. Then when I give the signal we all attack in turn. I'll Zoom! them until they're confused, then Yesterday and Mug go in with Wham! Bam! Pow! Boo-Boo, you just keep the Rabbits herded together — and *try* not to get in the way.'

'Me want to try secret weapon first,' rumbled Mug.

'*What* secret weapon?' demanded Princess Princess shortly.

Mug burped, sending a strong scent of fungus across the golden grass. 'It secret!'

'Oh, *great*,' muttered Princess Princess. 'A zombie secret weapon. I suppose you're going to throw your big toe at them or something. Okay, try your secret weapon. *Then* I'll give the signal.'

'You're a better W*ham! Bam! Pow!*er than any of us,' said Boo doubtfully.

'I can't do everything!' cried Princess Princess shrilly. 'It's just not *fair*, sending me out with three hopeless …' She took a deep breath. 'Come *on*. Let's get this *over* with.'

They strode through the thick gold grass. Boo supposed the sheep people ate it, although it would need millions of sheep people to munch all this.

'Over that hill, I think,' whispered Yesterday.

Princess Princess nodded. 'You go that way,' she muttered to Mug. 'Yes, that's *left*, you idiot zombie. Boo-Boo, you run over there. Yesterday, circle round with Mug then go on ahead of him. I'll climb the hill here. Don't do *anything* till I give the signal.'

They nodded. Boo began to circle the hill. If only I wasn't so clumsy as a human, he thought. It was so slow on two feet, and his jaws could hardly grab anything at all. And his hands were trembling and his skin felt all prickly with terror.

Some Hero, he told himself. How unfair is it that my friends are stuck with me?

And suddenly the Rabbits were there, lying with their paws on their noses on the grass. They were strange-looking creatures, with long velvet ears, pink noses and brownish white fur. They looked peaceful,

dozing in the sun — till you noticed the long feet for clubbing their enemies, the deadly claws and the razor-sharp whiskers.

Boo wondered where Mug and Yesterday and Princess Princess were. All at once he glimpsed Yesterday, a silent shadow across the far hill. And there was Mug, stomping across the hill opposite.

Boo bit his lip. There was no way Mug could ever be stealthy. The Rabbits were going to notice them any second. Even as he looked one of the Rabbits peered up at Mug. It snarled. Suddenly the whole horde was awake, their fangs flashing in the sunlight.

Where's Princess Princess? Boo thought desperately. Princess Princess had to start *Zoom!*ing now! The Rabbits would charge Mug any second! There was no way the zombie could protect himself from a horde of charging Giant Rabbits! They had to act!

But it was too late. Almost as one Rabbit, the horde began to hop towards Mug, slowly at first, then faster —

It was as though the world changed. Or have I Changed? thought Boo wonderingly. But when he glanced down he was still a boy. But the trembling had gone. The terror was still there, only now it seemed like a stone he could use to sharpen all his senses.

His whole life narrowed into a single purpose. To attack. He had to save his friend! Boo began to run …

And then he stopped. What was happening? The Rabbits had all stopped too. As Boo watched, one of them suddenly fell over and lay still. And then another and another …

'Me use secret weapon!' Mug yelled happily at Boo.

'But what is it?' cried Boo.

'Zombie sausage. See? It knocking them all out.'

Boo stared. Now he knew what to look for he could see it, a long, round sausage glistening with fat and maybe a bit of tomato sauce (at least he hoped it was tomato sauce), bouncing from Rabbit skull to Rabbit skull. And every time Mug's lunch bounced another bunny fell down.

Boo felt laughter well up inside him. A zombie sausage! Who needed Heroes when you had a zombie sausage? A whole mob of Giant Rabbits defeated by a secret zombie sausage! 'Look at it go!' he yelled.

The sausage was leaping madly now. Up, up, up it flew, then down, down, down …

'No!' barked Boo.

… into the mouth of the largest, fiercest-looking Rabbit of all. The Rabbit had swallowed Mug's secret weapon! The Rabbit grinned evilly, then looked puzzled. A second later it dropped to the ground.

Deadly indigestion, thought Boo. He gulped. The sausage had disposed of about half of the bunnies. But half a horde was still too many.

He looked around wildly. 'Princess!' he yelled. 'Where are you? Come on! It's time to *Zoom!* We have to attack the rest of the Rabbits!'

'It's … it's … it's …' came the echo. But Princess didn't reply.

What's happened to her? wondered Boo desperately. Had a stray Rabbit attacked her? But there was no time to hunt for her now. 'Mug! Have you got another sausage?' he yelled.

'Mum only packed one for lunch,' rumbled Mug.

'Er, anything else? A ferocious zombie apple? A deadly zombie tomato?'

'Only sausage today,' rumbled Mug. 'Wish me had zombie spaghetti too,' he added. 'Me hungry.'

'Oh,' said Boo. He tried to think. But it was

hard to think with a mob of killer Rabbits peering at you.

They were working out who to attack next. Boo had a sudden horrible vision of what a mob of maddened Rabbits might do to Mug. Or Yesterday's skull piled up with the others by the tents.

Suddenly the Rabbits began to break up into groups. Five of them hopped towards Yesterday, another five hopped after Mug, and a third group bounded towards Boo.

There's no way we can fight five Rabbits each, decided Boo, forcing his brain into overdrive. Their only chance had been with the four of them fighting together.

He had to plan! Fast! But all his training had fled. He had never felt right in his human body, and he felt even less right now.

Would it really make a difference if he were in werewolf form? Maybe not, said the human part of Boo's brain. Maybe the Rabbits would just think 'Cute little dog! Yum yum!' But his wolf mind was yelling *CHANGE*!

No time to concentrate. Just time to turn his back to Yesterday, tear off his clothes (he wasn't going to get tangled in his underpants this time) and …

PLUNG!

He was a werewolf again. The world was taller, its colours duller, its scents and sounds immeasurably more vivid.

Part of his mind said the Change made him no

better off at all. But the other part howled with joy. This felt good. This felt *right*!

All of which happened in perhaps two seconds …

Mug still slouched there, lost without his sausage. Yesterday stood her ground, her hands raised in the familiar Wham! Bam! Pow! opening defence position. She shot him a small smile. It wasn't a 'hey look at the fluffy puppy' smile. It was a smile of friendship and trust. It was the first time he had ever seen Yesterday smile. She looked … different, he decided.

There was still no sign of Princess Princess. She must have another plan, thought Boo. That was it! Any second now, Princess Princess was going to Zoom! in and do something *really* heroic …

But till Princess Princess arrived it was up to him.

But how? There was no way he could Wham! Bam! Pow! in his werewolf shape. He'd never learnt how to Wham! with hands and feet, much less Wham! with paws. Princess Princess would say he was *worse* than useless like this. And she'd be right.

Or would she?

What *could* he do in werewolf shape? Werewolf fangs were no match for giant bunny feet. And widdling wasn't going to stop a mob of Rabbits either.

So what was left? What could a werewolf do to save the day?

And then he had it …

He could run! He could tire out the Rabbits, so it would be easier for Princess Princess and the others to defeat them. How long can a Giant Rabbit run for? he wondered. It didn't matter. No matter how long it took, he'd keep on running. He could run forever to save his friends. For Mug and Yesterday, he thought. For the little girl Darlene and all her woolly people …

Boo sat back on his haunches and let his furry face stretch in a werewolf grin. 'Hey, bunnies!' he barked. 'Yap! Yap! Yap! Can't catch me! Can't catch me!' The largest Rabbit stared at him, as though it couldn't believe its eyes.

Suddenly the ground vibrated with the pounding of Giant Rabbit feet. Boo scampered forward a few steps, lifted his leg at the fallen leader Rabbit, and let out a small insulting drop … 'Pong Fu!' he barked.

'Take that, you furry fiends.' And then he ran.

Down the golden hill, away from the tents, away from the little lamb with her toy, away from his friends …

He glanced back. Were the Rabbits still following? Yes! A whole mob of Giant Rabbits thundered down the hill after him.

'Woof, you stupid Rabbits!' he called, and heard his challenge echo across the grassy hills. 'Woof! Woof! Woof!'

Where was Princess Princess? How long, thought Boo again, as he forced his legs to run even faster, will it take to tire out a pack of Giant Rabbits?

Up the next hill, down and up again … long grass brushed against his fur and whiskers, then doubling back and round again … he couldn't run too far from the others, Boo realised, or Princess Princess mightn't be able to carry out her plan.

Whatever it was.

Up another hill, around and down … Boo glanced behind again. Were the bunnies tiring? The gap between him and the nearest Rabbit was widening. They *were* getting tired!

Boo grinned, his tail wagging. He could run like this forever!

'Woof!' he yelled happily. Why had he ever tried to be a human? Four paws were so much more fun!

He could hear the bunnies panting. Ha! Even Giant Rabbits were no match for a werewolf's legs! This was great!

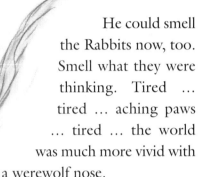

He could smell
the Rabbits now, too.
Smell what they were
thinking. Tired ...
tired ... aching paws
... tired ... the world
was much more vivid with
a werewolf nose.

'Boo! Over here!' Boo pricked
up his ears. Someone was calling
him. Yesterday! Princess Princess must be
ready to put her plan into action.

'Woof!' he yelled at the Rabbits again. He changed
direction and bounded back through the grass. There
was Yesterday, standing back-to-back with Mug. But
where was Princess Princess?

Boo skidded to a stop next to them. Behind him
he could hear the panting bunnies. 'Careful!' he
yelped. 'They're getting tired but they've got enough
strength to attack. Where's Princess Princess?'

'No Princess. No worries, either,' said Mug.
'Yesterday use *her* secret weapon now.'

'But she hasn't got a ...' began Boo. And then he
stopped.

Yesterday was yelling to the Rabbits as they

thundered across the hill.

'Grnt sff tch!' called Yesterday.

Boo glanced at Mug. 'Has she gone bonkers?' he whispered. 'I could have kept the Rabbits away for ages.'

Mug shook his head. 'That her secret weapon.'

'What secret weapon? Yesterday can't talk to Rabbits!'

Mug shrugged. 'Maybe we not know because it secret.'

'Cat guts! The Rabbits are going to be on us in another ten seconds! She's going to get herself killed!' He edged closer to her. Yesterday must be mad with fear, Boo decided and gave her bum an unobtrusive sniff. She didn't *smell* bonkers, he decided. She smelt … right.

'Sccft sppts?' cried Yesterday.

'She's talking nonsense …' growled Boo, then stopped. Because the Rabbits stopped pounding across the hillside too.

One by one they paused, their ferocious whiskery faces twitching in surprise, then sat down on their tails.

'Fsksp!' insisted Yesterday. 'Fcsppt spk? Sffgnt!'

'Spzx,' said one of the Rabbits in amazement. 'Lkxxzt zttz!'

'They understand her!' whispered Boo, stunned. 'What's she saying?'

Mug shrugged, sending a small cloud of flies buzzing. 'Dunno. Me not speak Rabbit.'

'Where's Princess Princess?'

Mug brightened. 'Oh, me know that. She went back to bus. Not feeling well.'

'By herself?! What if something had happened to her?! The Rabbits didn't get her?' barked Boo.

Mug shook his head, then felt it to make sure he hadn't shaken it loose. 'She okay. Yesterday checked,' Mug reassured him. 'Hey, what those bunnies do now?'

The first bunny had bent its nose down to the long golden grass. 'Vzzt?' it said uncertainly.

'Grzxpt,' insisted Yesterday. She bent down and pulled up a handful of grass and held it up temptingly. 'Mmm,' she said.

As Boo watched, the Rabbit took a reluctant mouthful of long gold grass. It chewed a moment, its giant nose wrinkled. And then it chewed some more.

The bunny looked thoughtful. 'Mmm!' it cried. 'Grnt slrrpt! Mmm!'

The second Rabbit took a mouthful, and then the others. Soon the whole mob was enthusiastically chewing the grass.

'Grnt slrrpt chppt!' said Yesterday.

'Fttt gp nggg!' agreed one of the Rabbits. 'Mmm!'

'Fttpp bfftd ztt!' cried the others. 'Fttpp mm bfftd ztt! Fttpp mm bfftd mm ztt! Fttpp bfftd ztt!'

Yesterday grinned. 'Hjkzx,' she agreed. Her whole face changed, thought Boo, when she grinned.

The first Rabbit blew her a kiss. It took a final mouthful of grass, then began to hop away, the other Rabbits following. Within a few seconds they had vanished over the hill.

'Wha—what was that all about?' barked Boo, sitting back on his haunches in amazement.

Yesterday grinned. 'That's *my* secret weapon,' she said. 'Mug has his zombie sausage. I can *Find* animals and talk to them!'

'What did you say?'

'I convinced them that salads are much healthier than all that meat — especially really stressed-out and frightened meat,' said Yesterday. 'Did they really want to be big fat bunnies, too out of breath to even catch a puppy dog? So they agreed to try eating grass instead. And they loved it! They're going to stay here and eat grass. There's enough here for the sheep people *and* the Rabbits. They never want to go back to the Ghastly Otherwhen again. They're not bogeys anymore! The Greedle has lost them!'

'You're brilliant!' cried Boo, wagging his tail happily. 'And you too,' he said to Mug. 'You've both got the most fantastic secret weapons in the universes. I wish I had a secret weapon. I'm not really a Hero,' he admitted. 'That thing with the Greedle, it was just luck. I don't have any Hero skills or secret weapons at all.'

'Yes, you do, you dingbat dingo,' said Yesterday.

'No worries,' agreed Mug.

'Then what are they?' demanded Boo, staring at his friends.

Yesterday laughed. 'You have Hero werewolf powers, of course! Who else but a werewolf Hero could outrun a pack of Giant Rabbits?'

'Or widdle in the Greedle's ice cream,' agreed Mug. 'Kung Poo!'

Boo shook his head. 'They weren't Hero powers. Lots of werewolves can run as fast as me.'

'Huh. Maybe,' said Yesterday, 'but you're the only one who can run when faced with savage Rabbits or was able to widdle all gummed up with Zurm jam. I was too terrified to do anything back there — and the Rabbits were too intent on eating us to listen to anything I said. You gave me time to work out what to say, and you exhausted the Rabbits so they were quiet enough to listen to me. And I know something else too.'

'What?' asked Boo.

'I know you're much happier as a werewolf than as a human.'

Boo blinked. Maybe she was right. There was no way he could have helped his friends get rid of the Rabbits in human form.

'But … but I look too cute to be a Hero!' he blurted out.

'What's wrong with looking cute? It doesn't make you any less a Hero.'

Boo shook his head. It was so good to let his tongue hang out again. 'Maybe … maybe I've been doing this all wrong. Maybe I should have stayed a werewolf, and not tried to be a human Hero at all. But Princess Princess said —'

He stopped suddenly. Princess Princess! How could he have forgotten Princess Princess! Was she all right? I have to Change, thought Boo. I can't let her see me like this.

'Turn your back!' he hissed to Yesterday.

'But, Boo …'

'Now!'

Boo concentrated.

PLUNG!

The ground retreated and the wind suddenly seemed cold on the naked bits that Princess Princess objected to. Boo ran over and picked up his pants then slipped his shirt on.

'Boo,' said Yesterday warningly.

Boo struggled with his zipper. 'We've got to see if Princess's okay!'

'Boo!' said Yesterday again.

'Mug said Princess wasn't feeling … what?' he asked.

'Look behind you,' whispered Yesterday.

Boo turned … just as the Giant Rabbit that had eaten Mug's sausage opened two very angry eyes.

'Zombie sausage only stunned it,' said Mug unnecessarily.

'Could you sort of stun it again?' asked Boo nervously.

'Sure.'

'You can?'

'Sure. When I gets another sausage.'

The Rabbit was getting to its feet now, its giant lethal feet …

'Jxtd fggb jnt!' said Yesterday quickly, pointing to the lush gold grass. 'Mmm Mmm!'

The Rabbit snarled. 'Ktx! Zplzq ftsphk jksspt!'

Yesterday gulped. 'It's got a tummy ache. The zombie sausage disagreed with it. It says it doesn't want to eat any ftsphk grass.'

'Um, what does it want?' asked Boo.

'Jxsnt?' asked Yesterday quickly.

'Lkt! Pklsppt svvsptt ktpppssst!' growled the Rabbit.

'It wants three Hero skulls to drink from and four Hero brains to …' Yesterday frowned. 'I'm not sure about that last bit. I think "ktpppssst" means "drink them like a milkshake" but it might mean "put them in my lunch box and"—'

'Never mind the translation!' yelped Boo, tearing off his pants so he could Change into werewolf form again. 'Tell it that it's a big furry wuss that can't catch a werewolf!' he added as he began to undo the buttons on his shirt. 'Tell it that you bet it can't catch me before …'

'Squeak!'

It was the mouse. Boo had quite forgotten that it had hidden in his pocket. 'Woof!' yelped Boo. 'Get back down in my pocket, you silly …'

'Squeak! Squeak! Squeak!'

Boo watched, horrified, as the tiny creature raced down his arm, down his bare leg and over to the

Rabbit. 'Squeak!' yelled the mouse again, peering up at the giant bunny.

'What's that?!' cried Yesterday.

'It's my mouse!'

'You have a pet mouse?'

'No! Well, yes. Well no, it's not a pet, it's …'

'Squeak!' called the mouse again, peering up at the Giant Rabbit. The animal grinned at it evilly. It raised one giant foot.

'No!' Boo prepared to leap.

But he was too late. With one final squeak the mouse jumped. It ran up the Rabbit's foot, up its leg, across its body and into one giant ear.

The Rabbit screamed! It lifted its giant foot and

with one massive twist in the air it hit the side of its head, right where the mouse had vanished.

The Rabbit's eyes widened in shock. Then they widened even more. Slowly, very slowly, the Rabbit fell with a thud onto the golden grass.

'It knocked himself out!' cried Yesterday.

'Mouse! Are you all right?' yelled Boo, quickly pulling his pants on again.

'Squeak?' The Giant Rabbit's ear twitched as the mouse peered out of the massive hole. 'Squeak?' it asked.

Yesterday laughed. 'Squeak, squeak, squeak!' she told him.

'What did you say?' demanded Boo.

'I said he was a Hero mouse!'

'Squeak!' said the mouse.

'And he agreed,' said Yesterday. 'His name's Squeak,' she added.

'Squeak, squeak?' Squeak ran — more slowly now — down the Rabbit's body. He stopped to give it one

final tiny kick with his hind paw, then ran up Boo's leg, and into his pocket.

'Well,' said Boo.

It was over.

'We did it! We did it! We did it!' cried Yesterday. She ran up to Boo and hugged him hard.

'Squeak!' protested Squeak, sticking his head out of Boo's pocket.

'Oh, I'm sorry! Squeak, squeak, squeak, squeak?' said Yesterday.

'Squeak,' said Squeak, but he sounded happier now.

'How did you learn to speak Mouse, too?' asked Boo, amazed.

Yesterday stopped in the middle of hugging Mug. 'I can talk to any animal. I'm not much good at the Wham! Bam! Pow! stuff. But most bogeys are so surprised to find a human who can speak their language that when I talk to them in their language they stop doing whatever it is they're up to. For a while, anyway.' She giggled. 'Do you know what Squeak said?'

'What?'

'That was a narrow squeak. Get it? Squeak. He's as bad as Dr Mussells. I think bad jokes must be catching. But, Boo, Mug, do you realise? We're the first Level 1s ever to beat a mob of Giant Rabbits! We're Level 2 Heroes now!'

'We really are Heroes!' said Boo, amazed.

Mug frowned. 'Two come after one? Not before?'

'No, two is after one,' said Yesterday firmly.

'You sure?'

'I'm sure,' Yesterday assured him.

A large fuzzy smile spread over Mug's face. 'That good,' he said. 'Me tell Mum n' Dad that me Hero level … what-you-say now. They be proud!'

'We're going to be the first in the class to reach Level 2!' crowed Yesterday. 'Me and you two and —' she stopped. 'Princess!'

Boo gulped. How could he have forgotten Princess Princess? Even for a couple of minutes? 'Princess!' he yelled.

He began to run. Down the hill and up through the long golden grass, past the bloodstained skulls to the tents. He pushed through the tent door. 'Princess, are you all right? Sorry, I mean Princess Princess!'

Princess Princess was huddled near the hammock. Her face looked pale. 'Wha—what's happening out there?' she asked tremulously. 'Are the Rabbits coming? We'd better get down the wormhole *fast* and …'

Boo beamed. 'Stop worrying! It's all done! Mug knocked out some of the Rabbits with his zombie sausage and I ran them till they were exhausted and Yesterday convinced them to turn vegetarian then Squeak got the leader to knock himself out again …'

'Who is Squeak?' said Princess Princess, with a trace of her old tone.

'Squeak?' said Squeak, poking his nose up out of

Boo's pocket again and peering down at Princess.

'A *mouse*!'

'It's okay,' said Boo quickly. 'It's a tame mouse.'

'Squeak!' said Squeak indignantly.

'Okay,' allowed Boo. 'He's a warrior Hero mouse and I'm going to tell Dr Mussells that he should go to the School for Heroes too. I mean as an official student because he's already been going to school in my pocket ...'

'Squeak,' said Squeak, satisfied. He dived down into Boo's pocket again.

Boo looked at Princess Princess with concern. 'Princess Princess, are you all right? I was so worried.'

Princess Princess sniffed. It sounded suspiciously like a crying sniff, thought Boo worriedly, and not her old contemptuous sniff at all. 'No, I'm *not* all right! I ... I ... my new sandal strap broke!'

'Is that all?' Surely she hadn't abandoned them just because her sandal strap broke?

'No! And I ... I've got a terrible blister! It's all *oozing* and ...'

'Where?' asked Boo, concerned.

Princess Princess shoved her foot out of sight underneath her. 'Never mind. I've bandaged it up now. I was just about to come out and save you all ...'

'Princess?' Yesterday appeared in the doorway, with Mug behind her. 'Why weren't you helping us?'

'I ... er ...' began Princess Princess.

'She couldn't,' said Boo. 'She was putting a bandage on her blister.'

'Yes, but —' began Yesterday. She stopped when Boo glared at her, then shrugged. 'Well, she'll just have to stay a Level 1 then. We'll tell Dr Mussells she had a good reason for not joining in and …'

'No!' cried Princess Princess. 'You can't do that to me! I'd die of *embarrassment*!'

'They might even make her leave the school!' added Boo. It was a dreadful thought — to never see Princess Princess again. 'Look, can't we say she helped us?' he added desperately. 'I mean, she was here. And we *did* vanquish the Rabbits. We just don't have to say exactly who did what.'

'Or didn't,' added Mug helpfully.

'Well …' began Yesterday.

'Please?' said Boo.

Yesterday shrugged. 'Okay,' she said.

'No skin off my bum,' said Mug.

'I think you mean "nose",' said Yesterday.

Mug checked his bum, and then his nose. 'Hey, that too!'

'But on one condition,' said Yesterday.

'What?' asked Princess Princess suspiciously.

'That you let Boo go back to being a werewolf. He can't be a proper Hero in human form. All his Hero skills are werewolf ones.'

'*I'm* not stopping him,' said Princess Princess.

'Yes, you are,' said Yesterday hotly. 'All those cracks about woof-woofs —'

'And boo-boos,' added Mug.

Boo looked at them, surprised. He hadn't thought

242

anyone else had noticed Princess Princess's remarks. Or had been angry or upset for him …

'Look, it's okay,' he began.

Yesterday folded her arms stubbornly. 'No, it's not! Princess?'

Princess Princess shrugged. '*Fine,*' she said shortly.

'Have you seen my mummy?'

Boo turned. It was the little lamb, Darlene. He'd forgotten all about her. He gulped. He wished he could ask the same thing. 'Has anyone seen *my* Mum?' Soon, Mum, he thought. Soon I'll be able to hunt for you properly …

The little lamb's silver lips trembled. She looked like her mother, though her fleece was a paler yellow, and fluffier. She clutched her toy closer. 'The Rabbits haven't got my mummy, have they? I was scared they'd get my lambie!' she added.

'Your mum is safe,' said Boo, forcing the picture of his mum from his mind.

'Yes,' said Yesterday gently. 'The Rabbits are all gone now.'

'Will they come back?' asked the little lamb.

'Maybe,' said Yesterday. 'But if they do they'll be nice friendly Rabbits, I promise. They'll just eat some of your long grass. And you've got plenty to share. You're safe now. All of you.'

'Yes,' said Princess Princess, sounding even more like her old self. 'We have totally solved your Rabbit problem!' Princess Princess gave a huge Hero-like kick into the air. 'Wham! Bam! Pow!' she cried.

The lamb looked impressed. 'Wow,' she said to Princess Princess. 'You must be the bestest Hero in the universes!'

Princess Princess did another spectacular twist, her leg held high. 'I'm the Totally Heroic Princess Princess of Pewké!'

'More like Pike, I'd say,' said Yesterday quietly. 'Not much heroism from *her*.'

Princess Princess put her hand on the lamb's yellow shoulder and began to lead her down the hill. 'Now, you just take me to this place where your mother and the others are sheltering and we'll tell them all about it. Come on!' she called back to the others. It's only fair to give the sheep people a chance to thank us properly. Hey, maybe they'd like to make us their royalty! Then I'd be Princess Princess Princess!'

'Squeak,' said Squeak. He sounded disgusted.

'I know,' said Yesterday. 'Well?' she added.

'Well what?' asked Boo, tearing his eyes away from Princess Princess's back. She looked incredible when she used *Wham! Bam! Pow!* like that.

'Are you going to Change back to werewolf form?'

'You really think I should?'

'Yes.' Yesterday gave her almost smile again. 'I like werewolves,' she added. 'Especially cute ones.'

'Me too,' rumbled Mug. 'Hairy is bit like fungus.'

Boo concentrated.

PLUNG!

The grass was closer and much more smelly. Boo took a deep happy breath and stepped out of his clothes.

'Squeak!' Squeak struggled out of his pocket and glared at him.

Boo grinned — a good drooly doggie grin. 'Woof! How about I ask Ms Shaggy to make you a special mouse bag? We can hang it on my collar.'

'Squeak,' agreed Squeak happily.

'Till then you can ride with me.' Yesterday picked Squeak up and set him on her shoulder. 'Come on. We'd better go and collect Princess Princess before she tells the sheep people how she single-handedly saved their world.'

'She wouldn't!' exclaimed Boo.

'Huh,' said Yesterday. She set off towards the cottage, Squeak riding on her shoulder.

Boo felt his tail begin to wag. Life was very, very good!

squeak squeak squeak squeak squeak squeak
squeak squeak squeak squeak?

squeak!

Translation: What do you call a mouse
who defeats a ferocious bogey?

Sir.

FROM SQUEAK SQUEAK SQUEAK BY SQUEAK
THE WARRIOR MOUSE

22

Orges, Ghhhhhhouls and Tttttttrollllllllllllls

'Doom! Doom! There will be flood and fire and great waves and horrible er, thingummies, the ones with six eyes and dagger-sharp toenails, I'll remember their name in a minute, and, you, Whatshisname, the werewolf puppy, if you don't stop whispering in the back there I'll send a plague of grasshoppers down your underpants ...'

The giant chicken flapped her wings indignantly at Boo as he stood on his hind legs, his front paws resting on the Finding lab bench. A few grey feathers fluttered down onto the Finding-room floor.

'My name's Boo,' said Boo. He must have reminded the school Finder six times already today what his name was. 'I was just explaining to Squeak what you said about Finding ... and wolves don't wear underpants.'

Miss Cassandra glared down her beak at him. 'Into your fur then. I have no objection to a mouse in my class, Whatshisname. But if it wants to ask a question it can ask me like everybody else.'

'Squeak?' asked Squeak, peering out of the red silk pouch that dangled from Boo's collar.

'Ah.' Miss Cassandra looked around the Finding room. 'Does anyone here speak Mouse?'

Yesterday put her hand up. 'Me, Miss. Squeak says he's got a problem.'

'Well? What is it?' clucked Miss Cassandra flapping her wings impatiently and sending another flurry of tiny feathers around the lab. 'Hurry up, Whoseamacallit. We have a lot of doom to cover this morning.'

'It's the computers. He wants to know if there are

special mice for mice. He doesn't think he can push the normal ones.'

'*Squawk! Squawk! Squawk!*' said Miss Cassandra crossly. 'If Thingamajig had been listening,' she said, 'instead of squeaking to Whatshisname down the back there, he'd have heard me say that Finding isn't reliable unless it's done properly. When you have more experience you will discover which way of Finding bogeys works best for you. Some Heroes use a radar system called Bogeydar, linked by satellite receiver to a laptop. But as you five know all too well, Bogeydar can give a false reading if bogeys are lurking just out of range.'

Boo wagged his tail politely. He was beginning to wonder, though, if the Finder hadn't simply made a mistake when she'd sent them to face the Giant Rabbits. She was the most forgetful teacher he'd ever come across. But surely, he thought, the school wouldn't keep Miss Cassandra as a Finder if she made mistakes like that. And in any case he was glad she had!

It turned out they weren't to be Level 2s, after all. Dr Mussells and the Teachers' Council considered the matter, and decided that as the four of them had faced not just three bunnies, but a whole horde of Giant Rabbits, they should be made Level 3s immediately.

'It would have been Level 4,' said Dr Mussells, showing his matchless teeth and passing them each a banana as he swung slowly from the top of the whiteboard in his office. 'But we felt that none of you had enough experience for a Level 4. But it was an excellent effort. A good deed indeed, in fact! Get it? He-he-he.'

Dr Mussells hadn't mentioned Squeak. Boo wondered if Squeak was a Hero Level 3, too. Dr Mussells had never actually said Squeak was officially a student at the School for Heroes. But then he hadn't said he wasn't, either.

Squeak seemed happy anyway, in his little pouch dangling from Boo's collar. Boo brought him a few crumbs of cheese every morning too. But Squeak still hopped out and went back into the wormhole each afternoon. It seemed the wormhole was his home.

Boo found the School for Heroes easier now. Level 3s had privileges. To begin with, the five could choose which classes they went to (except for Squeak, who basically had to go where Boo went). There wasn't much writing, either, so there was no trouble holding a pen with his teeth.

They didn't even have to go to classes at all, if they didn't want to. But most Level 3s went to as many as they could: after all, that was why they were there, to learn all they could about Heroing. And most of the Level 3 classes were small, like this one, with only the five of them in it.

There were other differences too, now that Boo was in wolf form. No more clumsiness in *Wham!* *Bam! Pow!* — his paws weren't much good for the traditional blows, but his fangs and werewolf jaw

250

were excellent for grabbing and holding on tight. He mightn't be much good at recognising what bogeys *looked* like, either, but he never forgot a smell. (It turned out that the school had a smellevision set that showed bogey DVDs just so that Heroes with more nose-talent than eyesight could learn what each bogey smelt like.)

But mostly it was different just being in a group. Somehow he and Mug and Yesterday (and Squeak) were a gang now. They'd been friendly before, but these days they did almost everything together.

To Boo's surprise Princess Princess hung around with them sometimes too. She still had her group of admirers — even more now that she was a Level 3. But most times she chose the same classes that Boo, Mug and Yesterday did.

Boo sometimes wondered if Princess Princess was worried that they might change their minds and tell Dr Mussells what had really happened the day of their Hero test. (Of course, it wasn't Princess's fault she got a bad blister, he added hurriedly to himself.)

Maybe she'd decided she liked him, he thought hopefully, even in werewolf — well, puppy — form. Or maybe she just wanted to hang around with the Heroes who'd vanquished the Rabbits.

Because somehow the entire school knew that there had been a whole horde of Giant bunnies. Not only that, but word had seeped through the universes that *all* Rabbits, not just the ones Yesterday had spoken to, were turning into vegetarians.

On every world in the universes — well, every one that had Rabbits — they were changing from ferocious, fanged predators to fluffy bunnies, only interested in grass and the occasional carrot or lettuce leaf … and other Rabbits, of course. One of the Greedle's most faithful flesh-guzzling bogeys had been changed into a sort of cuddly toy that hopped — and all because of them.

Even some of the ancient Heroes stopped to say hello to Boo now. And no one had 'accidentally' thrown a spear at him for weeks.

'Are you listening to me, Whatshisname?' clucked Miss Cassandra.

Boo jumped guiltily and pricked up his ears. 'Yes, Miss Cassandra.'

'As I was saying then, if your mouse doesn't want to use a mouse then he can use a crystal ball.' Miss Cassandra flapped her wing at the crystal balls on each desk next to the laptops. 'He *can* read a crystal ball, can't he?'

'Squeak,' agreed the mouse.

'I'm taking that as a yes,' said Miss Cassandra, before Yesterday could translate.

Boo put up his paw. 'But how do they work?'

'Cluck cluck cluck!' Miss Cassandra was growing impatient. 'If you want to know the science behind crystal balls, just go to the library. I think it's hiding behind the girls' toilet. You'll find the book you want in the science section, unless it's still off on its "Bold Brave Book" course. But better take a bucket of sand with you — some of those science books can be explosive. Now, what was I saying before I was so stupidly interrupted?'

'How to Find bogeys, Miss Cassandra.' Princess Princess sounded bored. She'd been staring out the window at the sparks rising from the volcano all morning. Boo supposed Princess Princess knew all this already. It must be great, he thought, to have Hero relatives who could help you with your homework.

'Of course. Thank you, Princess, er, Thingummy. Well, many Heroes' special skills help them locate evil all in their own special way. Dr Mussells, for example, uses a banana.'

Yesterday put up her hand. 'How?'

'I believe there's something about the taste when evil is nearby. I like to consult octopus guts. It's old fashioned, I admit, but as I'll now demonstrate, octopus guts can be very reliable.'

Boo drooled on the Finding-lab bench as Miss Cassandra emptied out a Thermos of ripe-smelling octopus guts. It had been a long time since breakfast. His tail began to wag against the bench …

Princess Princess nudged him. 'Hey, woof-woof, put your tongue back in your mouth. You're making a puddle.'

'Sorry,' whispered Boo. He shut his mouth again.

'Ah, yes,' said Miss Cassandra, thoughtfully.

Yesterday leant forward. 'What do you see?'

'An Orge on Bandicoot World 4. But he's just digesting a meal of …'

'Innocent peasants?' suggested Princess Princess.

'*Clawk! Clawk! Clawk!* Good suggestion! No, a carrot and cashew burger. The Greedle adores burgers, and the bandicoots make superb carrot and cashew ones. I've even had a few myself — wormholes are very useful for inter-universe take-aways. But Orges are the most useless bogeys in the universe — only really useful to send out for take-aways. They can pick up the burgers but they won't try to slaughter the bandicoots. Although, as in this case, they tend to eat the meal you've sent them to fetch. No Hero duty needed.'

'Shouldn't that be Ogre?' asked Yesterday politely.

Miss Cassandra shook her head. 'Orges are notoriously bad spellers. Right,' she continued, jumping up onto her vacuum cleaner (she'd explained that vacuum cleaners were much faster than broomsticks) and grasping the handle with her claws. 'Tomorrow I'll show you how to recognise Ghhhhhhouls and Ttttttrollllllllllllllls using a sack of marbles. In case you're out of crystal balls.'

Boo put his paw up. 'Are Ghhhhhhouls and Ttttttrollllllllllllllls bad spellers too?'

'I think they just have a malfunction on their word processors.' Miss Cassandra pressed the start button on her vacuum cleaner and Broom!ed out of the classroom. Boo sighed and grabbed the pen in his jaws to make a note in his homework diary.

'How do you spell Ttttttrollllllllllllll?' he asked.

'Seven ts, r o and fourteen ls,' said Yesterday helpfully.

Mug opened his eyes, then popped them back into his skull. 'Me hungry,' he said.

'You're always hungry,' growled Boo, scratching an itch behind his ear.

'Digestion not good when stomach decomposes,' agreed Mug.

'Yuck,' said Princess Princess. She was wearing red today, embroidered with tiny emeralds. Boo had been feeling lately that Princess was really starting to like him. She was even sharing his lab bench! Maybe she's realised how brave and daring a cute wolf puppy can be, he thought, scratching his other ear.

Princess Princess got off her stool and stepped quickly away. 'I hope you don't have fleas?' she demanded.

Or maybe not, he thought. 'Er, maybe.' He'd stopped having (yurgh!) baths ever since they came back from fighting the Rabbits. There didn't seem to be much point now he was in wolf shape all the time. Wolves were supposed to smell wolf-like! There was no Mum around to remind him any more, either. Mrs Bigpaws would never dare to suggest that a Hero — even an apprentice Hero — was getting whiffy, he thought a bit sadly. 'You don't have any flea powder, do you?' he added.

'No!' said Princess Princess flatly. 'I don't have fleas, either. It's amazing how often you don't need flea powder when you don't have fleas!' She stamped out of the classroom.

Boo put his head on his paws. The School for Heroes Dance was next month. He'd been trying to get up enough courage to ask Princess Princess if she'd go to it with him. But it seemed that even being a Level 3 wasn't enough to make up for being a were-puppy. And there were plenty of other Level 3s who'd love Princess to go to the dance with them, or that Level 4 Hero who could juggle battle-axes and *Zoom!* at the same time ...

'Never mind,' said Yesterday sympathetically. 'She does like you, you know.'

'No, she doesn't,' said Boo, standing up and starting to trot after her and Mug out of the Finding lab.

'She likes you as much as anyone else, anway. It's just ...' Yesterday hesitated. 'Well, it's just the puppy thing,' she finished.

'But our Principal is a monkey! And there's Mr Hogg too ...' said Boo, helplessly. 'Half the Heroes on the mountain are animal shapes!'

'I don't think she'd go out with them either,' said Yesterday. 'Even if they were a hundred years younger. It's a handsome heroic prince with only two legs or no one for Princess.'

'Oh,' said Boo glumly. He felt his tail droop.

'Squeak,' said Squeak. He sounded sympathetic too.

'Lunch,' rumbled Mug hopefully, as they made their way out of the cavern and onto the ledge by the volcano. 'Hey, look out!'

'Let me by, you old varmint!'

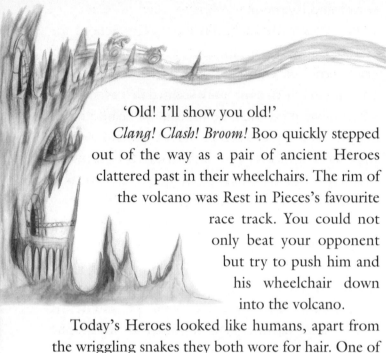

'Old! I'll show you old!'

Clang! Clash! Broom! Boo quickly stepped out of the way as a pair of ancient Heroes clattered past in their wheelchairs. The rim of the volcano was Rest in Pieces's favourite race track. You could not only beat your opponent but try to push him and his wheelchair down into the volcano.

Today's Heroes looked like humans, apart from the wriggling snakes they both wore for hair. One of them waved at Boo as the wheelchair thundered by. 'Good bit of Hero work on those bunnies, wolf boy!'

'Thank you, sir,' said Boo politely.

The gang wandered down to the skinning pool. Princess Princess was sitting on a big black boulder with a whole mob of Level 4 hunks, Boo noticed gloomily. One of the hunks had only two legs, too, if you didn't mind green scales and thought fire-breathing was cool.

Was the fire-breathing Level 4 a prince back in his own universe? Boo wondered. Had there ever been any werewolf princes? There were no princes at all in Werewolf World these days. Maybe if he did something incredibly heroic the Council of Werewolves might make him a prince …

'Me got cold slug pizza and zombie spaghetti,' observed Mug, lowering himself carefully onto their favourite boulder. He had almost lost a foot into the crater the day before, though he'd assured Boo he'd sewn it back on extra tightly. 'What you got?'

'Chicken-neck sandwiches,' said Boo, hauling Yesterday's bananas out of his bag and dropping them on her lap. Old Ms Shaggy was still bringing him nice stinky chicken necks every few days. He bit off a bit of crust for Squeak.

'Squeak!' said the mouse, taking the crust in his tiny paws.

'Hey, me just remember,' rumbled Mug. The zombie spaghetti wriggled a bit in his mouth. 'It my birthday this Saturday. Mum said, you like to come to party?'

'Hey, cool.' Boo wagged his tail.

'Squeak,' agreed Squeak, cleaning the last of the crust off his whiskers.

Yesterday looked up uncertainly from her bananas. 'I … I'm not sure …' she began.

'Hey, why not?' barked Boo.

'I … I have work to do. At home.'

'What sort of work?' asked Boo curiously. Yesterday never talked about her home. Princess Princess talked about her world all the time, and even Mug had pictures of his sister (she looked pretty much like him, except her fuzz was blonde, not green). But Yesterday never said anything about her world at all.

Yesterday shrugged her thin shoulders. 'Oh, things.'

'It important birthday.' Mug sounded hurt, though it was hard to tell with a zombie. 'Me four hundred.'

'Hey, wow,' said Boo.

'Mum been cooking special.' Mug slapped one of the flies that buzzed around his fuzz.

'Not zombie spaghetti?' asked Boo. He hadn't tried zombie spaghetti yet, even though Mug kept offering him some. There was something about the way the zombie slugs had squirmed in his stomach that made him uneasy.

Mug inspected the fly, then crunched it between his crumbling teeth. 'Zombie parties *always* have zombie spaghetti. But we haves other stuff too. Zombie lamingtons. Slug toast. Also meringues. Not zombie ones. They stay puts when you eats them. Have games too,' he added temptingly.

Yesterday bit her lip. 'Okay,' she said at last. 'I'd love to come. And they'll understand,' she added hopefully, almost to herself.

'Who? Your mum and dad?' asked Boo. Yesterday had never talked about her family.

'Sort of,' said Yesterday. 'How do we get to your place?'

'No worries,' said Mug. 'You come here, then all go in wormhole with me. I bring you all back here, then we goes back to ours universes. Unless,' he added, looking hopefully at Boo, 'me have slapover at someone else's place that night.'

'Er, slapover?' Boo wondered if this was a Hero technique he hadn't come across yet.

'You know. You stays at friend's house. Me never had a slapover,' he added sadly.

'You mean *sleepover*.' Mrs Bigpaws would probably be proud to have another apprentice Hero stay the night, he thought, even if he is a two-metre-tall zombie. He'd just have to make sure the puppies didn't gnaw on any stray Mug bits they found lying around. 'You can have a sleepover at my place after the party if you like,' he offered.

'Hot lake!' said Mug happily.

'You mean "damn",' corrected Boo. 'I've told you before.'

Mug shook his head carefully in case it fell off. 'No hot dam here, only hot lake.'

Boo grinned. That was real brain work from Mug. But what, he thought suddenly, do you get a giant blob of fungus for his birthday?

Hey, you want to hear a joke? They used to crack up when I told this joke at school. 'What did one flea say to another flea after the party?

"shall we walk home or take the werewolf?"'

Hilarious, isn't it? I mean it was really funny because there was this puppy in our class ...

THE MEMOIRS OF THE TOTALLY HEROIC HER ROYAL HIGHNESS PRINCESS PRINCESS SUNBEAM CARESSE OF PEWKÉ

23

A Zombie Birthday Party

It hurt a bit, thinking about birthdays. Boo couldn't help remembering his own birthday last year. Mum had given him a remote-controlled backscratcher and the biggest ice-cream cake Sleepy Whiskers had ever seen, with squished lizard icing. There'd been Kitten Icypoles and Choc-Fly Sorbet and Frozen Moose Mousse or Mouse Mousse, too.

What will my next birthday be like? thought Boo dismally, as he plodded a bit unsteadily along the wormhole the next Saturday to meet Mug and the others. He was in human form again today, hoping to impress Princess Princess. He was pleased that Mug had invited her too. It was amazing how hard it was to balance on two feet after being on four paws. And even the thought of Princess Princess failed to lift his spirits.

How could he be thinking of going to a party?

But it wouldn't help Mum if he didn't go. He'd already done an hour of *Zoom!*ing practice today and raced up and down the creek, as well as two hundred doggie leaps, which Boo reckoned was just as good as push ups. And Mug was his friend *and* a Hero, in his own fungusy zombie way. And if Boo was ever going to be able to rescue Mum — if he ever made it to Level 4 — he'd need all the friends he could get …

'Student approaching!' he yelled, as he stepped out of the wormhole.

Someone cackled happily by the portal. 'Student? Best not look at me then, sonny.'

Boo stared at the ancient Hero. She was as tall as Mug, with masses of bright yellow hair, a thin scrap of gold and purple striped fabric over a skinny body, and 126,000 wrinkles. 'Er, why shouldn't I look at you?'

She beamed at him, showing brilliant white false teeth. 'Because I'm Gloria the Gorgeous, sonny. And I'm not just gorgeous, I'm drop-dead gorgeous. One look at me and bogeys keel over. Everyone keels over when they look at me!'

'But I've already looked at you!'

Gloria the Gorgeous peered down at him. Her bright blue eyes were heavy with eyeliner and false eyelashes. 'Don't feel faint? World spinning a bit?'

'No,' said Boo honestly.

'Bother. Better go and put on some more lipstick. That should do it.' She began to totter up the mountain path to Rest in Pieces on the highest heels Boo had ever seen.

Boo gazed around. School looked weird on a weekend. The bats hovered over the lava pit, zapping at sparks, and the lava glugged and bubbled. From up at Rest in Pieces came the sounds of elderly Heroes yelling 'Biff! Bam! BINGO!' and hitting each other with their walking sticks. But the ledge itself was silent.

The school looked curiously empty.

The hot wind blew up from the cauldron, tasting of fire and rock. The ground shivered again, as the volcano shifted in one of its tiny earthquakes.

It still feels like the Zurms digging, thought Boo. It smells like Zurms, too, sort of strawberry and volcano, he added to himself, absently trying to scratch an itch with his hind leg and realising he was in human form just as he started to fall over. But that was impossible. Why would Zurms dig yet another tunnel to the Heroes' volcano, the worst place for bogeys in the universes?

And anyway, there was nothing special about the food here, nothing that the Greedle might want. Mr Hogg had said that the food up at Rest in Pieces was mostly tentacles — tentacle kebab, roast tentacle, or tentacle sushi. The retired Heroes had spent their working lives eating whatever they could get — which was mostly bits of defeated bogey, grilled on an open fire or, where there wasn't any firewood, raw. And even the Greedle would stay away from a volcano full of Heroes.

'Squeak?' said Squeak, poking his head out of the pouch around Boo's neck.

'Can you smell danger too?' asked Boo.

'Squeak,' the mouse replied.

Which doesn't help much, thought Boo, as he hadn't learnt how to speak much Mouse yet. He must just have been imagining the strawberry smell. It was so hard to smell properly in human form. Or maybe the ancient Heroes were having strawberry and tentacle muffins for morning tea.

'Toorootoorooo!'

Boo stared. Something was thudding through the wormhole. Something massive that shook the ground with every tread! Something that stank so bad it even cleared his nose in human form …

'Toorootoorooo!'

He'd been right! he thought. Bogeys from the

Ghastly Otherwhen were invading the school!

What should he do? Scream for help and hope someone up at Rest in Pieces heard him? No! A Level 3 Hero couldn't yell *help!* He'd just have to face whatever it was till the others arrived.

Is there time to Change? he thought frantically, just as the something lurched out of the wormhole.

'Toorootoorooo!'

Boo jumped back as an elephant surged past him. A large *zombie* elephant, he realised, as a bit of its foot landed on his nose.

'Hi,' called Mug, waving from the elephant's back. 'Me brought smelephant to carry us all to my place! Like bus but zombie!'

The zombie elephant skidded to a halt, with a three-and-a-half-leg landing.

Mug slid down the smelephant's trunk and hauled his duct tape out of his pocket. He expertly taped the severed foot back on, patched up the trunk, then turned to Boo. 'You look greats,' he announced.

Boo flushed. He hadn't known what zombies wore to a party (or for that matter what other guests wore to a zombie party), and he wasn't going to wear what werewolves wore to parties, which was just a collar, not when he was in human form, anyhow.

So he'd looked up 'Handsome Princes' in the library to see what *they* wore to parties. It took a few hours to track down the library (it had been hiding under the stairs yesterday) but he'd finally found 'Handsome Princes' in *The Book of Instantly Everything*, which was an unusually polite book and had considerately stopped its sword practice so he could look it up. According to the book, Handsome Princes wore silk and velvet to parties. Ms Shaggy had sewed all night to make the best Handsome Prince outfit Boo reckoned the school had ever seen.

'You don't think the green velvet cloak is too much?'

Mug grinned. 'No. It cool fungus colour. White silk shirt good too. Sleeves look like big saggy maggots.'

'Er, thanks,' said Boo doubtfully. Actually he was so hot in all the silk and velvet that the sweat was dripping down his back. But it was worth it if Princess Princess thought he looked like a Handsome Prince. If she came at all …

'You look pretty good, too,' he offered. 'Sort of ... neat.'

Mug beamed. 'Me combed fungus. Special for party,' he said.

Boo pulled a package out of his pocket and handed it to Mug. 'Hey, happy birthday!' he said. 'From me and Squeak.' He watched as Mug unwrapped it.

'Hey, cool. Scent,' rumbled Mug.

'It's "Instead of Shave",' said Boo. 'It's made from essence of dead cow, and old tortoise dung. Mr Bigpaws says it's great. He uses it all the time.'

'Cool,' rumbled Mug.

'And this,' said Boo. He thrust another package into Mug's fuzzy hands. 'It's ice cream. I made it myself. It's the Best Ice Cream in the Universes. I thought we could eat it at the party.'

He'd spent all morning starting up the machinery and mixing the ingredients and finding a freezer pack to keep the ice cream cold all the way to the party. It had felt funny, working at the ice-cream shop without Mum there singing to herself. Sort of sad. But good too, as though she was almost with him.

'Eat what?'

Boo's world went bright again as Princess Princess strode out of the wormhole. 'Princess! Sorry, I mean Princess Princess. I wasn't sure you were coming!'

'Well, I am. What's that thing? It stinks.'

'It a smelephant,' said Mug.

Princess Princess was wearing a tiny gold vest

today, and a tiny blue-and-gold-striped skirt with 'Hero' embroidered around the hem. Even her shoes were gold — lacy sandals with high gold heels. 'You look wonderful,' said Boo before he could stop himself. He wondered suddenly if even Gloria the Gorgeous had looked as good as this when she was young.

Princess Princess shrugged. 'I wasn't going to come. But people might have asked why I wasn't going to Mug's party, after all we went through together.' She stared at the elephant. '*What* is a smelephant?'

'It's a zombie elephant,' explained Boo. 'It's going to give us a lift to the party.'

'Oh, *great*. If I get any zombie yuck on my new clothes I am going to be *seriously* angry.' Princess Princess looked at her diamond-studded watch. 'Come on, let's get going.'

'Yesterday's not here yet.' Boo hesitated. 'Princess Princess, Mug …'

'Mmm?' said Princess Princess impatiently.

'You don't think … I mean, can you feel something strange?'

'What?' demanded Princess Princess.

'Oh, nothing,' said Boo.

'The only strange thing here is a zombie elephant,' said Princess Princess. 'Oh good, here's Yesterday. Oh, no, it's you, sir.'

Mr Hogg suddenly appeared before them. He was wearing a tiny spangled vest — pink — and spangled sunglasses. His tail looked freshly curled. 'Good

morning!' he trilled. 'And how are we all this merry Saturday morn?'

'Is my birthday,' rumbled Mug. 'We off to birthday party on smelephant.'

'Enjoy yourselves!' carolled Mr Hogg. 'I'm just ducking back to pick up my speech. I'm trotting off to a Warrior Pig conference for the week.'

'Ha-ha, sir,' said Princess Princess.

'I beg your pardon?' said Mr Hogg.

'Your joke, sir. Trotting off. Trotters …'

'It wasn't meant as a joke,' said Mr Hogg stiffly. 'Well, enjoy yourselves. Don't eat too much birthday cake!'

'Here's Yesterday,' said Princess Princess in relief, as Yesterday stepped out of the wormhole, still in her old tattered tunic. '*Finally*!' Princess Princess stared at Yesterday in disgust. 'Is *that* what you're wearing?

Erk. Come on, you lot. Let's get this *over* with.'

Mug had brought a ladder so they could climb up onto the smelephant. He'd even strapped on a seat, though it was a bit of a squash fitting them all on it.

To Boo's relief the zombie smell wasn't so bad up on the smelephant's back. He didn't want Princess to get car-sick — or smelephant-sick — before they got there. And the seat would stop any zombie yuck seeping into his new pants.

Not that Princess had commented on them, he thought. Or said he looked just like a handsome prince. He sighed. Maybe she was so used to handsome-prince-type gear that she took it for granted.

'Toorootooroooo!'

The smelephant gave a stumbling run, then galloped into the wormhole. The volcano's glow vanished as the wormhole's gloom settled around them.

Boo gave a sigh of happiness. He was squashed up next to Princess Princess! What could be better than that?

Well, actually, he admitted to himself, I can think of several things that might be better. Princess Princess playing catch with him on a deserted beach, just her and him and a ball and the waves rolling in to chase and maybe some dead seagulls to roll in.

And Mum back at the Best Ice-Cream Shop in the Universes, said a small voice in his mind. A family to come home to.

'Something stinks,' said Princess Princess. 'And I
don't just mean decomposing elephant.'

Mug smiled happily. 'Thanks.'

'That was not a compliment,' said Princess Princess.

'Dat's good,' said Mug. 'What's one of those
anyway?'

Princess Princess sighed. '*Okay*, you lot. Which
one of you has rolled in the chookie-doo-doo?'

'Um, me,' said Boo. 'Do you like it? Mr Bigpaws
says he always rolls in chook-doo before a party. And
he's the best-stinking werewolf in Sleepy Whiskers.
Everyone says so.'

'Boo-Boo's boo-booed,' said Princess Princess. '*Again.*'

'Um — whose bed are we going to come out under in your universe?' asked Boo, trying to change the subject. He hoped it wasn't going to be Mug's sister's. It would be embarrassing to come out under a girl's bed.

'It come out under Graunt Doom's bed,' said Mug.

'Graunt?' asked Yesterday.

'She great. She Great-great-great-aunt Doom,' said Mug. 'She got cool fungus carpet!' he added.

'Oh, *great*,' muttered Princess Princess, as the smelephant came to a stop. 'Come on. Put the ladder down so we can get off this dopey thing and up into your universe.'

'No need,' said Mug happily. 'Smelephant will rise up with us under the bed.'

'How can an elephant fit under a bed?' demanded Princess Princess.

'Me made smelephant that stinks. No, me mean shrinks.'

'It stinks too,' muttered Princess Princess. Her eyes opened wider. 'Hey, you mean you *made* this elephant? That's impossible. You're *dumb*!'

Mug grinned, showing his crumbly green teeth. 'Yeah. Me dumb with words. Me dumb with numbers. But me not dumb with DNA and zombie stuff.'

The smelephant began to rise … and shrink. Suddenly they were all tumbled together under a bed

on something cold and fuzzy, with a small smelly
elephant in the middle.

'Erk!' yelled Princess Princess. 'Get me out of
here!' She crawled out over the moist fungusy carpet,
kneeing Boo in the ribs as she went, then stood up.
Boo followed her, then stared.

He was in a room ... or was he? The walls were
white ... but when you looked closely there was a
tracery of what looked horribly like veins. The walls
seemed to bounce like a heartbeat ... and the floor
went up and down.

'What's *happening*?!' shrieked Princess Princess. 'This place is weird! It's *moving*!'

Mug grinned. 'You inside zombie house. No worries. House just swimming.'

'It's *what*?!'

'It hot today. House swimming in lagoon. Come on. Come and meet my family!'

✳ ✳ ✳

It's a beautiful lagoon, thought Boo, gazing out from the living room. The water had a pink sandy beach on three sides, and pink palm trees, and pink zombie swans gliding in the shallows.

'Mum like pink,' said Mug proudly. 'House pink too.'

'Yes, it's very … pink,' said Boo weakly.

'Pink feathers good insulation,' said Mug.

'And the feet?' asked Yesterday.

'How house move around without feet? Hi, Mum! They here!'

Mug lived in a giant pink zombie duck, if ducks had doors under their beaks and windows all around where their wings should be, and a roof garden on their backs.

Mug's mother was big and fuzzy, like Mug, but her fuzz was pink instead of green. She stood up as they came in. 'Welcome!' she called. She leant out the window and peered up at the house's beak. 'Gee-up, house!'

'*Quack*,' said the house obediently. It began to

paddle in to shore, the swans gliding silently away as it approached.

'This Dad,' said Mug.

A big brown lump looking like a bigger, older Mug grinned at them from the sofa.

'And this little sister, Glug. She decided to become zombie two years after me.' Mug grinned, showing green crumbling teeth. 'She see it much more fun being zombie in our family.'

A blonde lump of fuzz jumped up from a small pink chair. She smiled at Boo, showing long pink teeth. 'Him cute,' said Glug, waving fingers held on by duct tape. The fingernails and toenails had pink polish on them.

'Er, thanks,' said Boo.

'And this Graunt Doom,' went on Mug.

'Hiya,' boomed Great-great-great-aunt Doom, tapping her stick on the floor. She was sitting on what Boo supposed was a chair, even if it did have four fuzzy feet and was eating what looked like an over-sized apple. She looked just like Mug, except her fungus was grey and her nose was wrinkled. A single grey tooth showed when she grinned.

Boo felt a lump rise in his throat. They all looked so happy. Mug was lucky, having a family like this to belong to.

What if everyone's right? he thought suddenly. What if Mum's gone for good? If he was just kidding himself, refusing to believe she'd never come back …

'*Told* you a werewolf was coming. *Told* you him sad for mum, too,' boomed Graunt Doom to Mug's dad.

Boo woke up from his dream, embarrassed. 'Didn't Mug tell you I was a werewolf?'

'Me tell her,' said Mug. 'But Graunt Doom know anyway.'

'*Told* you he'd misunderstand,' boomed Graunt Doom.

'Graunt Doom was teacher at the School for Heroes,' explained Mug proudly.

'When I young, of course,' Graunt Doom boomed modestly. 'When I turn a thousand I think, hey, me getting on a bit. So me retired for a while. But not at Rest in Pieces. Me don't like eating tentacles. Me likes food that fights back.'

'*You* taught at the School for Heroes?!' said Princess Princess. 'You … you *can't* be a Hero! You don't look like a Hero at all!'

'What did you teach?' asked Yesterday quickly.

'Finding!' said Graunt Doom. '*Told* you Princess Pea Brain not believe me been teacher,' she added to Mug, poking him in the stomach with her stick.

'That's Princess *Princess* Sunbeam Caresse of Pewké,' muttered Princess Princess. For once she looked slightly awed.

'*Told* you Pea Brain have too many names!'

'Graunt the best bogey Finder in the universes,' said Glug proudly.

'Finding's not *really* being a Hero, is it? Finders don't Wham! Bam! Pow! bogeys much.' Princess Princess peered out of the windows. 'Can we go swimming?' she asked, hurriedly changing the subject.

Mug's dad shook his head as thunder suddenly growled above them. 'Too wet,' he said.

'*Told* you rain coming,' said Graunt Doom, bashing Mug's dad lightly on the head with her stick. Boo blinked. Were there eyes peering out of Graunt Doom's stick?

'But —' began Princess Princess.

'House swim instead!' said Mug's mum.

And it did.

It was impossible to be sad at Mug's place. The house rocked and swayed as it splashed in the lagoon (and the various items of furniture frantically shifted from one leg to another to keep their balance) as the rain poured down.

At least the rain wasn't pink, thought Boo. But despite himself, he was having fun.

At lunchtime the house waddled up into the greenest patch of fungus Boo had ever seen. There were other fungus growths too, tall giant pink and yellow ones, almost like trees. And a strange rotting smell ...

'Dead slugs,' said Glug proudly, patting her straggly hair. It had a pink bow in it. 'This where Giant Slugs tried to invade island.'

Princess Princess stared out at the decomposing

slugs. 'Why would the Greedle bother sending bogeys *here*? There's nothing worth eating!'

'Ha!' roared Graunt Doom. 'It want zombie spaghetti! But Mug here send zombie pizza to tap them on the head! Them slugs *really* dead now. No zombie-ing for them!'

'Why would *anyone* want to eat zombie spaghetti?' began Princess.

'*Told* you she not like zombie spaghetti,' boomed Graunt Doom, poking Princess Princess with her stick.

'*Huh.*' Princess Princess gave a triple whirl out of the stick's way. 'You don't need to be a Finder to predict that.'

Mug's mum laughed, showing green fuzzy teeth like her son's. 'We got lots eats. Slug pie, slug quiche ...'

'You see, I'm on this *really* strict diet,' began Princess Princess.

'*Told* you she on diet!' roared Graunt Doom.

'Also lemon meringue, chocolate birthday cake, pizza with everything …'

'Um, everything?' asked Yesterday cautiously.

'*Told* you she'd want to know,' rumbled Graunt Doom.

'Everything except rat, cockroach, skunk and slug or zombie anything,' said Mug's mum. 'Now we open presents.'

'*Told* you what was in presents …' began Graunt Doom.

'Shh,' said Mug's mum. 'It not polite …'

'Can you really tell what's in the presents?' asked Yesterday, fascinated.

Graunt Doom nodded. One eyeball fell out. Glug kindly grabbed it and pushed it back in.

'Let's see,' hollered Graunt Doom. 'That one.' She pointed her stick at Princess Princess. 'She brought sicks.'

'No, I didn't!' said Princess Princess indignantly. '*Vomit?* Yuck.'

'Sorry, me mean socks. *That* one.' She pointed her stick at Boo. 'He bring Best Ice Cream in the Universes. And "Instead of Shave". Smell great!'

Boo held out the freezer pack. Mug opened it and took a fingerful. 'It Best Ice Cream in the Universes!' he announced.

'*Told* you,' said Graunt Doom.

'Huh,' said Princess Princess. 'Socks is easy to guess. And Boo's mum had an ice-cream shop, so that's easy too.'

Graunt Doom grinned, showing her long grey tooth. '*Told* you she say that,' she declared. 'You try guess then what her bring.' She pointed her stick at Yesterday.

'Handkerchiefs,' said Princess Princess.

Graunt Doom shook her head.

'Bath salts.'

Another shake. Something flew off from behind her ear.

'Duct tape,' offered Boo, joining in.

'She *told* us you say that,' said Mug.

Princess Princess wrinkled her perfect nose. 'I give up then. This is *silly*, anyway. Who cares what's in the parcel?'

'Well?' asked Boo.

Yesterday held out the package. Mug took it and began to unwrap it. 'It little cage ...' he began. 'Hey, it tiny flying lizard!'

'*Told* you it be fly-catcher lizard,' boomed Graunt Doom, tapping Yesterday approvingly with her stick.

'It can sit on your shoulder and catch the flies before they lay maggots,' explained Yesterday hesitantly.

Mug beamed. 'Me hate flies!'

Yesterday nodded. 'I know. Now you don't have to use fly-spray so you won't sneeze so much. You really like it?' she asked anxiously.

'Best present in universes,' said Mug. 'Now me never have to blow boogies into handkerchief again.' He held up the sodden bit of rag then threw it out the window.

'Should have asked me,' Graunt Doom told Yesterday. 'Would have *told* you he'd like it.'

'Where did you get a lizard that eats flies?' asked Boo.

'Oh, nowhere in particular,' said Yesterday. Yesterday doesn't look happy often, Boo thought. But it's worth the wait when she does.

Mug put the tiny lizard gently up on his shoulder.

'*Chip!*' it said, flapping its tiny wings and picking a couple of flies out of the air. It burped happily.

Mug beamed. 'Wow! Me love listening to burps! Now *you* get presents,' he added.

'Why should we get presents?' asked Yesterday.

'Zombie custom,' said Mug. 'Oldest zombie give all visitors present. Not "thing" present. Word present.'

'Oh,' said Princess Princess. 'Is *that* all? My dad gives visitors ruby and gold cups. *Important* visitors anyway. And he …'

Graunt Doom peered at Princess Princess through her grey fringe of fuzz. 'Here gift for you,' she grunted. 'You want handsome Hero prince. But your Hero prince nearer than you think.'

What does she mean? thought Boo, suddenly hopeful. Was *he* the prince Graunt Doom meant? Except he wasn't a prince … though he was wearing prince-type clothes.

Graunt Doom turned to Yesterday. She shut her eyes for a moment. She opened them and she shook her head. 'Strange. Strange,' she said. 'Can see strange things around you. Have never seen things like this before. But know one thing …'

'What?' asked Yesterday quietly.

'You good girl. One day you be best Finder school has ever had. Better than me even. You get what you want — one day. But it may not be what you think you want.'

'*Huh*,' said Princess Princess sulkily. 'That doesn't mean anything.'

'It mean a lot, girl!' said Graunt Doom sharply. She looked at Boo. 'And young werewolf,' she said.

'Let see …' Suddenly Graunt Doom's eyes grew wide. 'Danger!' she whispered. 'Danger! Danger! Danger!'

'Where?' cried Mug.

Graunt Doom blinked. She shook her head a few times to clear it. 'What I say?' she demanded.

'You said "danger",' said Yesterday quietly.

'Huh,' said Princess Princess. 'That's not Finding! Of *course* there's danger. We're at the School for Heroes. So I'm going to get a prince, big news. And Yesterday is going to get something she wants — one day. Yeah, yeah.' She glanced at her watch. 'I've got to get going. Mum's getting the court dressmaker to make me a new Hero costume. It's got sapphires all along the skirt,' she informed everyone.

None of the zombies looked impressed. 'Sapphires taste good?' asked Glug.

'You don't *eat* them, you dumb zombie,' said Princess Princess sweetly. 'They just look pretty. Come *on*, everyone.'

Boo sighed. He didn't want to go yet. But they'd all arrived together, so he supposed they had to leave together too.

'Um,' said Yesterday. She crossed over to Mug's mum and whispered in her ear.

Mug's mum smiled. 'No worries!' she said. 'You take as many dead Giant Slugs as you want!'

'What!' cried Princess Princess. 'No way am I travelling with dead slugs.'

'But you don't like eating slugs!' exclaimed Boo to Yesterday.

Yesterday flushed. 'They're just a ... a souvenir,' she said shortly.

'Me fix trailer to carry slugs behind smelephant,' said Mug's dad kindly. 'You can keep trailer too. No worries.'

'No worries,' agreed Yesterday.

PLEASE wipe your shoes before coming back to school after Hero work. Because if you think doggie-doo smells bad scraped off your foot, you should smell bogey entrails in the corridor ...

JONES THE JANITOR
SCHOOL FOR HEROES WEEKLY NEWSLETTER

24

On the Scent of Danger

School was just as deserted as it had been that morning. The same bats were zooming after sparks down in the lava pit. The only difference was the smell — those long-dead Giant Slugs on Yesterday's trailer smelt really *interesting*, thought Boo, even though he was still in Two-Leg form.

There was no sign of Gloria the Gorgeous. Boo wondered if she was still putting on more make-up.

Princess Princess slid off the smelephant and waved her hand in front of her nose. 'Those slugs *pong*!' She turned to Mug. 'I-had-a-very-nice-time-thank-you-for-having-me,' she chanted as she strode back into the wormhole. 'Not! Bye!'

Boo sighed as he slid down the smelephant's trunk too. Princess Princess hadn't even noticed his prince clothes. He may as well have stayed in wolf shape. And at least if he Changed he'd be able to smell things properly.

PLUNG!

It felt like a hiccup with indigestion. The world wobbled … and suddenly he was a wolf again.

Yesterday bent and picked up Boo's finery and began to fold it for him.

'Thanks,' said Boo, absent-mindedly lifting his leg on the smelephant and raising his nose to sniff the air. He could smell the same strawberry scent that he smelt that morning. But it was much, much stronger now he was in wolf form. And there was another scent as well, one that raised the hair on his neck. 'I'll give you a hand to your place with the slugs if you like,' he added, still sniffing. 'I don't have to be home till dark.' Yesterday still hadn't mentioned what her universe was like. Suddenly he was curious.

'I'll manage,' said Yesterday shortly.

'Are you sure?' How in all the universes was Yesterday going to pull a trailer-load of dead slugs by herself? 'Why do you want dead slugs anyway?'

Yesterday shrugged. 'I just do.'

It was the only answer he was going to get, Boo realised. The ground shivered under his paws again. He sniffed the breeze from the volcano.

What *was* that smell?

I've smelt that scent before, he thought. And then he realised. It wasn't just a strawberry smell.

It was the scent of danger.

Why had he never realised danger had a smell before? It was the same scent he'd smelt when the Greedle invaded Sleepy Whiskers, underneath the stink of strawberry jam and popcorn. It had accompanied the smell of death on the breeze on the World of Golden Grass.

And the school had the same smell now. Impossible, he thought. It *has* to be safe here. He gazed down at the pit as another flame leapt up towards the afternoon shadows.

Shadows ... surely there were more shadows than before?

Boo glanced at Mug and Yesterday. Mug was waiting for him to take him back for his 'slapover', and Yesterday — well, she seemed to be waiting for him and Mug to leave first. 'Can you smell something?' he asked suddenly.

'Dead slugs,' said Yesterday, shifting impatiently from one foot to the other. 'Shouldn't you and Mug be going now?'

'No, I mean ... something dangerous.' He felt silly as soon as he'd said it. How could he expect a human to be able to smell as well as him? He was probably imagining it, anyway.

Another burst of flame leapt up from the pit, as if the volcano knew what he was thinking. The air crackled around them.

Yesterday looked at him strangely. 'I ... I don't know,' she said.

'You mean you *can* smell something?' said Boo eagerly, his tail wagging.

'No ... more like there's a shadow behind me I can't quite see. It's just a silly feeling.'

'A feeling, or a Finding?' demanded Boo.

'I … I don't know.' Yesterday bit her lip. 'I've only had a few Finding lessons, remember. Just like you.'

'But you're a natural Finder!' said Boo excitedly.

'Graunt Doom said you be the greatest Finder school ever had,' rumbled Mug.

Yesterday shook her head. 'But I'm not a *trained* Finder yet! I just … well, *feel* things sometimes. But mostly I don't know what they are. Or what to do about them.'

'Mug?' demanded Boo. 'Do you feel anything — or smell anything?'

The zombie shook his head. 'No. But you Hero werewolf. You smell things. Yesterday Hero Finder. Me just Hero zombie.'

Boo hesitated. It sounded crazy to say the words aloud. 'It smells like there're bogeys around,' he admitted. 'But that's impossible! Isn't it?'

Yesterday stared at him. 'This is the safest place in the universes! No bogey would invade the School for Heroes. There isn't even anything interesting for the Greedle to want to eat here. Unless it's decided it likes dead slugs,' she added.

'I know,' said Boo miserably. He lifted his nose and sniffed again.

The hackles rose on his neck. Something was wrong.

'Could you do a Finding?' he asked urgently. 'Please, Yesterday, I know it sounds crazy! But Find as hard as you can. Please?'

'Well … okay,' said Yesterday quietly. 'If you really want me to.' She shut her eyes.

She stood there, unmoving, for so long Boo was worried.

'Can you Find anything?' he demanded.

Yesterday opened her eyes. 'No,' she said. 'I don't see anything.'

'Well, that's all right then,' said Boo in relief.

'No, you don't understand!' whispered Yesterday. Her face was white under her tan. 'I don't see *anything*! I can't even Find the volcano. It's just a blank.'

'Maybe … maybe you're tired after the party.' And after eating twenty-four mini pizzas and three slices of birthday cake, thought Boo, but he didn't like to mention that. He'd never seen anyone eat as much or with such enjoyment as Yesterday.

'You're probably right,' said Yesterday doubtfully. 'But … Boo, Mug, there's something strange about the … the nothingness. When I Found the school some bits were more nothing than others. Does that make sense?'

'I don't know,' said Boo slowly. His fur still prickled with the sense of danger. *Yesterday can feel it too*, he thought. *It isn't just me.*

'Graunt Doom trust your Finding,' said Mug. 'Me do too.'

'Maybe if we walk towards where it should be but it isn't … I don't know,' said Yesterday desperately. 'It all just feels weird! But can we try?'

'Sure,' said Boo quietly.

He watched as Yesterday shut her eyes again.

Suddenly she began to move. It was eerie, thought Boo, as Yesterday unerringly swerved to avoid a rock. She can't see, but she can!

He tugged at Mug's fuzzy paw. 'Come on,' he hissed. 'We need to follow her.'

Slowly, steadily, Yesterday stepped through the doorway into the mountain, then along the corridor towards their classroom. Her bare feet padded silently on the steaming stone. Mug's fungus feet went *slap, slap, slap*. Boo's werewolf claws clicked. His ears were pricked to catch any sound. His nose alert for any changes in smell. But the danger scent seemed no stronger.

Suddenly, Yesterday stopped and opened her eyes. 'No,' she whispered. 'This is the way it wants us to walk ...'

'What's *it*?'

'The nothingness.'

Boo nodded. He felt calm suddenly, just as he had when he faced the Rabbits. This was what he had to do ... 'Let me try smelling again.'

He sniffed. For a moment the danger smell seemed to ooze all around them. Then slowly he realised where the scent was greatest. 'That way.' He pointed with his nose down the black stone corridor to the gymnasium cave.

Yesterday turned and shut her eyes again. She began to walk where he was pointing, stepping slowly and hesitantly across the hot rock. Her face was pale and sweat beaded on her forehead. Boo and Mug moved cautiously at her side.

'Boo? Can you smell anything else?' she said urgently, her eyes still closed.

'No. Nothing else.' Just bats, talcum powder and old school lunches, he thought. The ordinary school smells. But Yesterday didn't mean those.

'There's something here,' said Yesterday quietly. 'Something that shouldn't be here.'

'A bogey?' Boo felt his fur prickle again.

'I don't know.'

'How can a bogey invade the School for Heroes? Someone would have noticed! Are you all right?' he added, looking at her pale face.

'We've got to keep walking.' Yesterday was struggling to speak now, her eyes were squeezed shut. 'We have to keep on going!'

Boo padded next to Yesterday now, his nose raised to capture the scent, while Yesterday stumbled beside him, forcing her body to follow whatever her mind could see. Mug thudded behind them. Boo was glad that Mug was there. No matter what was in front of them, he knew the zombie would guard their rear.

They kept walking, Boo's ears pricked, his jaws half open to grab his prey. Past the Finding lab, past the library (temporarily perched opposite the gymnasium cavern, the books doing sit-ups or sharpening their fangs), past the …

Yesterday stopped by a thick wooden door, scorched by years of heat and ash. 'Here,' she whispered, opening her eyes. 'Boo, Mug … it's in here!'

'But that's the staffroom! There's no one there at the weekend!'

Yesterday shook her head stubbornly. 'Yes there is. I *know*.'

What should we do now? Boo thought. Try to burst in the door? Or find Jones the Janitor, with his deadly screwdrivers? But would Jones believe three students?

The thick wooden door creaked open. Something lunged out towards them.

'Ah, Boojum Bark. And Mug and Yesterday.' It was Dr Mussells, hanging from the lintel by one paw and munching a banana in the other. Behind him the rest of the staff were gathering their papers and preparing to leave.

Boo stared. He felt Yesterday shiver in shock beside him. Mug stood there speechless.

'What brings you three here on the weekend?' asked Dr Mussells pleasantly, still swinging from the lintel.

'Mug's birthday party, sir,' said Boo quickly, to give Yesterday time to catch her breath.

'Ah, the old transport swap,' said Dr Mussells, as the other teachers came out behind him. Ms Snott was in black and gold lycra today. Miss Cassandra clucked past them, her grey feathers ruffled. 'Used to do that when I was a student. We've been having a staff meeting. Just getting the class timetables sorted out. Here, have a banana.' He handed them each one, patted Boo on the head, then knuckled along the corridor after the other teachers. Somehow he'd found another banana for himself too.

'Yesterday?' whispered Boo.

'It's still there,' said Yesterday. 'The feeling ... it's still there.'

Boo shivered. For one horrible moment he'd been afraid that the Greedle had taken control of the teachers. But these are old Heroes, he told himself. If there was any way the Greedle could get control of one of them, it would have done it years ago.

'What's *making* the nothingness — there's no sign of anything wrong here at all!'

'I don't know! It's still there. But there're more patches now, not just one here at the staffroom. Boo, we haven't imagined it, have we? The feeling?' said Yesterday desperately.

'No,' said Boo softly. 'I've smelt that danger smell before. I've felt that kind of vibration, too. But it's only when I've been in wolf form. I just didn't realise what it meant till now. Everything about school's been so different ...'

Yesterday gave him one of her rare smiles. 'You didn't believe in yourself, did you, Boo?'

Boo shook his head. 'I didn't seem cut out to be a Hero.'

'You Hero,' said Mug gruffly. 'Me seen you be Hero.'

'So what do we do now?' whispered Yesterday. 'How can we possibly convince the teachers — and all the other old Heroes too — that there's danger here?'

'I don't know.' Boo tried to keep the quiver from his voice. 'But we have to try!'

⚹ ⚹ ⚹

The three of them moved down to their favourite boulder by the skinning pool, almost without thinking about it. They sat in silence for a while, watching the water plop and bubble. Boo scratched his ear, trying to think. Suddenly he brightened, 'Bum sniffing.'

Yesterday blinked. 'What do you mean, bum sniffing?'

'Bum smells tell you *everything*,' explained Boo. 'Or they do if you're a werewolf. If the teachers sniffed our bums they'd know we were telling the truth.'

'Um, Boo,' said Yesterday tactfully.

'What?'

'Don't you think there's a faint chance you might be expelled if you tell any of the teachers to sniff our bums?'

Boo's furry forehead wrinkled. 'You think so?'

'I think there's a good chance,' said Yesterday gently.

Boo sighed. Humans were strange.

'Me could ask Graunt Doom to come here. She Find danger,' rumbled Mug.

'Of course!' Yesterday gave another of her almost smiles. 'Why didn't I think of that? But we don't need to go all the way back to your universe. We'll ask Miss Cassandra!'

'But why hasn't Miss Cassandra Found the danger already?' demanded Boo.

Yesterday shook her head. 'It doesn't work like that. She may be looking everywhere else in the universes for danger, but not here! Why would she ever think to do a Finding on the school and Rest in Pieces? Come on! If there's any danger around, Miss Cassandra's sure to Find it once she starts looking!'

Was she right? Boo waited for his tail to wag. It still stayed determinedly between his legs, even though what Yesterday said made sense. The giant chicken *was* the person to help them. There was only one small problem.

'The teachers have all left,' he pointed out. 'And it's against every school rule to go up to Rest in Pieces.'

Yesterday raised her chin. 'Then we'll just have to break the rules,' she said calmly. 'Coming?'

Mug nodded. Boo gave a small whine. But he stood up and padded after her.

※ ※ ※

Down below them the lava frothed and bubbled. The path was narrow, and rutted by centuries of wheelchair tyres. There was no safety rail. Boo supposed that old Heroes didn't do safety rails. Or safety anything.

The path wound its way upwards. On either side were narrow terraces, on which ancient Heroes dozed on banana lounges or in their wheelchairs, or indulged in a little *Zoom!*ing in the dim reddish sunshine that found its way through the volcano smoke.

Boo bit his lip. He hadn't realised there were quite so many old Heroes on the mountain. There *couldn't* be any danger here!

Could there?

'Miss Cassandra not snozing over there, is she?' muttered Mug.

'It's snoozing,' Yesterday whispered back. There was something intimidating about so many ancient Heroes, thought Boo, that made you want to whisper. 'And no, she's not over there.'

'How you sure?'

'Because it's hard to miss a three-metre-tall chicken,' hissed Boo.

The path twisted around a giant pile of boulders, shining black rock and glittering yellow crystals. A big sign hung from the top. 'Rest in Pieces', it said, and then in smaller letters: 'Beware of the Heroes! They bite. And other things too'.

And there it was.

Boo wasn't sure what he expected a retirement village for Heroes to look like. A palace, perhaps, built out of the hard volcanic rock, with craggy battlements. But instead, Rest in Pieces looked pretty much like the school below it — a wide, not-quite-level rock ledge ending in a sheer drop down to the volcano, and a giant cave mouth, yawning blackly in the cliff face, with smaller windows staring blankly out at the rising sparks. From deep in the cliff came the muffled sound of cackling laughter and Wham! Bam! chops.

'Oi!' yelled someone. Boo stared. It was the elderly Hero who had tied him up in her pink knitting on his first day at Hero School. She hobbled out of the cave, her knitting still in her hands. It was yellow wool today. It looked like it might be going to be a bootee, though Boo wasn't quite sure what a baby with that shaped foot would look like.

'What do you three think you're doing?' she demanded, puffing up to them.

'Woof!' began Boo politely. 'I'm Boojum Bark.'

'And I'm Dahlia the Dazzler!' snapped the old woman.

Mug snickered. 'Good joke.'

Dahlia the Dazzler glared at him. 'That was no joke, sonny. I was the most dazzling Heroine in fifty universes. Bogeys just had to get a look at me and they stopped in their tracks.'

'Like Gloria the Gorgeous?' asked Boo incautiously.

Dahlia the Dazzler snorted. 'I was a hundred times more dazzling than Gloria! Of course the lasso helped,' she added. 'And I had my own hair and teeth in those days too. Now what do you three want? You know it's against school rules for you to be up here.'

Boo tried to stop his tail melting between his legs. This woman was ferocious! 'We need to speak to Miss Cassandra.'

'Old Chookie? What about?'

Boo gulped. There was no point lying. 'I can smell something — something new and dangerous. And Yesterday here is a Finder and she thinks something is wrong too.'

Dahlia the Dazzler cackled. 'What about you,

sonny?' she said to Mug. 'You think you have some Hero sense that says there's danger?'

'Me come because me their friend,' said Mug.

Dahlia the Dazzler snorted again. It sounded a bit like an elderly pig grunting. 'Sounds like you're the only one with a good reason to be here. Look,' she added to Boo and Mug. 'Do you know how old I am?'

Boo shook his head.

'I'm 156. I'm a *very* old Hero. And you know how I got to be a very old Hero?'

'By being very, very good at it,' said Yesterday softly.

Dahlia the Dazzler looked at her sharply. 'Maybe you're not so dumb after all. Look, kids, I like a bit of adventure as much as anyone. Give me a Vampire Viper and I'll rip its fangs out any day, and crochet a border around them too. But if you want to find your own adventures you're just going to have to wait till you're Level 4 Heroes. Understood?'

'But —' began Boo desperately.

Dahlia the Dazzler fixed him with a stony gaze. 'Son, I don't think you understand. I'm on look-out duty today. Which means I'm up here with my binoculars watching for anything — *anything* — that might endanger the school. Mutant octopus. Eruption. Kids who don't obey school rules. And if you think I might have missed something — well, that means you think I can't do my job. And you know what that means?'

'What?' whispered Boo.

'I get very, very angry,' said Dahlia the Dazzler softly. 'And you *don't* want to make me angry.'

They had to go, thought Boo. It would just make Dahlia the Dazzler even angrier if they stood their ground. She was right. They were young and silly and imagining things and …

'No,' he heard himself growling.

'No?' growled Dahlia, baring a fine set of false teeth. They'd been shaved to points, Boo realised, and gleamed red in the light of the volcano.

'No! We want to see Miss Cassandra.'

'That's right,' rumbled Mug.

Yesterday nodded.

Suddenly Dahlia the Dazzler let out another cackle of laughter. 'Good for you!' she roared. 'A true Hero never gives in! Come on! I'll take you to Chookie. Of course, she might try to peck your eyes out for disturbing her on a Saturday night. But hey, a bit of risk is what heroing is all about!'

'What she do Saturday night?' rumbled Mug. 'Her practise Wham! Bam! Pow!?'

'No. There's this cop show she likes. Come on. You'll find her in the TV room.'

Dahlia the Dazzler began to hobble into the cavern.

LOST AND FOUND COLUMN

Lost: During last week's Biff Bam Bingo Tournament, a set of drinking skulls. Great sentimental value. Also my contact lenses. Reward or a good kicking, whichever is most appropriate. Apply Marvin the Marvellous, Room 76, Rest in Pieces.

FROM THE 'REST IN PIECES' NEWSLETTER

25

Rest in Pieces

'Wait for my Go, people. Steady … okay! Go! Go! Go! Go! Go!'

'Reeeeeeeeekkkkkkk!!!!' Police sirens sounded in the distance as a brave-looking human in police uniform commando-rolled across the screen.

The Rest in Pieces TV room was the biggest cavern Boo had ever seen. Its ceiling stretched up into darkness. It was hard to make out the rough stone walls at all. The only light was blue and flickering, and came from the giant TV set bolted high on one of the walls.

'Oi, Chookie, some kids to see you.' Dahlia the Dazzler paused. 'Well, not kids as such,' she amended. 'No goats at all, in fact. One human in a tatty tunic, one puppy dog, and a zombie.'

'I'm a werewolf,' said Boo firmly.

'And I'm the Queen of Wonderland,' said Dahlia. She grinned at him. 'Don't snarl at me, sonny. I really am the Queen of Wonderland. They made me honorary queen when I saved them from a plague of bogey ants. The Greedle wanted their recipe for honeydew nectar. Lovely stuff, that nectar, but it always made me fart.' She turned on the lights then pressed a remote control on the wall. The TV screen went blank. 'Chookie! Are you awake?'

'*Clawk! Clawk! Clawk!* Of course I'm awake.' Miss Cassandra stood up, ruffling her feathers and blinking at them vaguely. 'I was just closing my eyes there for a second till they got to the exciting bit.'

'Excuse us, Miss Cassandra,' said Yesterday politely from the doorway.

Miss Cassandra swung round, flapping her wings. 'I see lumps of rotten chicken meat! Maggots! Vile stenches!'

'I think that my lunch,' rumbled Mug. 'We just had good party.'

Miss Cassandra blinked her tiny chicken eyes. 'Ah, yes, I knew they were there somewhere. How can I help you all?'

'I'll leave you to it,' said Dahlia the Dazzler. 'I'll see you around, kids. Even if you don't see me.' She tottered off down the corridor.

Boo gulped, trying to ignore the gooseflesh under his fur. 'We think the school is in danger.'

'What? Here? From what?'

'From the Greedle.'

'*Clawk! Clawk! Clawk! Clawk!* Are you crazy?!' clucked Miss Cassandra. 'Why would the Greedle come here?'

It was a good question. Boo shook his head. 'I don't know.'

'The Greedle is interested in only one thing.' For once the big chicken seemed alert. Perhaps the nap had refreshed her, thought Boo. 'That's food. And I can't see him going for our tentacle cheesecake.'

'But the Greedle and his Zurms must have come here once,' put in Yesterday. 'Otherwise there wouldn't be a wormhole here.'

Miss Cassandra nodded her feathered head. 'True.

Once upon a time this whole world was covered in grass and thingummies. You know, the things that smell nice …'

'Old chicken necks?' offered Boo.

'Flowers?' said Yesterday.

'Flowers, that was it. You've heard of the vanilla orchid?'

Yesterday and Boo nodded. Mug just looked blank. 'You get vanilla flavouring from the vanilla orchid. But this mountain grew the Fuffuf flower — even more delicious than vanilla.' Miss Cassandra sighed. It was a chickeny sound, but still a sigh. 'There were Heroes in those days, too. But not here. There was no School for Heroes. And no Rest in Pieces. Heroes lived in our own universes and did the best we could. But then the Greedle invaded this world, killed the inhabitants, took the Fuffuf flowers and made the Zurms dig so deeply that molten rock burnt up from the centre of the world to make volcanoes erupt so no one else would ever get Fuffuf flowers again. The destruction of a whole world shocked the universes. At the next Conference of Heroes we decided to have a Hero centre here, on the world the Greedle had tried to destroy. Old Heroes could retire, and teach young Heroes. The universes need more Heroes. And here we are.'

'So there's no reason for the Greedle to come here,' said Yesterday slowly.

Miss Cassandra shook her feathered head. 'No nice yum-yums any more. Nothing but a bunch of

Heroes. Why would the Greedle want to waste its monsters fighting us? All of us have defeated its minions many many times.'

'Could you still look again?' asked Yesterday quietly. 'Please? A proper Finding of the whole school. I know there are lots of Heroes on lookout. But a Finding uncovers hidden evil, too. You don't do Findings of the school, do you?'

Miss Cassandra stared down her beak at the three of them for a moment. Then she nodded. 'Very well. I must admit I hardly ever bother to do a Find at the school. There's already too much Finding work locating bogeys in the otherworlds. You did very well with those bunnies, by the way. I was having a Find yesterday and do you know what? Kids in one universe are actually keeping them as pets! Rabbits! That could never have happened before you tamed them.' She shook her head thoughtfully, making her feathers fluff. 'Come to think of it, it has been at least six months since I did a Find over the school … Well, we'll see. Come on.' She began to strut out of the TV room.

Boo hurried after her. 'Where are we going?'

'Down to the thingummy!'

'Do you mean the Finding lab?' said Yesterday helpfully, dodging round an ancient Hero on a knife-edged skateboard.

'Of course. Now keep up!'

✶ ✶ ✶

The school corridor was dark. It smelt like bats and burning rock. Miss Cassandra switched on the light. At least the shadows have gone, thought Boo. But the strange vibration in his paws and the scent of danger were just the same.

'Owwwww!'

He jumped. 'What was that noise!'

'Just Ms Punch practising Book Fu,' said Miss Cassandra casually. 'She and those books can get a bit savage on Saturday nights. Right, here we are.'

They strode into the Finding lab. Boo felt his spirits rise as Miss Cassandra looked over the apparatus on the benches.

'Now, let's see … crystal ball, laptop, bogey octopus guts … I'll use the laptop for this, I think. There's been a bit of interference in the crystal ball lately and I want to keep the octopus guts for tonight.'

'You Finding other bogeys tonight?' rumbled Mug.

'No. Making soup,' said Miss Cassandra. 'Once you've done a Find with octopus guts they lose most of their flavour, and soup makes a nice change from tentacle kebabs. Now let's see.' She opened her laptop and stared at the screen.

Nothing happened for long seconds, then something flickered. The shape grew firmer. First there was an image of the school, or rather lots of images, flickering here and there — the classrooms, the school hall, the library (perched up by the boys' toilets tonight). Then gradually the pictures lost their focus. The screen fizzed. Suddenly a picture flashed onto the screen.

Miss Cassandra's eyes widened in horror. 'Ah,' she clucked quietly. 'So there *is* something strange about. My apologies, er, Whatareyournames. It seems that you were right.'

Long white things wriggled and squirmed among bright red liquid on the screen.

Yesterday gasped. 'What is it? Is that red stuff … blood?'

Mug peered at the screen. 'I think that my snack,' he rumbled. 'Mum packed me snack in case me gets hungry in the night at Boo's place. It spaghetti and tomato sauce.'

'But spaghetti doesn't wriggle!' cried Miss Cassandra.

'Zombie spaghetti do,' explained Mug.

'*Clawk! Clawk! Clawk! Clawk!*' Miss Cassandra snapped the laptop shut. 'Well, that's it.' She sounded annoyed. 'Nothing more terrible than zombie spaghetti, though that does sound pretty horrible. Plus the overactive imaginations of a couple of apprentice Heroes. The whole school is totally, absolutely clear.'

She patted Yesterday's hand with her wing. 'I'm sure you'll make a fine Finder one day, when you learn to do it the professional way. And as for you, young Whatshisname,' she said to Boo. 'Learn to think with your brains instead of your nose. The smell of danger indeed. I've never heard such nonsense. And I'm sure Dr Mussells will say the same.' Her claws clicked on the stone as she stalked out of the lab.

✹ ✹ ✹

'Well,' said Boo, as he padded down the corridor between Yesterday and Mug. 'That went well, didn't it? Now we're a joke. Boo-Boo does another boo-boo.'

Yesterday sighed. 'It'll be all over school. Dr Mussells will tell everyone on the staff. The whole school will be laughing at us. We're the kids who thought the School for Heroes was under attack.'

'Ha-ha-ha-ha,' said Mug gloomily.

The strawberry scent was still there, and the smell he'd thought was danger, too. It just goes to show how much I have to learn, thought Boo glumly.

He felt his tail droop towards the ground. 'Why did it have to happen *now*?'

'Why just now?' asked Yesterday. She still looked pale, her eyes shifting uneasily at the shadows as they came out onto the ledge.

'Oh, nothing,' said Boo sadly. Even his ears felt droopy.

Yesterday glared at him. 'No, go on. Why?'

'I was going to ask Princess Princess to the dance,' said Boo, scratching his ear miserably. 'But there's no chance at all she'll say yes now.'

'Oh,' said Yesterday. She stared down into the volcano, avoiding his eyes.

'You come to dance with me,' said Mug. 'That what best friends for.'

'Um, Mug, Boo might like to take a girl to the dance,' said Yesterday diplomatically.

'I suppose I could bring Spot,' said Boo doubtfully. 'She's my friend from home. But she won't know anyone except me.'

'No worries. Boo take my sister Glug,' said Mug cheerfully. 'She think Boo totally hat.'

'I think you mean hot,' said Yesterday.

'That too.'

Boo gulped. 'Does she?' He suddenly imagined trying to dance with a two-metre lump of blonde fungus. A friendly lump of fungus who thought he was hot …

'Boo's going to take me. Aren't you, Boo?' said Yesterday.

'Am I?' asked Boo, surprised.

'Yes, you are,' said Yesterday firmly.

'You don't have to ask me just because I can't go with Princess Princess,' began Boo.

'I want to go with you. I like you,' said Yesterday simply.

'You do?'

'And I like you both, so me and Glug will come with you too,' added Mug.

'Right,' said Yesterday. 'That's settled. Come on.' She gave a sudden shiver, her eyes darting to the shadows again. 'I need to get my slugs home before they stink up the school. And you and Mug need to go for his slapover.'

Boo said nothing. But despite the smell of strawberry jam the world no longer seemed as droopy after all.

✳ ✳ ✳

It was fun having a slapover, sorry, sleepover (Mug's mistake was catching), decided Boo, as the two of them settled down in his room at the Bigpaws's. Mug didn't fit in a doggie basket, of course, but most werewolves kept a bed *and* a basket in their bedrooms, in case they felt like Changing at bedtime, and Mug could just squeeze himself into the bed in Boo's room.

Spot had really liked Mug, too. Even if he wasn't a wolf, he had a good strong smell. And he was a Hero, too. Boo had thought the Bigpaws might even have put up a sign, they were so happy to have two Heroes under their roof: 'We Have Heroes Here Tonight!'

It should have made up for the embarrassment of the afternoon. But it didn't. How could he have been so stupid?! Of *course* there was no such thing as a scent of danger. He'd just imagined the smell of strawberry jam. Or maybe one of the tarts at Mug's party had been strawberry, and the scent had lingered on his fur. And all volcanoes vibrated a bit …

Boo snuggled down in his basket and tried to sleep. Mug snored comfortably in the bed next to him, the container of zombie spaghetti on the bedside table, in case Mug felt like a snack in the night. Though after six poodle pizzas and a third helping of corgi crumble and ice cream, Boo didn't know how he'd be able to fit any more in.

At least it's Sunday tomorrow, he thought drowsily. We can sleep in, then maybe play Catch the Frisbee with the gang down at the creek. Mug would like that, and Spot too.

Yes, it was good to have friends. And slapovers … his eyes closed.

He didn't know how long he had slept when suddenly his eyes flashed open. The moon was hanging in the sky like a pizza with corgi topping. A small pig snored from its nest in the branches outside, though more softly than Mug.

Something was wrong.

The danger feeling was back again. It wasn't just

a smell, this time, or a feeling in his paws. This was like ice water washing through him. Like a rope on his collar pulling him, leading him ...

He struggled to his feet, trying to push the last remnants of sleep away, and bounded over to Mug. He stood on his hind legs and licked Mug's fungus face. It felt strangely rough against his tongue. 'Wake up,' he barked.

'Um ooopf,' rumbled Mug sleepily.

'Come on! We have to go!'

'Go where? Bathroom?'

'No! Back to school! There *is* danger there! Now!'

For a horrible moment Boo thought the big zombie was going to argue. But he didn't. He just staggered to his feet. Boo scampered out the door and down the stairs. Mug lumbered behind him.

They had to *hurry*, thought Boo, racing down the moonlit street towards the ice-cream shop. He didn't know how he knew, or why. It was as though his body was compelling him. Or his instincts perhaps. Not just his werewolf instincts, but his Hero instincts too. The ones he'd never known he had.

He pushed the door of the ice-cream shop open with his nose, and padded down the hallway.

A faint memory of strawberry jam stopped him in his tracks. He scampered back into the kitchen and rolled the bottle of rat essence from the cupboard with his front paws. Mug helped him slip it into the mouse pouch that hung from his collar, then they both ran back to the bedroom and slid under the bed. The floor dropped.

Why did the floor have to drop so slowly? Hurry! thought Boo, as they finally landed in the cold gloom of the tunnel.

'Squeak?' It was the mouse.

'Sorry, your bag's got stuff in it,' said Boo, as the small creature leapt onto his back. 'Can you hold on there instead?'

'Squeak!'

Boo supposed that was a 'yes'. He wondered if the mouse had felt the danger too, or if he and Mug had woken it from wherever it slept in the tunnel. But there was no way he could ask it without Yesterday to interpret.

And it was time to run!

Boo bounded down the tunnel, Mug thundering at his side. They had to go faster! Faster! Surely the tunnel was never as long as this before …

At last the red glow appeared in front of them, growing brighter as they pounded towards it. And then they were there. 'Students approaching!' yelled Boo, as they burst onto the school ledge above the volcano.

He skidded to a stop.

There was nothing there.

'Where danger?' panted Mug, trying to catch his breath.

'I — I don't know.' Boo sniffed. Nothing — just the scent he'd smelt that afternoon. Just the same earthquake-type vibration, though it was even stronger now. But something *had* woken him. There *was* something here …

'Boo! Mug! What are *you* doing here?'

Boo stared. It was Princess Princess. She wore pink silk pyjamas with tiny gold crowns on them. Her slippers were pink and fluffy. 'What are you doing here?' he replied.

Princess Princess flushed. 'I … I lost my necklace this afternoon,' she said unconvincingly. 'I came back to get it. Mum will give me heaps if I lose it. It's an *heirloom*, you know. My aunt wore it when she gave the dragon indigestion,' she added, gaining confidence. 'It's got a row of diamonds and —'

'You no wear necklace this afternoon,' rumbled Mug.

Princess Princess flushed even deeper. 'I … I don't know why I'm here. I just had to come! *All right*?!'

'Maybe you *are* a Hero then,' said someone softly.

Boo turned. It was Yesterday. She had stepped out of the wormhole so quietly that even he hadn't heard her. 'Yesterday!' he cried.

Yesterday wore the same tattered tunic as she always did. Had she changed before coming here, he wondered, or did she wear it even to sleep in?

'I did another Finding,' she whispered. 'Miss Cassandra was wrong. She's so vague — I should never have trusted her to Find properly. She couldn't even get our Rabbits right. Come on! We have to go up and warn the Heroes!'

'Warn them about what?!' Princess Princess looked as though she might cry. 'Why did I *come* here? I should be in *bed*! I just had this *feeling* …'

'A Hero feeling,' whispered Yesterday. 'Come on! There isn't any time to lo—'

'—lose.' That wasn't Yesterday's voice, thought Boo. He'd heard that voice before!

The scent of popcorn wafted across the ledge. There was the stench of overcooked strawberry jam, too. The vibrations grew stronger still.

It was the Greedle.

There is only one SURE way to survive an attack by the Greedle and all its vile henchmen. Just make sure you never, ever meet them.

COUNT TTOO-TTEN'S GUIDE
TO THE GHASTLY OTHERWHEN

26

Zombie Spaghetti versus the Greedle

'Too late, little puppy,
Ah, fate! How unlucky!'
'Though "puppy" and "unlucky" don't really rhyme, do they? said the Greedle. 'You know, I'm so excited that my poetic skills are deserting me.'

The Greedle looked the same as it had back in the ice-cream shop, thought Boo. The same gaping mouth and long white fangs, the same sagging belly.

Behind him lurked a pack of octopuses but with thousands of tiny staring green eyes, and little shoes on every tentacle. A row of Zurms lurked behind them, the strawberry jam oozing from their rears and bubbling slightly in the heat of the volcano.

Boo wanted to leap at the Greedle's throat. But he couldn't move. He was frozen, just as he had been all those months ago. Yet this time no Zurm had oozed its jam anywhere near him.

Why can't I move?! thought Boo. Out of the corner of his eye he could see Mug and Yesterday, immobile too. Already one of the Zurms was covering Mug with strawberry jam.

'How can I put this poetically?' mused the Greedle, rubbing its stomach happily. 'It's finding a rhyme to "Hypnopus" that's so difficult. "Slip so ruse?" "Flip, oh Bruce"? I think — yes I really do think it's best not to be poetic at all if you can't do it well, don't you?'

Where's Mum? Boo wanted to shriek. What have you done with her? What are you doing here?! Leave my friends alone!

But he couldn't.

The Greedle chuckled. 'But of course you can't answer me! Can't talk, can't walk, can't balk, can't stalk. Those are the Hypnopuses over there.' The Greedle gestured at the octopus creatures, with their staring eyes. 'They are such *useful* bogeys. They paralyse anyone they stare at.' The Greedle shook its head regretfully. 'The strawberry jam just didn't work with you, did it? But never mind. The Hypnopuses and the Zurms between them have got every Hero on this silly mountain nicely jammed — including that big chicken. Oh yes, I was quite clever there!

Never never never never,
Has any villain foul or fair,
Been so clever clever clever.

My Hypnopuses, multi-talented beasties, lurked in the Zurmhole under the school and hypnotised that silly chicken Finder so she couldn't see us.'

Suddenly the vibrations grew even stronger. The whole ledge shook.

The Greedle rubbed its hands. 'Dear dear,' he said.

It seems to me,
That soon you'll be,
Shaken right down
Into the ground.
And waiting below?
That volcano!

'You and the whole school and Rest in Pieces. My best plan ever! To tunnel with a hundred Zurms under the school and bring the whole thing crashing down forever, first thing Monday morning. No more Heroes! All the old Heroes gone, and all the young potential Heroes too. No one will ever dare to be a Hero again! Every universe and everything delicious in it — pizzas, cherries, ooooh, yummy yummy banana cake with chocolate icing — everything I want, all just for me! I'm too excited to even make a poem about it. Maybe later,' it added gaily.

When all this is over ...
And you all are dead dead dead,
I can find nice rhymes,
In my head head head.
When you are black and crispy,
And the school has gone all wispy,
Then maybe I ... Oh, forget it. It's time to turn this place into lava forever!'

He *had* to be able to move, Boo told himself. It wasn't even as if he was gummed up with strawberry jam this time! It was just mind control! Surely he could break away.

But you're a Hero wolf, said a whisper in his mind. *You're good at smelling, biting, widdling. Not brains.*

It was as though his paws were set in rock — cold rock, that was freezing his bones. He would have whimpered, but his throat was frozen too.

One of the Hypnopuses handed the Greedle a tray covered with a white cloth. The Greedle lifted it up. 'Oooh, yummy. Scones and jam and cream. *Just* what I need to make tonight totally perfect.' The Greedle gave a sweet smile as it bit into the scone. It flicked a shiny finger at the Hypnopuses, who slowly, terrifyingly, started slithering towards Boo and his friends.

Ashes to ashes and rust to rust,
All you fine Heroes will turn to dust.

'Bye-bye now!'

Boo strained to move, but it was impossible. Out of the corner of his eye he could see Mug and Princess, frozen too. The mouse was a frozen lump on his back. Nothing in the world moved except the Greedle, munching its scone, the bubbling lava down in the pit, the advancing bogeys and …

Something shifted next to him. Even more slowly, slowly, something moved.

Yesterday.

Her eyes were shut. But she still walked towards the Greedle, her arms extended. The Hypnopuses stopped, confused.

'What …?' began the Greedle, around a mouthful of scone. Then its smile deepened. 'Oh, I see what you're doing,' it said.

You clever child.
I'm quite beguiled!

'You've put yourself into the Find trance, haven't you?'

'Yes,' said Yesterday's voice, strangely distant. 'My mind is far away. My mind can move my body despite the Hypnopuses, as long as I'm in the trance.'

The Greedle laughed. It was almost a pleasant laugh, laced with genuine amusement.

Almost.

'You think you can possibly beat *me*, you shabby little girl?

Your precious ancient Heroes,
Are all frozen through.
And any time I want,
I can kill you, too.

'Maybe you can kill me,' said Yesterday dreamily. But I'll tell you one thing: I'll die before I let you hurt my friends.'

The Greedle laughed again as it licked the last of the jam and cream from its skinny red fingers. 'How long do you think you can keep that up? A few minutes will exhaust you.'

Yesterday said nothing. She was concentrating on moving in her trance.

Boo pushed frantically against the Hypnopuses' control. Yesterday was walking so slowly, he thought, like she was trapped in jelly. How could she manage to walk at all, with her mind in two places?

But she was too slow! he thought. There was no way she could fight the Greedle in her trance, much less tackle the bogeys. All the Greedle had to do was call over one of the Zurms, and they'd have her. Yesterday might be able to walk through the Hypnopuses control, but she'd be trapped in the Zurms' strawberry jam.

Then Yesterday would die.

How could anyone be as brave as that? Be able to control her body even as she faced death? And all to try and save her friends ... Already Yesterday's lips were turning blue. Her fingers were white. But she kept on going.

And suddenly Boo realised where she was going. She wasn't trying to attack the Greedle at all! She was heading into the wormhole.

The Greedle stared as Yesterday moved past it, without even an attempt to Wham! Bam! it.

'You see,' whispered Yesterday. Every word seemed torn from her body. 'I am going for help.'

'But there *is* no help!' screamed the Greedle.

'Yes there is! Mr Hogg is at a Warrior Pig Conference. I'm going to get him — and his friends. A whole conference of Warrior Pigs! We'll be back!

We might even find some student Heroes on their way to the school.'

'Zurms! Dig! Dig now!' The worms vanished down into solid rock in a hundred directions. 'The school will be in ruins by the time you get here!' shrieked the Greedle. Even as it spoke the ground began to shatter. A boulder bounced down the cliff, and then another ...

Yesterday hesitated at the mouth of the wormhole.

Boo gazed desperately at Yesterday, at Mug, at the frozen Princess Princess. A few seconds more, he thought, and I'll be bounced down into the lava. You'll be the last thing that I see. My friends ...

The mountain shuddered again. The whole peak began to topple down, just as the ledge below them cracked.

Something moved. Something white and wriggling. It zoomed from Mug's pocket and began to swirl through the air. Faster, faster ... suddenly the loops began to wind around the cliffs and boulders, round and round and round, like giant white rubber bands holding everything in place.

Zombie spaghetti, thought Boo in wonder. Mug's overnight snack! He must have brought it with him. Even though Mug was trapped in strawberry jam, his zombie spaghetti was tying up the school, saving it from disintegration.

'Heroic pigs!' shrieked the Greedle again, too furious even to rhyme. 'I'll show you Warrior Pigs! What chance have they got against my Hypnopuses and my Zurms!' He turned to his remaining bogeys. 'Come on!' he screamed. 'The strawberry-jammed heroes here are going to starve anyway! We have to get the girl — and the pigs! The rest of the brats will arrive just in time for the main collapse. Then I'll be free! Free to have every yummy in the universes all to myself!' The Greedle dashed after Yesterday as she vanished into the blackness of the wormhole.

The Zurms oozed back through the rock to join the Hypnopuses. They all began to follow their master into the wormhole, loping, snaking, sliming, lurching.

Boo had a sudden vision of what Yesterday must look like, a lone thin girl with bare feet and a tatty tunic, stumbling in her trance down the wormhole, while the Greedle and the bogeys of hell followed her.

Would she get to Mr Hogg and his Warrior Pig Conference in time to warn them? Who could run faster, Yesterday on her bare feet or the Greedle and his bogeys?

Then suddenly he realised.

Yesterday *couldn't* be going to Mr Hogg's Warrior Pig Conference. The wormhole would take her back to her own universe!

And she was taking the Greedle with her.

He couldn't let her face the Greedle all alone! He had to help her! He had to break free! There was no room to worry about himself any more. There was no room for worry at all. Just a determination to save his friend.

It was as though the hopes of a million universes met in his body. We need a Hero, they cried. And suddenly he was that Hero. He heard a growl, deep in his throat.

All at once he found he could move.

Mug and Princess Princess were still jammed. But there was nothing he could do for them now, he thought frantically, or the jammed-up Heroes up at Rest in Pieces.

Suddenly he remembered the bottle in his pouch. He *could* help them! He could find a bucket, fill it with water, add drops of rat essence, throw it over Mug and Princess …

… and by then the Greedle and its bogeys would have destroyed Yesterday.

How could he choose? he thought desperately. Or maybe …

Almost before he had time to think, he shook the pouch off over his head and nosed out the bottle of rat essence. He grabbed it with his teeth and lifted it up, then threw it as hard as he could down into the bubbling volcano.

Suddenly the smoke was filled with the scent of dead rat.

Would the rat-filled smoke be enough to dissolve the jam? He couldn't stop to find out! He could only hope, just as he could only hope the zombie spaghetti would keep holding the school and the mountain together.

Boo growled again as he raced down the tunnel.

Was he close enough behind Yesterday to be drawn into her universe too? Or had he lost them in those few seconds when he stopped to throw the rat essence? Would he find himself under the bed at the ice-cream shop?

For a few seconds he thought he was too late. Then all at once he saw them — the Greedle, running in a weird and horrible shuffle, with Yesterday pounding ahead. She seemed to have escaped the Hypnopuses' power as soon as she got into the tunnel, thought Boo. Behind them the bogeys raced to catch up — the Hypnopuses in a nasty sort of eight-legged dance, and the Zurms, still spreading a thin trail of strawberry jam.

Boo growled again.

The Greedle glanced back at him. 'Oh no, you don't,' it called.

You can't!

You won't!

No more widdling, little Hero!

Just take this,

And you'll be zero!

Something flashed from the Greedle's hand. Boo glanced down to where it had landed. It was a small, fanged cockroach. The Roach bit deep into his paw, and kept on biting.

Boo yelped. He shook the cockroach off, but the agony remained. It wasn't just pain. It was sharper, deeper and more horrible than anything he'd ever felt. He rolled on the ground, trying to control his body, then forced himself up onto his paws again. Only three paws worked now. Well, three would have to be enough.

Blood dripped onto the tunnel floor as he limped forwards again, avoiding the deadly stickiness of the jam.

It was almost impossible to balance. Even harder to hobble forwards with three legs. But he could do it. He could do anything! Ignore the pain. Ignore everything but Yesterday and the monsters that pursued her. He was nearly there!

Could he manage to leap over the bogeys and snap the Greedle in his jaws? Impossible even with all four paws. But he was going to try!

Boo leapt, his teeth bared, just as the Greedle and Yesterday rose up and through the wormhole. A second later the floor rose again, taking the other bogeys with it.

His jaws met nothingness.

The real point to remember, darlings, is that your costume has to be practical. When you're dashing out to save a world you can't stop to iron your cloak or wash tomato sauce stains from your top. Oh, and watch out for horizontal stripes, too. They're so unflattering.

A HERO'S GUIDE TO FASHION,
MR PG HOGG

27

The Dinosaurs of Yesterday

Suddenly he began to rise as well. In a few seconds he'd be ... where? Sleepy Whiskers or ... What *was* Yesterday's world? What universe had she taken the Greedle into?

The world changed. Dirt beneath his fur. A smell of ...

Boo blinked and wrinkled his nose. The stink filled his nostrils. A smell of burning! Were they back at school? But this wasn't the smell of a volcano. This was like the smell of a road on a hot day, as the tar melted under your paws.

He scrambled out from under the bed and peered around. But it wasn't a bed, he realised. It was just a sheet of ragged leather stretched between four rocks.

What *was* this place?

He was in a hut, as small as a cupboard back home, made of roughly piled rocks. Above him a sheet of leather was stretched over the walls to make a roof. There was a large rock for a table, a small rock for a chair, and that was all. The door was just an opening in one wall.

There was no sign of Yesterday, the Greedle, or the bogeys.

Boo staggered out the door, then stopped, his teeth bared. This couldn't be Yesterday's world! Not this!

This world was rock. Flat rock and blue sky, unchanging as far as he could see, bordered only by the horizon, a thin line between the grey and the blue. Only two things broke the monotony — the stone hut, and the small lake below it, bubbling silver and smelling of salt and sourness.

It was like a page from a history book. A prehistoric world, before grass, before trees, even before seas or mountains or volcanoes, when the world was rock and tar … The ground shivered under his paws. For a moment he thought it was the Zurms, digging again, then realised it was the earth itself.

How could Yesterday live in a world like this?! But there was no time to think about that now. He gazed around frantically. Where were they all? And then he saw them.

Four of the octopus bogeys held Yesterday by her arms and legs. One had wrapped two of its tentacles around her throat. The Zurms stood ready to spread their jam if needed. The Greedle stood in the middle of them all, smiling gently.

Welcome, little wolf!
I have to say
This wasn't the way
I hoped we'd meet again today.
But now you're here,
My puppy dear,
We can begin to play!

'Let go of her,' growled Boo, then realised how dumb he sounded. Why would the Greedle bother to let Yesterday go now?

The Greedle rubbed its hands together.

Let's play a game!
You be tame
A wolf to make my ice cream.
And in return
You get to learn —

'Stop it!' howled Boo. He showed his fangs. 'Let her go, or I'll go for your throat.'

Oh! Now, now! gloated the Greedle.

That isn't how

A mannered pup behaves.

'I'll give you to the count of three,' growled Boo. 'And then I'm coming for you.'

You'll have to bite

With all your might,

To get through all my slaves!

'Then I will,' interrupted Boo. 'I'll Wham! Bam! Pow! every one of your bogeys. Then I'll bite you.'

No wolf's won wars

With just three paws, said the Greedle calmly. Its plans might have gone astray, but at least it seemed to be enjoying its poems too much to focus on killing its captives — yet.

'Boo.' It was Yesterday's voice. She'd woken from her trance, Boo realised. This was her real voice — weak, but awake. 'Boo, go back into the wormhole. Now!'

'No!' he yelled. 'Not without you!'

'Boo, please! You have to listen! Go back to the school,' Her voice was just a gasp, so he had to strain to hear it. 'You have to save yourself! Ahhh!' Yesterday screamed as the bogey octopuses pulled at her arms and legs.

'One,' said Boo.

'Boo, please … please just go! I'll be all ri—'

'Two.'

'Boo —'

'Three!' Boo leapt.

The world was a muddle of arms and fangs, tentacles, strawberry jam and pain. Underneath it all was the laughter of the Greedle and the smell of tar and ancient rock.

'Kill h—' began the Greedle. Was it going to say Kill 'her'? Or 'him'? But before it could finish, the Greedle began to choke.

'Squeak! Squeak! Squeak!'

It was the mouse! Boo had forgotten that the tiny animal had still been on his back. He must have clung to his fur all the way down the wormhole. And now, by the sound of it, Squeak had jumped down the Greedle's throat.

You stupid mouse! thought Boo, as his claws ripped at a monstrous face, and his jaws bit through one tentacle, then another. A mouse can't attack the Greedle!

'Squeak!' The sound was muffled but determined.

Something changed. The Hypnopuses and Zurms still tore at him. But suddenly they seemed … distracted. A distant thudding sound grew louder. It wasn't an earthquake or tunnelling bogeys. It was …

The tangle of bogeys around him began to shriek. The world was suddenly black with blood and scraps of skin and feathers. This is it, thought Boo. This is the end …

'Yesterday! Squeak!' He tried to yell to them — not to call for help, or to apologise for not helping them. But because he didn't want to die alone. Didn't want them to die alone. If you have to die, he thought, it's best to die a Hero, doing what you have to do. And it's better to die with your friends around you.

Though living, he thought, would be a heck of a lot better …

Suddenly he realised that nothing was trying to bite him, strangle him, rip him apart, smother him with jam or behead him. Instead, the bogeys were dark dead-weights on top of him, piled so high he couldn't see the sky or light.

A dead weight. Dead.

Until they began to move again …

Boo struggled up out of the quivering pile of Hypnopuses and Zurm corpses — and stared.

Creatures — all enormous, with small heads and leathery wings, with fangs that gleamed, and shrieks that tore the world — pulled at the mass of bogeys around him, stuffing bits of tentacle or leathery foot into their mouths. For a moment he thought the Greedle had called up reinforcements from the Ghastly Otherwhen.

Then he saw the Greedle was gone. There was only him, a small bloody puppy among the slaughter, and Yesterday, lying breathless on the rock.

'Yesterday!' He limped over to her, and licked her face. 'Yesterday, are you all right?'

Behind him the ripping, squelching and gulping sounds continued.

Yesterday struggled to sit up. 'Yes,' she gasped. 'Boo, what about you?'

'I'm fine,' he said, though he wasn't. His leg was a thread of fire, one ear felt like it had been torn off, and his fangs felt like they'd been tugged by a dozen giant octopuses. Come to think of it, he thought, they had.

The mouse! Where was he?

'Squeak!' cried Boo. Perhaps, he thought desperately, the little mouse had survived, just as he had. 'Where are you?'

'Squeak?' The mouse peered out of a pile of bloodstained bones. It looked scared, and its whiskers were bent, but it was otherwise unhurt. It jumped up onto Boo's shoulder and grasped Boo's fur as though it would never let it go.

Yesterday stared in horror at the pile of bogeys. Suddenly she began to cry. 'It isn't fair,' she sobbed.

'No! They should never have attacked you —'

'I don't mean that! The Zurms and the Hypnopuses didn't start out being evil. They were taken over by the Greedle. Maybe they were happy on their own worlds! Maybe I could have convinced them to change — just like I convinced the Rabbits. But now they're dead! And it's all my fault!'

Boo stared at her. He wanted to lick the tears off her cheeks, but was afraid she might scream *yuck*.

'It's not your fault,' he began.

'Yes it is! I brought the bogeys here!'

'You didn't make them evil! The Greedle did that! You just did what you could to save us all!' He shivered. 'Come on, we have to go, before those creatures get us too.'

'They won't,' said Yesterday.

'You can't be sure of that! Come on!'

'They won't,' said Yesterday. 'Because they're mine.'

That was when the school minibus arrived.

Heroics are all very well. But who has to clean the minibus or mend the fang marks in the doors when they get back? Me.
And you try polishing 1,000 bloodstained drinking skulls.

JONES THE JANITOR

28

Yesterday's Secret

The bus exploded through the hut doors, widening them considerably. Rocks sprayed out either side.

The bus doors flashed open. Dr Mussells swung by his tail from the doorway, his white teeth bared in a grimace of rage, a banana in both hands.

Dahlia the Dazzler and Gloria the Gorgeous burst out beneath him, arm in arm. Gloria wore a pink feather boa around her neck, her knitting raised ready to strike, her face calm, her eyes alight with the joy of battle. Boo blinked. Suddenly the two ancient Heroes were dazzling: so bright they hurt his eyes.

Ms Snott leapt out next, a vision in turquoise lycra, a dozen daggers in her fists and mouth, then Mrs Kerfuffle, wielding *The Atlas of all the Universes*, the biggest, most heroic book in the library. Jones the Janitor followed with his screwdrivers, then Ms Punch, wafting above them all, and Mug, waving more of his zombie spaghetti around his head like a lasso.

A mass of ancient Heroes scrambled out behind him, in a tangle of wheelchairs, walking frames, wooden legs and hearing aids.

'Let me at 'em!'

'No pushing at the back!'

'Last one to get a bogey is a tentacle muffin!'

'Boo!' rumbled Mug. 'Is you all rights? Yesterday? Squeak?'

'Squeak!' yelled the mouse, still clinging to Boo's fur.

Boo tried to speak, but no words came. Pain, exhaustion and horror washed through him, draining him almost as thoroughly as if the Greedle had sucked him dry. He tried again.

'I'm all right.' The words were almost a whimper. 'I'm all right,' he said more loudly.

'The Greedle!' yelled Dr Mussells. 'Where is it?'

Boo pointed. The creatures were still a swirl of fangs and claws and leather. Now and then one shrieked in triumph, then bent again to its meal. On the ground at their feet were a few white scraps and a faint stain that may have once been the Greedle.

'What in all the universes are those?' Dr Mussells stared at the monsters, his bananas still ready to strike.

Yesterday forced herself to her feet. 'They're mine,' she said softly.

'But, girl —'

Yesterday clicked her fingers. The creatures looked up from the remnants of the bogeys.

'Greeed Kneet!' crooned Yesterday softly. One by one the monsters rose. A couple fluttered above Yesterday on their leathery wings. One giant with spines along its back stepped tenderly towards her, and sniffed, as though checking she was all right.

'Pteeed, neeel?' cried Yesterday gently.

The spined monster glanced towards Dr Mussells and the others, then, seeming reassured they weren't going to attack Yesterday, took wing.

Once again the air was full of leather and strange high-pitched squeals. Then they were gone.

'What … how …?' began Boo. The world swam around him. His paws felt like marshmallows.

Tears rolled down Yesterday's cheeks. But she didn't bother to wipe them away. 'They're dinosaurs. My dinosaurs. That's who I am — Yesterday of … Yesterday.'

'I don't understand …' began Boo. His brain was mush. He didn't know what to say, or how to say it. The energy and desperation that had driven him had seeped away, leaving him as cold as the Greedle's glance.

Dr Mussells swung down onto rocky ground. 'I think,' he said quietly, 'that we can assume the Greedle is no longer a threat. Even if it's managed to escape — and I profoundly hope it's lying there with the rest of its bogeys — it can't hurt us now. Come on, lad. You too,' he added to Mug and Yesterday. 'Well done, the lot of you.' He tossed his bananas to Boo and Yesterday, then reached into the bus, pulled out another and threw it to Mug.

'Come on, now,' he said firmly. 'Back to school.'

'But, sir —' began Boo. The world shivered once again and everything went black.

✳ ✳ ✳

It was cold in the sick bay, despite the *glop glop glop* of the hot lava below the window, and the tendrils of steam from a crack in the walls. Boo lay under a blanket on the bed, his nose to his bum, and shivered. He didn't think he'd ever be warm again. The coldness of the vision of death lingered in his bones.

But the chill of despair was worse. He could never follow the Greedle or its monsters back into the Ghastly Otherwhen now. Mum was trapped there forever! And it was all because of him.

He wanted to whine. He wanted to howl, or hide under his blanket forever, shutting out the world. A world without Mum.

But he couldn't. He had friends who relied on him, just as he relied on them, people who needed him …

Life had to go on, no matter how much it hurt.

A shadow appeared by the door. 'Boo? Are you okay?'

'Ms Punch say he got broken leg and torn ear and ...' The booming voice could only belong to Mug.

Yesterday sighed. 'I meant are you okay enough for visitors?'

'I'm okay.' Boo's voice sounded flat, even to himself.

'Me brought you bone to eat,' offered Mug, pulling out a big meaty lump from somewhere in his fungus. 'It not a zombie bone, though. Zombie bone too wriggly when you not well.'

'Um, thanks.' Boo tried not to look at the bone. It reminded him too much of the bloody scraps that had been all that was left of the Greedle and its monsters. He might never gnaw another bone again, he thought. 'What's been happening?'

Yesterday pulled up a chair by the bed. Mug squatted next to her.

'We all unfroze soon as your rat stink dripped all over us.' Mug rumbled. 'That rat smell good! Princess unfroze too, but she couldn't come help rescue you on account she left her electric blanket on back at palace. Her had to run back and turn it off.'

'Oh,' said Boo.

'And Mug's zombie spaghetti is still holding the mountain together ...'

'Zombie spaghetti never let go,' said Mug proudly.

'Dr Mussells is busy organising repairs. He's got to make a report to the Interuniversal Council of Heroes, as well as the parents.'

Boo nodded. It wouldn't be easy, he thought, to find a way to tell parents that their kids' school had been nearly destroyed by the Greedle and his bogeys.

'Dr Mussells say me and Yesterday Level 4 Heroes now! Him announce it tomorrow at Speech Day!' added Mug proudly. 'He say to tell you "well done," and him see you tomorrow too.' Mug frowned. 'You be okay for Speech Day?'

'I'll be fine. Level 4 ... congratulations! You deserve it.' And they did, thought Boo. The whole school would have vanished without Mug and his zombie spaghetti. And he bet Yesterday was the bravest Hero the school had ever known, leading the Greedle and its monsters away by herself. He looked up at Yesterday, sitting so quietly by his bed.

'Is that really your world?'

Yesterday nodded without looking at him.

'It was ... wild. Horrible,' said Boo.

Yesterday turned her face away. 'So now you know,' she said softly. 'I'm not a golden princess, like Princess. I never will be. I'm just — Yesterday, from a dead world.'

Boo wanted to whimper at the pain in her eyes. 'I don't understand. How can you live in a universe like that? Survive there with those creatures?'

'I look after them,' said Yesterday simply. 'That's my job. That's why they attacked the bogeys and left you alone — they could smell me on you, so they knew you were my friend. The bogeys were attacking us. So they …'

'Yes,' said Boo. He shivered again. It was going to be hard to forget the shriek of despair and the wet gurgling sounds as the creatures ate the bogeys.

'They're dinosaurs,' said Yesterday. 'Pterodactyls. Pteradons. All the creatures that have vanished in other universes are still alive on Yesterday.'

'But why are you there with them?' cried Boo.

'I'm … I'm a slave. It's my job. Yesterday — the world, not me — is a …' She frowned. 'I suppose you'd call it a zoo. Or a museum. It's owned by the Guardians. They own me too. They visit Yesterday to show their children the animals that are extinct everywhere else. Slaves like me look after the animals. Every one of us is called "Yesterday". I don't even have my own name. I look after the animals in Quarter 15, distribute them food.' She shook her head. 'What there is of it. The Guardians don't realise how much dinosaurs need to eat … or maybe they think they put on a better show if they're hungry and attack each other.'

'So that's why you took the garbage and the slugs?' said Boo wonderingly.

Yesterday nodded. 'For them. They're always almost starving. And me,' she added softly. 'You have no idea how hungry I get sometimes. I … I'm very good with the animals. Better than any of the other slaves. I can Find them if they're in trouble. I can even talk to them, so the Guardians sent me here. They thought that I'd learn useful skills here, to make me a better keeper. And besides,' she added bitterly, 'a Hero slave is valuable. Maybe when I graduate they'll sell me for even more money. You can do anything you want to a slave.'

Boo struggled to sit up. 'But why didn't you tell us?' he barked. 'I'd have brought you a lot more than a few bananas,' he added guiltily, thinking of all the food he'd eaten while Yesterday had watched, hungry.

'What? That I'm only a slave? Less than the dust? Not a princess like Princess. Just … nothing,' said Yesterday bitterly. 'Nothing at all.'

'You Hero,' said Mug. 'And friend,' he added firmly.

'That's right,' said Boo. 'Yesterday, look at us! Don't turn away! You're our friend. And you're going to be a brilliant Finder. Those Guardians don't own you! No one can own another person. They just think they do! And — and somehow we'll find enough money to buy you from the Guardians … or find another way to free you and —'

'What?' Yesterday was almost smiling again through her tears. 'You … you don't mind?'

'Of course we mind!' said Boo fiercely. 'We mind that you've been lonely. We mind that those Guardians think they can use you! We mind that you've been *hungry* —'

'Have idea!' rumbled Mug. The others looked at him in surprise. 'All bogeys that Heroes kill, we send to Yesterday. Then dinosaurs have lots to eats!' said Mug triumphantly. 'No worries!'

'And we'll find some way to free you,' said Boo, still fierce.

'I'll cost a lot,' warned Yesterday. She really was smiling now. 'Especially with all my Hero training —'

'We'll manage somehow,' growled Boo. 'One day. But for now — friends. Okay?'

He held out his paw. Yesterday took it, while Mug took her other hand. 'Friends share things,' said Boo. 'Good things as well as danger. Friends together.'

'Together,' echoed Yesterday.

'No worries,' rumbled Mug.

'Squeak,' said Squeak, sticking his nose up over the blanket. And, for the first time ever, Boo saw Yesterday laugh.

And another thing to remember too:
if you see a sign that says
'Wet paint' … don't!

THE WEREWOLF GENERAL'S ADVICE TO YOUNG
WEREWOLVES SEEKING A HERO CAREER

29

A True Hero

Boo stared at his reflection in the mirror. His fur was brushed. His collar was polished. He'd even had a (aaaaagh!) *bath* last night without anyone telling him to. He looked as good as a werewolf pup could look, except for his leg, which was still in plaster. Even his torn ear looked dashing.

But he still looked more like a puppy than a Hero.

He sighed. He should be happy. He was glad that his friends were going to be made Level 4s at today's Speech Day. They deserved it! And the school dance next week with Yesterday … that was going to be good too. Then school holidays and next term.

Boo glanced at his reflection again. Was that puppy in the mirror really a Hero? He'd only gone to the school to work out how to rescue Mum. And now …

No, he thought. He did want to go back to school next term. He'd make it to Level 4 somehow. And then he *would* find a way to get to the Ghastly Otherwhen. He didn't know how … or when. But just for a moment he felt as he had when he had the Greedle in his jaws again, and knew he could never let it go.

'Are you ready, Boo? You smell *hot*!' Spot galloped up the stairs. She gazed at him, her tongue lolling to one side. 'I wish I could come to Speech Day with you. But Dad says students only get one ticket for someone who's not their parents. The Werewolf General's waiting for you downstairs,' she added.

Boo looked at her. So much had happened in the last few months. He used to be like Spot, happy playing Frisbee by the creek. And now … Boo limped down the stairs.

The Werewolf General's fur was brushed. His medals hung from his collar. Even his wooden leg was polished.

Boo had tried to tell the Werewolf General that there was no point in his coming to Speech Day. Boo wasn't going to get an award, and he'd be fine by himself. But the Werewolf General had insisted.

They limped through the living room together. At least I still have all my legs, thought Boo, glancing down at the Werewolf General's wooden paw. And it was good to have someone by his side, even if they weren't family. Friends can be family too, he thought.

'Bye, Boo!' called Mrs Bigpaws. 'You do look smart! A perfect Hero.'

'Thanks, Mrs Bigpaws,' muttered Boo.

'We're proud of you, young pup,' added Mr Bigpaws.

Boo and the Werewolf General limped up the street to the Best Ice-Cream Shop in the Universes. The winter's slush had vanished now. Spring flowers dotted the gardens. A couple of little pigs fluttered above. Boo snapped at one halfheartedly, and watched as it flapped up and landed on a branch of blossom.

'Oink,' it said reproachfully, sending a tiny dropping onto the footpath below. The pigs were wearing little hats today, to protect them from the spring sun.

Boo pushed the shop door open with his nose. The ice-cream scents were fading. He could hardly smell Mum these days, either.

'Do you still miss her?' asked the Werewolf General, as Boo traced his paw through the dust on one of the churns. 'Sorry. Stupid question. Of course you do.'

Boo shrugged. What did it matter if the shop grew dusty, and the churns stayed still and empty? Boo padded after the Werewolf General into the bedroom, then slunk down to follow him under the bed.

The floor sank below them into the wormhole.

'Squeak!' The mouse scampered along the tunnel, then leapt down into the pouch on Boo's collar.

Boo tried to feel happy as they limped towards the school. But all the other kids would have parents at Speech Day. Well, except for Yesterday …

Yesterday had no one. At least he had an adopted family. Mrs Bigpaws had even made him poodle pancakes for breakfast. And the Werewolf General cared enough to come with him today.

No, thought Boo, as the red glow of the School for Heroes appeared at the end of the wormhole, compared to Yesterday's my life is —

'Student and ex-student approaching!' barked the Werewolf General.

Boo stared as they came out of the wormhole, all other thoughts forgotten. Who would have thought the School for Heroes could look like this?

The school had been transformed!

Red and yellow balloons floated above the heat of the lava pit. Jones the Janitor had even managed to stick tiny red and yellow skulls on the cliff above the dark entrance to the school. More tiny skulls and needle daggers dangled from the strands of zombie spaghetti that still held the volcano together.

But the people! thought Boo. He hadn't realised the universes held so many creatures as this! The ledge was crammed. Heroes in wheelchairs with fangs or furry whiskers, Heroes on walking frames with flames for paws or leathery wings and Heroes with walking sticks roamed about the school ledge, peering at the students and making the occasional disparaging comment.

There were more lassoos, swords, ancient shields, tiaras, hearing aides and pairs of glasses than Boo had thought existed. Ms Snott looked particularly heroic in a dress made entirely of daggers crocheted together, with two more daggers thrust into her hair.

Parents wandered through wisps of steam with their would-be Hero kids. Parents with three eyes, six legs or butterfly wings, parents who looked human till you saw their forked tongues or claw-like hands. And there were Mug and his parents and Glug and Graunt Doom, by the trestles covered with plates of food and big urns of tea, nectar, embalming fluid, blood, and various other fluids preferred by creatures from even stranger universes.

The School for Heroes suddenly smelt of scones and tea kettles as well as lava. *Click, click*, went the Werewolf General's wooden paw on the hot rock. *Thud, thud, thud*, went Boo's plaster leg.

'Good to see you looking better, sonny!' cackled Dahlia the Dazzling. She was still arm-in-arm with Gloria the Gorgeous, each splendid in new spangled skirts and six tonnes of lipstick.

'*Told* you we'd see the werewolf puppy!' boomed Graunt Doom, poking at Boo's coat with her stick. She was wearing a hat today, green with a feather in it, though when Boo looked at it again he thought he saw a pair of eyes blink at him.

'Of course you'd see him,' muttered Princess Princess. It was the first time Boo had seen her since the night the Greedle invaded. She was looking particularly heroic today, in tiny silver pants trimmed with diamonds and an even tinier diamante-studded top, and a tiara in her curls. 'He goes to school here, doesn't he?' She was with a man Boo supposed was her father, tall and striking in a dark blue velvet suit with white fur around the cuffs, and a gold crown on his head.

'Good show, what?' the King said vaguely. 'Lots of animals here. Always liked animals. Eaten a lot of them in my time. Terribly hot, though. Time they turned the air-conditioning up.'

'*Told* you he'd bring Widdles,' roared Graunt Doom.

'Who's Widdles?' asked Boo.

'Me,' said the Werewolf General meekly. 'It was my nickname at school. Miss Doom here was my teacher.'

'Hmmph,' boomed Graunt Doom. 'You widdled on classroom doorpost in my class.'

'Sorry,' said the Werewolf General. 'I hadn't quite got the hang of bathrooms.' But he was grinning, and looking keenly at the food selection.

'Graunt Doom coming back to teach,' rumbled Mug.

'Me replace Miss Cassandra,' thundered Graunt Doom. 'She remembered she getting too forgetful to be good Finder any more. *Told* you I was just retired for a while. Could have *told* you all that Greedle going to invade, too.'

'Why didn't you?' demanded Boo.

Graunt Doom grinned, showing her crumbled teeth. 'Worked out best like this. You see. Me *knew* it would.' She picked up a scone and inspected it. 'Boring,' she boomed in what she probably thought was a mutter. 'Food no fun if it don't wriggle.'

'Would you like a scone, sir?' Boo asked the Werewolf General. Somehow he didn't feel like one himself, not after seeing the Greedle eat a trayful as the school rumbled and shivered. Maybe he'd never eat a scone again.

'Always ready for a scone,' barked the Werewolf General, sitting on his haunches. Boo sat too in the shade of one of the trestles while the Werewolf General wolfed down a scone with apricot jam (Boo was glad there was no strawberry) and a chicken and chutney sandwich and a small cheese and lettuce roll, and lapped a cup of tea that one of the old Heroes had considerately put into a doggie bowl.

'Squeak!' said Squeak.

'Oh, all right.' Boo bit off a crust of cheese sandwich. Squeak took it in his tiny paws. Then all three trotted after the crowd to the school hall: the big cavern deep in the mountain where Boo had widdled on his first, terrible day.

'Over here!' It was Mug, waving at him from the back of the hall in the seat just behind Princess Princess and the King. 'Me mind you seats!' rumbled Mug. 'No one minds zombie smell here at the back.'

Graunt Doom nodded thoughtfully as Boo and Squeak and the General squeezed into their seats. 'That girl Yesterday — she make great Finder one day.'

'Are you *telling* us that?' asked Boo. He looked round for Yesterday. Yes, there she was, on the other side of the hall. She caught his eye and waved and started to come over to them.

'Too right. No worries,' pronounced Graunt Doom, bashing her hat to stop it making rude faces at the ancient Heroes in the row behind.

'All stand!'

Boo stood with the others as the teachers filed in behind Dr Mussells, knuckling his way up the hall and onto the stage.

The school choir sang while the teachers watched. Ms Snott coolly juggled her daggers and Dr Mussells leapt high and swung from a thick rope suspended above the stage. Everyone sat again as Dr Mussells read out the names of all the students who were going up a level. Boo wagged his tail as hard as he could against the back of his chair to join in the clapping as Mug and then Yesterday went up on stage to have their hands shaken and get their Level 4 scrolls.

Princess Princess snorted in the row in front of them. 'It should have been me up there, Daddy,' she muttered. 'If I hadn't left my electric blanket on I'd have defeated the Greedle all on my own. I just didn't want the palace to burn down.'

'Really? Good show. Well done,' said the King vaguely. 'Who's that chap with the banana? I say, is there any chance of a nice cold sorbet and a few serfs waving fans?'

Dr Mussells had finished the lists of students who were going up a level, but he didn't sit down. Instead, he looked around the hall.

'And now,' he said loudly. 'The School Medal for Outstanding Heroism. This medal is only awarded once every ten years. But this year the staff have unanimously decided it is time to award it again — to Yesterday, Mug and Boojum Bark!'

Boo blinked. Surely he'd misheard. 'What?!'

'*Told* you all get medals,' bellowed Graunt Doom happily.

Mug gave him a gentle pull. 'Us supposed to go up now!'

'But … but I didn't —' Boo's paws were leaping off the chair even while his mind was saying no.

Boo padded up to the stage in a daze, with Mug and Yesterday beside him. Dr Mussells held out a tiny furry hand. His other hand held a large gold medal and a banana. 'Congratulations, Boojum.'

'But, sir, I can't take this!' cried Boojum, as he held his paw out automatically.

'But I thought you liked bananas,' said Dr Mussells.

'I mean the medal!'

Dr Mussells stared. 'I don't think we've ever had a student refuse a medal before. Have we, Ms Snott?'

Ms Snott casually threw a dagger into the ceiling, where it pinged into the rock. 'Not a single belly-bouncing, ear-wax-dribbling pile of lizard-doo one of them.'

'Well, Boojum? Why can't you accept the medal?'

'Because I haven't been a Hero!' cried Boo. 'I've never been a Hero! It was just luck the first time, and the second time the mouse did more than I did.'

'Squeak,' agreed Squeak, peering out of his pouch and twitching his whiskers.

'And last time — that was luck too. Mug and Yesterday did the real Hero stuff. I was just there!'

'Really?' Dr Mussells turned to face the audience. 'This is a School for Heroes. But can any student tell me what a Hero is?'

'*Told* you he'd ask that question,' roared Graunt Doom from the back row. She was sitting on her hat now, to stop it misbehaving.

No one put up their hands.

'Boojum?' asked Dr Mussells.

Boo's forehead wrinkled. 'Well, someone who fights evil.'

'And did you do that?'

'Yes, but ...'

'Someone who fights evil,' said Dr Mussells. 'Someone who doesn't run away no matter how great the danger. Someone who stands by their friends, who does their duty. Someone who is *there*. And you, Boojum Bark, were truly *there*.'

Dr Mussells clipped the medal onto Boo's collar.

'I … thank you, sir,' said Boo. He offered Dr Mussells his paw.

The cheers nearly lifted the roof.

'At least he hasn't widdled on the stage this time,' said Ms Snott. But she was smiling too. Her wrinkles wiggled in strange ways when she smiled.

'And I also have very great pleasure,' said Dr Mussells, 'in advancing you, too, to Hero, Level 4.'

Boo stared as the cheers rose again, then stumbled off the stage and padded down to his seat in a daze as the choir started singing the school song.

Oh, Heroes we
All try to be.
As you can see
It's destiny!

He could lead a search party for Mum now. There had to be some way to find the Ghastly Otherwhen! He could —

'*Told* Mug you'd get Level 4, boy,' hollered Graunt Doom. 'Told him not to tell you, too.'

'Shhh,' bellowed Mug's mum, even louder than Graunt Doom. 'Singing still going on!'

Yesterday pressed a quick kiss on the top of Boo's furry head, then blushed. 'I'm so proud of you!'

The choir had finished now and the teachers were marching out. The parents and students stood, then followed them.

One by one Boo's classmates stopped to clap him on his furry shoulder.

'Congratulations, Boo.'

'Yeah, man, congratulations!'

'Well done!'

'Oh, Boo.' It was Princess Princess. She smiled at him ... Princess Princess actually smiled at him. 'I'm so glad you're taking me to the dance, Boo,' said Princess Princess.

'But ... but —' said Boo.

'You *were* planning to ask me, weren't you?' cooed Princess Princess.

'Yes, but ...'

'That's *settled*, then. Human form, of course!' added Princess Princess.

'Fine heroic-looking girl, that,' barked the Werewolf General, as Princess Princess sashayed back to join her father.

'Yes, but ...' said Boo. He glanced at Yesterday. Had she heard?

She had! She was watching him, an expression in her big brown eyes that was hard to read.

'*Told* you today be difficult,' boomed Graunt Doom, putting the now well behaved hat back on her head.

'Squeak,' agreed Squeak.

Boo scratched his ear with his back foot. He had everything he'd wanted! He was a Level 4! He could lead a rescue mission to the Ghastly Otherwhen — just as soon as he worked out how to find it! And the most gorgeous girl in the school had asked him to the dance!

How in all the universes was he going to get out of this one?

✳ ✳ ✳

Author's Note

There may be other universes and wormholes, though you may not find one under your bed. But if you hear a strange noise in the night, and a feeling of danger seeping up your toes ... well, are *you* ready to be a Hero?

PS: See you in the next book!

School for Heroes Book 2

Dance of the Deadly Dinosaurs

Boojum Bark, student Hero and werewolf, along with Yesterday and her troupe of dancing dinosaurs, the reluctant but gorgeous Princess Princess Sunbeam Caresse of Pewké, Mug the zombie, and Squeak the warrior mouse, head into the Ghastly Otherwhen to rescue Boo's mum.

But the Ghastly Otherwhen isn't what Boo expects.

Why do the villagers scream in horror every time Boo lifts his leg?

What excuse will Princess Princess give this time for refusing to Wham! Bam! Pow! the bogeys?

When *will* Mug get his mutant zombie spaghetti under control?

And how exactly *do* you dance with a dinosaur?

A flood of deadly pus is oozing out of the Ghastly Otherwhen towards the sleeping village of Fluffy Botham. You have 47 seconds to save its innocent inhabitants!

Do you:

1. stop to change into a smart suit of red lycra, with cape, boots and helmet?

2. quickly take some pics to send to your friends?

3. open your laptop to look up 'Deadly pus: 101 methods of removal'?

4. just do your best?

SCHOOL FOR HEROES ENTRANCE EXAM,
QUESTION 56

/

'You want to *what?*' Princess Princess Sunbeam Caresse of Pewké stamped her royal foot. The silver sandal made a squelching sound in the whale's digestive juices.

'Shh!' Boo looked round cautiously. All he could see was the dark red wall of whale's tummy quivering around them, and Yesterday and Mug sloshing through the ooze in front. But his wolf nose told him lots more. He could smell blood, and fear. The flea bogeys on the whale were just ahead, carving out chunks of whale guts. 'The bogeys will hear you!'

'Ha! There aren't even supposed to *be* any bogeys any more! Not since the Greedle vanished.'

Yesterday didn't bother to turn round. 'The Greedle controlled lots of bogeys to find its food. These are probably just left over. And of course we're going to help Boo find his mum. That's what friends do.'

'Oh, *right*. So *now* we're inside a whale's yucky tummy hunting leftover bogeys instead of getting ready for the school dance. My new dress is pure gold thread, you know! My dad's had every gnome in the kingdom spinning it for weeks! And *now* this crazy werewolf puppy wants us to try to find the Ghastly Otherwhen to rescue his mum …'

'Ghastly Otherwhen okay now Greedle gone,' boomed Mug. 'Maybe,' he added. His zombie fungus glowed in the darkness of the whale's belly. Which is useful, thought Boo, as now we don't need to use torches to find the flea bogeys who are attacking the whale.

'Huh! Well I just want to get *out* of here and get my hair done and … *eeeeekk!*'

'There they are!' yelled Boo. He splashed towards the team of tiny bogeys, busily trying to carve out a section of the whale's liver. The giant animal quivered in pain again sending the ooze sloshing up aound Boo's tummy.

'Stop!' barked Boo.

'Here, let me.' Yesterday could speak to any animal. Even bogeys, thought Boo gratefully.

'Snnnoooommoooppfoo?' groaned Yesterday, in what Boo supposed was fluent Flea. He scratched his ear automatically. That was the problem with fleas. You only needed to think the word 'flea' and your ear began to itch. And that awkward bit above his tail.

'Voooommooooo?' squeaked one of the fleas, in an unexpectedly deep voice. It sounded surprised. 'Gooo?'

'Noooocooooooodooooo!' moaned Yesterday reassuringly.

'Cooo! Dooo dooo foo!' The little fleas gazed up at Yesterday, their antennae twitching in delight.

Suddenly they began to dance around the whale's belly, splashing as they went. 'Dooo dooo foo! Dooo dooo foo!'

'Let me guess,' said Boo, as the fleas danced off into the darkness. 'They're yelling that the Greedle has gone and they're free.'

Yesterday smiled. Yesterday didn't smile often, but it was worth it when she did. 'Yes. They're happy. But they don't know the way to the Ghastly Otherwhen,' she added. 'They say the Greedle always sent other bogeys to fetch the stuff they collected.'

Boo nodded sadly. He'd hoped that maybe *these* bogeys had come from the Ghastly Otherwhen, so he could follow them back there. But he wasn't going to give up. 'We may as well head back to school then.'

'At last!' Princess Princess pushed back her golden hair, leaving a trail of whale slime. 'Let's get *out* of here fast so I can get my *hair* done! Which way now?'

Mug pointed.

Princess Princess stared. 'But *that's* …'

'Out whale bum,' boomed Mug. 'We can't go out of mouth in case we tickle throat and whale sneeze. Whale sneeze crush us all. So out through bum.'

'Out its *bum*? Its actual *bum*?! There's no way I'm going to go out a whale's bum. I'm …'

Suddenly the blubbery walls began to contract. It was like being squeezed out of a tube of toothpaste, thought Boo, as the walls closed about him. The giant whale's sphincter muscles began to push, push, push …

The world grew dark. Boo took a breath, then wished he hadn't. *Hurry up, whale*, he thought frantically, as he tried to snort out a noseful of whale-doo doo. How long did it take for a whale doo doo to pass through a whale bum? Hurry uuuuppppp …

And then they were free, whirling in a mass of brown and blood stained water. He tried to dog paddle, but the current was too strong. He swirled along, a tumble of fur, tail and paws.

Suddenly he felt Yesterday grab his tail. She began to pull him, swimming strongly. He was vaguely aware of Mug and Princess Princess swimming beside them. His jaws longed to open and gulp in air. But there was only water. And at last he felt his back scrape under the big ledge of rock that Boo supposed was the closest the Universe of Glug came to a bed. Wormholes in every universe came out under a bed. It was traditional.

His paws felt rock as well. All at once they were sinking again. Down, down, down — but not into water.

For suddenly the water was gone, and the whale-doo too. They were back in the wormhole between the universes they'd just used to travel here, the smooth rock ceiling high above them, the cold air smelling just faintly of strawberry jam.

Boo breathed in a giant lungful. He'd never thought he'd be so glad to smell strawberry jam again. 'At *last*!' Princess Princess wiped whale gunk from her eyes. She began to march down the wormhole. 'I'll see you tonight!' she yelled back at Boo. 'And don't forget to Change!'

Boo nodded as he tried to lick the worst of the whale-doo off his fur. Princess Princess would never go to a dance with a puppy dog — not even with a werewolf who'd just been given the School for Heroes medal for Outstanding Bravery and made a Level 4. He'd have to Change into human form. And wear pants, which he hated, and underpants, which were just plain dumb. *And* try to balance on two feet when he danced …

Actually he wasn't sure that he wanted to go to the dance with Princess Princess Sunbeam Caresse Von Pewké at all. He'd been going to go with Yesterday, but it was impossible to say no when someone as heroically gorgeous — and royal — as Princess Princess Sunbeam Caresse Von Pewké expected you to do something.

He glanced over at Yesterday guiltily. 'I … I got you something for the dance,' he said shyly. He picked up the package. He'd left it in the wormhole before they'd travelled up to Glug.

'What is it?'

'A dress. I … I asked Ms Shaggy to make it. She's the best sewer in the whole of Sleepy Whiskers. I thought you mightn't have a party dress.' Yesterday was a slave, sent to improve her skills at the School for Heroes by her masters, the Guardians. She didn't own anything, he thought, except her tatty tunic snd her rock hut. He gazed up at Yesterday anxiously. Had he offended her? But Yesterday was smiling again.

'Oh, Boo,' she said. A tear rolled down her cheek.

Boo stared. He'd never seen Yesterday cry before. Even when she'd dragged the Greedle back to her own universe of rock and dinosaurs she's never cried. 'I've never had a proper dress.'

She fumbled with the packet, then held up the dress. It was silky green and silver spangled.

'D—do you like it?'

'I love it. I love green!'

'My sister Glug wearing pink fungus,' boomed Mug, making the wormhole echo. 'Also pink spangles.'

'She'll look lovely.' Yesterday still sounded tearful as she gazed at her dress. 'She'll be the most gorgeous zombie in the world.'

'I'm sorry I'm not going with you instead,' said Boo quietly.

Yesterday lifted her chin. Suddenly she was the old Yesterday, full of dignity and courage. 'That's okay.' She shrugged. 'I'm going with someone else.'

'Who?' Boo was surprised at the spark of jealousy he felt. He didn't know Yesterday *had* any other friends except for him and Mug. And Squeak, of course, though the mouse hadn't come with them today. Boo supposed it was washing its whiskers for the dance.

'A friend,' said Yesterday.

'What friend?' persisted Boo.

Yesterday smiled. 'A dinosaur, of course. Who else would I go to a dance with?'